Requiem in La Paz

REQUIEM IN LA PAZ

Jonna Gjevre

Storyador
Wooden Stake Press LLC

Text copyright © 2014 Jonna Gjevre
Jacket art copyright @ 2014 Damon Za
All rights reserved.

Published in the United States by Storyador, an affiliate of Wooden Stake Press LLC.
http://www.woodenstakepress.com
http://www.storyador.com

ISBN-10: 1940936004 (trade)
ISBN-13: 978-1-940936-00-0

For my family

PHANTASMA

Wednesday night in La Paz, I heard the voices of the dead. At first, I thought I was hearing music.

I was in a gated community near the Valley of the Moon, dizzy with altitude sickness and soldiering my way through the reception honoring my quartet. The guests were mostly Bolivian bureaucrats or embassy types from Fairfax, Virginia.

"CIA, of course," Lucia whispered on her way to the bar, leaving me with Mikhail, our second violinist, who was of course already drunk.

Empty phrases circulated with the empanadas. *Investor confidence. International community.* I'd been trapped at parties like this since I was twelve, with no choice but to endure. So I stood patiently with my illicit cocktail, waiting for Lucia to return. But the music crept into the room instead: low, faint, and urgent. Impossibly familiar.

I turned my head, spotted the angels, and ducked into the entrance hall.

Beside the curving staircase were two large paintings of angels, each one set in a gilded frame. With smooth, untroubled faces, they were waiting and listening.

I inched closer to the angels, and the polite chatter of the reception dissolved. A deep, ambient drone pulsed. I looked around for the source of the music, drawn to a horned figure on a pedestal. Then I heard Lucia's voice hissing my name.

"Izzy! There's a godlike Norwegian archeologist in the library. He's talking about ancient ruins. Too old for you, but you've *got* to see him."

She was still hung up on my age. But with the strange music worming its way into my brain, I couldn't care less. "He's all yours. And the next one, too. I can barely stand."

Usually, I had no trouble keeping up with Lucia. But this morning, when we started our South American tour, I noticed a change. It wasn't just altitude sickness: it was something more. I'd begun to feel slow, as if weighed down by earth and stone.

Lucia raised a graceful brow. "When you come to La Paz, *camina lentito, come poquito, y duerme solito.* Until you're used to the altitude, of course."

"Hey ladies," said Mikhail, trailing me into the foyer. "The party's that way. What are you doing out here?"

Lucia rolled her eyes. "Godlike Norwegian," she reminded me and glided away.

"What did she say?" Mikhail asked.

I shrugged. "We're supposed to walk slowly, eat lightly, and sleep all alone." A thin half-circle of lemon floated in my cocktail like a disapproving frown. "And maybe not drink so much."

"Yeah, right." Mikhail approached the clay figure on the pedestal, sipping his bourbon. "Angels and devils in the same room? Is that even legal?"

I stared at the crude statue. It squatted on goat feet, with a giant barbed tail, a pointed beard, and twisted horns curving into an arc. It really *was* a devil.

Mikhail reached out to touch the grotesquely painted face. I shot a glance at the ambassador's reception next door. "Idiot idea, Mikhail."

He peered at me over the top of his glasses, his narrow forehead oily and pale.

"You know," he said, with a touch of disdain. "There's a long history of violinists who sell their soul to the devil. Tartini. Paganini. Dude down in Georgia. But never any stories about a little viola player."

"Guess I'm safe then."

Mikhail grinned. "Nah. You just miss out."

The music surged, and I realized the drone was coming from the statue itself. The pulse filled the room like a dying heartbeat, drawing my gaze to the eyes of red clay. It was calling out to us, seeking a response.

A chill prickled my arms. "We should go now. We've gotta meet and greet."

"Just a minute." He took a step closer, his voice fallen to a whisper.

"Mikhail!"

Ignoring me, he dragged a finger across the statue's forehead, making a sign of the cross. The drone abruptly changed, becoming less like music, more like a human voice distorted with rage. I *knew* that sound.

I grabbed Mikhail's arm, but it was too late: the moment I touched him, something passed through us, dry and cold. A crack splintered across the devil's body, pitching the entire room into silence.

Slowly, my vision cleared. My cheek was resting on the hard terrazzo floor. Broken shards of clay lay everywhere. Mikhail lay beside me, in a bourbon-soaked heap of fine wool. His eyes were open and unfocused, his mouth slack. A blood vessel forked in a lightning bolt across his left eye.

I swallowed and tried to raise my head. "Mikhail?"

Words were forming slowly, thoughts beginning to unblur. There had been a man watching us from the staircase, a man with pale, tight skin and a chilling smile. Eyes like an empty grave. I tried to hold onto him, but he faded, and the dead thing in his hand—shriveled and gruesome and gray—withered into oblivion.

Mikhail's shoulders abruptly twitched, as if something inside him were crashing into a wall. He struggled to sit up. "Izzy? What the hell did you do that for?"

He's blaming me, I thought with relief. Just like he does in every rehearsal.

I nudged a piece of clay from my gown, relief turning to horror. "Oh my god. We've destroyed a priceless artifact."

"We? You're the one who broke it."

"It's not priceless." The speaker entering the hall was a young Bolivian dressed in black tie, the only guest I'd seen who was under twenty-one. He had a broad, appealing face, with strong indigenous features. His hands were slender and graceful, his hair completely black. "And it's not an artifact."

"Can't hold her liquor," Mikhail explained, with unsurprising cowardice. "She passed out and knocked it on the floor."

I started to protest, then stopped. Mikhail wasn't lying: he really seemed to think he was telling the truth.

We all looked at the remains of the horned statue.

"Oh, shit," I breathed.

"*El Tio,*" the young man said, almost sadly. "The uncle."

I tried to stand, but my head filled with prisms, and a band of nausea collared my throat. More guests filtered in, curious and whispering. After a childhood spent onstage, I was used to being the center of attention, whether I wanted it or not. But not like this.

"I'm Enrique. Enrique Rodriguez." He bent down to support me, saw my face, and reacted at once. "You aren't well. I'll find Dr. Paulsen."

"No need," someone said. "I'm already here."

Unmistakably, it was Lucia's godlike archeologist. With sun-streaked hair that fell to his shoulders, Dr. Paulsen appeared to be Mikhail's age, or maybe even in his thirties. But faint lines weathered the corners of his eyes, making him seem almost ageless.

"Let's get you off the floor." In one swift move, Paulsen lifted me up.

"I'm fine," I protested, vaguely aware that my skirts were bunching obscenely around my thighs. "Really, I'm okay. Put me down!"

"Please," Enrique said, his voice quiet. "Let us help you."

I relented, and somehow we made it to the library.

"*Soroche* is a serious condition," Paulsen said, settling me onto a leather sofa. "Acute mountain sickness, we call it. Did you see all the oxygen tanks at the airport? This city's at twelve thousand feet."

"What's going on here?" Lucia pushed through the crowd, a nervous mother hen in a strapless silver gown.

Mikhail gestured gracelessly at the entrance hall. "The usual. Viola player messing up."

"You're playing the viola now?" Enrique asked, easing a pillow behind my back.

I offered him a weak nod.

"I have all your violin concertos, and the unaccompanied Bach." He abruptly ducked his head, smile flashing white.

"You do?"

Encouraged, he crouched beside my sofa. "You look so much younger, in all the photographs."

I winced, thinking of my old album covers: blonde pigtails and freckles, Peter Pan collars, mouth full of braces. "Well, I was younger. When I was thirteen."

Why couldn't I breathe? And why couldn't I remember? Had I really fainted and broken the statue, as Mikhail claimed? It occurred to me that memory loss was probably a sign of impending suffocation.

I'll die a virgin after all, I thought bleakly. And be sent home in a virgin body bag. *That's just great.*

Each successive breath seemed more empty and futile, and Paulsen's hand burned like acid as he brushed a few stray hairs from my eyes.

"There are drugs that can ease altitude sickness," he told us. "Diamox, for example. But it can cause blurry vision, and make your fingers numb."

"Numb?" Lucia was appalled. "We have concerts to play. What kind of a stupid side effect is that?"

Enrique stood, straightening his jacket with a practiced hand. "May I recommend coca tea? It always helps me when I return from the States."

Seeing my hesitation, he smiled. "It's just tea, you know. I'll make sure of that."

He slipped through the French doors to the entrance hall, where the ambassador's maids stood hovering over the wreckage of the statue, agitated voices protesting in a language that wasn't Spanish. Quechua, perhaps. Or Aymara. Whatever they were saying, it was clear they didn't want to touch the thing.

Enrique murmured a response in the same language, then knelt down in his tuxedo. I watched him pick up the broken pieces of the devil, and I wondered what a boy my age was doing at a party full of diplomats.

"Coca tea? That sounds pretty old school to me." Mikhail was standing too close to Paulsen, the broken blood vessel gleaming bright in his left eye.

"It's just a mild stimulant," Paulsen said, then turned to me. "Let's check your pulse, okay?"

He bent to take my bony wrist in his hand, eyes searching my face. I pressed my other wrist against my gown, so he wouldn't see my scar.

Paulsen abruptly stiffened and let go of my wrist. "*Phantasma*," he muttered, his face hard and cold. He didn't look into my eyes again.

Phantasma? Bewildered, I watched him walk away.

Mikhail followed like a duckling. "So you're a doctor, then?"

"I'm a pathologist." Paulsen filled a tumbler with bottled water and retrieved a glass of scotch from the sideboard. "A paleopathologist. My South American patients have been dead for a long time."

Lucia's eyelashes curled upward. "So you're not digging up ruins, you're digging up skeletons."

"Mummies," Paulsen said, returning to my sofa and bringing a small group of gawkers with him. "I'm digging up mummies."

He held out the water, not quite making eye contact. "Drink this please, Miss . . ."

"Linden," supplied Mikhail. "Isobel Linden."

"You study mummies," I repeated, not sure if I should be fascinated or repulsed. I clutched at the glass, my hands as weak as wet paper, and took a sip.

"Natural mummies." Paulsen was watching me drink, and I saw that his eyes were the same gray as his suit. Like ashes edging a banked fire, both faded and bright.

I slid to the edge of the sofa and pulled myself halfway to my feet, before a wave of nausea spiked in my throat and knocked me back into the pillows.

Damn. I swallowed, tasting bile.

"Are you sure she's all right?" Lucia asked, apparently torn between fawning over Paulsen and trying to replace my mother. She paced back and forth, all cleavage and stilettos.

Paulsen said something reassuring. In the foyer behind him, I caught a glimpse of our host, Ambassador Melton. He was looking down on Enrique and the wreckage of the devil's statue, his muscular body completely still. In my experience, stillness usually meant rage.

"I knew it was a mistake to fly right into La Paz," Lucia fretted. "I feel responsible, you know. Isobel's only seventeen."

"Seventeen," Paulsen repeated softly. He looked past me with such intentness that I followed his gaze, wondering what he was seeing. Just a wall of leather-bound books. "You're a prodigy, I suppose?"

"No," I said, hairs prickling on the back of my neck. "No, I'm not a prodigy."

"But you *are* a prodigy," said Ambassador Melton, coming in with Enrique and a housekeeper bearing tea. "Enrique's been following your solo career for years."

"You're very kind," I said, with my best professional smile. "But that was a lifetime ago. I play chamber music now." It *was* a lifetime ago. It was almost four months.

Enrique handed me a steaming cup of coca tea.

"An ancient remedy," he said, slender fingers brushing my hand. "*Mate de coca.*"

"Thank you." Hearing the word remedy, I felt oddly

comforted. Altitude sickness could be treated. But hearing voices and going mad like my mom? Not so much.

The ambassador's watery blue eyes blinked rapidly. "I do hope you'll be all right for the concerts. My wife is very eager to hear your quartet."

"Nothing to worry about," Lucia intervened. "Isobel's *never* missed a concert."

"I'm so sorry about your statue," I blurted in a rush of dread, knowing that Mikhail would never deliver an apology himself. "I don't know what happened."

Mikhail looked on, not a trace of guilt on his face. Why didn't he remember what he'd done?

"Don't trouble yourself." Ambassador Melton held up his big hands, forestalling my apologies. "It's no great treasure. It's just an idol, from an abandoned mine."

"Do the miners worship the devil?" Mikhail asked, finding this as interesting as the mummies. I wanted to kick him into silence, but that would have required standing up.

"Worship him?" Enrique frowned. "Never. Outside the mine, they're good Catholics. But mining is so dangerous, when they go underground they hedge their bets. *Dios Padre* is their father above; *Tio* is their uncle underground. He has authority there, in the mine."

Beside him, Paulsen shifted slightly, and exchanged a glance with Ambassador Melton.

"So maybe Izzy just got herself cursed," Mikhail said with complacent enthusiasm. "If she wasn't cursed already."

I glared at him. I didn't make any Faustian bargain to become a concert violinist when I was a kid. I just gave up my childhood. Every minute of it. And to get out, I gave up my family.

"*Tio* would never curse the innocent," Enrique insisted. "The miners bring him offerings: alcohol and coca. In return, he protects them from death."

The ambassador laughed. "A local religious tradition, of course. Many Bolivians conflate the earth mother Pachamama with the Virgin Mary, and some even find room in their worship for the devil. Their adaptive approach to Catholicism is really quite fascinating."

The ambassador went on in his condescending way, talking about folk beliefs and regional superstitions. Enrique's eyes darkened. He took a breath and said nothing.

I sipped the pale amber-green tea. It was an ancient remedy, Enrique had said. It was an offering.

I could feel my strength and my focus beginning to return, and I caught hold of a single spiraling thought before it spun away and was gone. The pale man on the staircase: I'd seen him before.

THE MOTHER'S STONE

On the way home from the ambassador's, I realized that drivers in La Paz don't always use their headlights at night.

"Why are we driving in the dark?" I asked, glimpsing a jagged strip of darkness cutting through the heart of the city. An ancient riverbed, surrounded by city lights.

"More economical," Lucia said, steadying herself against the door as we made a sharp turn. "Saves on light bulbs."

This made no sense to me, but I knew I wasn't processing information well. Too much had happened that I didn't understand: the strange music coming from the statue, the pale man standing on the staircase, Mikhail's failure to recall what he'd done.

Perhaps Mikhail blacked out. It wouldn't be the first time.

"You're such a lightweight," he snorted when we arrived at the Hotel Miranda, watching me fumble with my bag. He rubbed at his eyebrows and released a flurry of dandruff. "It's 'cause you don't eat. You need to eat more."

"Sure," I said with an eye-roll. "So I can drink more."

Our cellist David Weiss was waiting for us outside the hotel. Unshaved, dressed in black leather, wearing a scowl.

"That's enough, Isobel," he snapped, helping Lucia out of the limo. "You and Mikhail can chill out."

Mikhail slunk off, looking sullen. I said nothing.

"Did they find my other bag?" Lucia asked David, stepping

carefully over the cobblestones.

"It's in your room." David held out his arm, but she didn't take it.

It was late, the winter air cold and still. We'd been among the last to leave the ambassador's, saying goodnight to all the guests, listening to endlessly similar good wishes for the upcoming concerts. Mikhail headed for the hotel bar, and David and Lucia exchanged a look, Lucia frowning.

"Keep an eye on him," she whispered. David gave a short nod.

"I think I'll join you," he called to Mikhail, tugging off his leather coat.

Lucia marched across the glass-walled lobby, shoulders knotted together. Her velvet shawl was tightly pulled around her, her hands curled into fists under the fabric.

I stumbled after her clattering stilettos. "You're wrapped up like a mummy, Lucia."

"Me?" Lucia wasn't too cold to turn the tables on me. "You're the one who's wrapped up," she said, and spun to walk backwards in her heels. "I saw you staring at that Norwegian doctor. He had you wrapped around every one of his fingers. Each of which is lacking a ring, as I'm sure you noticed."

This would have been an acceptable bit of girlish teasing, had a tall Norwegian doctor not appeared in front of the elevators just as she got to the phrase 'Norwegian doctor.' She continued on, oblivious.

"Lucia!" I finally hissed. She spun about, saw Paulsen, and recovered with the same professionalism she would have brought to a memory lapse in a recital.

"Dr. Paulsen! We were just wondering what brought you to the party. How do you know Ambassador Melton?"

Paulsen began to respond, then stopped, as if he'd just become aware of my presence. He blinked, his eyes following the line of my neck, the vein pulsing in my throat.

"The ambassador has been quite helpful," he finally said. "There are a number of complex policies involving the use of pre-Columbian artifacts."

"Like mummies," Lucia said, a bit breathlessly. "And you study them."

Paulsen smiled, then turned the full force of his gaze on me. "I'm one of those who interrogate the dead."

I began staring at the button for the elevator, punching it a second time. The button stared back, its light unchanging.

"And what do the dead tell you?" I heard myself ask.

"If I'm lucky, they tell me how they died."

"I already know how your mummies died," I said, unsettled for no reason I could understand. "They were murdered. Victims of human sacrifice. Like that Inca girl they found whose head was compressed into a cone. Left to die on a mountaintop."

"Ooh, horrible!" Lucia shuddered theatrically. "She was probably a slave, taken from an enemy tribe. Being punished or something."

Paulsen brought his hands together in front of his chest. An odd gesture, as if he were warding off an invisible blow. On his right hand, a long white scar stretched from his knuckles to the base of his thumb. "A terrible punishment, don't you think?"

"Punishment? *You* don't know what she did. Maybe she was completely innocent. Maybe they even tried to convince her she was lucky. Maybe she even believed them."

I was surprised to hear myself talking again.

"Maybe." Paulsen was looking seriously at me, and I sensed that I was somehow framed in his vision as if on a slide or a screen, slowly being pulled into sharper focus.

The elevator doors opened, and he followed us in. The conversation died. I focused my attention on the doorplate, which had the word 'Schindler' written into the brass. We got off on the third floor, and as the doors were closing, he said:

"Miss Linden, I'm looking forward to hearing you play *Death and the Maiden*."

Lucia and I stood for a moment in the quiet hallway.

"Miss Linden," she finally said. "Not Miss Baigorria, Miss Linden. Naturally, he remembers *your* last name."

"Lucia, please. It's not like that."

"He cannot have failed to notice how interesting I am. But it's your hair, I suppose. That whole Nordic genome of yours."

"Lucia, please."

"And does he realize you're just a kid?"

"Just a kid? Really?"

"Okay, then." She withdrew a plastic card from her clutch and opened our door with a sigh. "Well, I guess he likes Schubert."

Our room was just as we'd left it, comfortingly bland and teetering between cluttered and tidy. I pulled off my shoes and collapsed onto the bed. The burgundy polish had chipped off the ends of my toes, and after awhile I began picking at the polish, wondering why my nails still didn't need to be trimmed.

Faintly, as if coming through the air vents, I heard a low, muddled drone. I reached over to open the viola case resting on my bed.

"You're *not* going to practice now," Lucia said. "It's almost midnight."

"It's so dry here. I just want to make sure it's okay." I unlatched the case, revealing the Stahler viola inside.

My viola wasn't much to look at. Barely a hundred years old, with a garish coat of shiny orange varnish. Only the leaf-like tendrils at the ends of the f-holes marked it as anything more than ordinary. That, and the fact that no matter where we were, its strings were always perfectly in tune.

I picked it up and plucked a series of chords, and Paulsen's cold gray eyes took shape in my mind. I was used to people staring. I was a performer, and scrutiny came with the territory. But I wasn't used to aversion. As if he were seeing some kind of freak.

"The viola's fine." Lucia emerged from the washroom smelling like rosemary. "You're the one I'm worried about."

I brushed away a tiny fleck of rosin. "I'm feeling better."

Lucia put down her skin cream and sat on the bed. "Is something wrong? You've been different, quieter, ever since we got to La Paz. It's almost like you're not here." Her eyes found mine. "We're in this for the long haul, you know. The four of us, we're like a family. We need you to be happy."

My throat tightened, and my calloused fingers curled around the scroll of the viola. I didn't have a family anymore.

I *am* happy, I wanted to say. But Lucia would know it was a lie.

"Isobel? What's wrong?"

How could I tell her about the man on the staircase? Or the eerie music worming its way into my brain? How could I tell her that everything, even the air that filled my lungs, seemed to be straining with the effort it took, just to keep on going?

"I'm fine," I said, looking up with a smile. "Really, I am."

A few hours later, I woke up cold, struggling to breathe. It was happening again. Sliding to the edge of my bed, I rolled weakly off the mattress. *I might not wake up next time.*

The room was quiet and still, a dull ray of meager light shining in through the gap in the curtains. Shivering, I folded my arms across my chest, trying to remember when I'd last woken feeling joyful, feeling hope.

It was before, I decided. Before the funeral. Before the razor blades. Before I found the Stahler.

I stole a look at Lucia, whose skin shone like amber in the dim light. She had pieces of white tape flattening the invisible lines on her forehead, foam earplugs wedged into her ears. She wouldn't hear a thing.

I clamped a heavy chrome mute over the bridge of the Stahler and snuck into the bathroom. Once inside, I tightened the bow and played a single plaintive note. With its hard metal stranglehold on the bridge, the mute flattened the life out of the viola, leaving only a pinched, tinny imitation of its real voice. But it didn't matter. I was playing again.

It's hard to say what happened after that. Whenever I plunged into the music late at night, I never remembered it afterward. Not what I'd played, nor for how long. I only knew I felt stronger.

Eventually, I stopped to pull a broken hair from my bow,

and I realized I was sweating, the fabric of my T-shirt sticking to my back, darkening the shallow space between my breasts. How long had this been going on?

Pushing open the bathroom window, I stuck my sweaty head out and breathed in the cold night air. After years of being home-schooled in lonely hotel rooms by my mom, I was finally in a new city, with a new life. Just for moment, I felt limitless and free.

Then I saw them. Next to the hotel was the National Archeology Museum, where a pair of stone beasts guarded the courtyard gates. Two men stood beneath the carved sentinels: a stiff, brick-shaped figure and a tall man with long golden hair. I watched them standing in the streetlights, and the minutes passed.

At first, I couldn't hear anything. Their voices were three stories down, muffled by the sounds of the city. But not beyond my reach. I closed my eyes and stretched into the darkness, and then by some power everything faded—the distant nightclubs, the barking dogs, the traffic from the nearby Prado—and I caught the thread of their voices at last.

"Are you satisfied?" the man asked, his voice rasping like a lit match. "I'd rather not wait here all night."

Paulsen's voice was cold. "Do you have the Mother's Stone?"

"It's yours, for a price."

"I've paid you, Hurst. Just hand it over."

"But you haven't used it," the man said. "There's another price you'll pay for that."

Harsh laughter filled the courtyard. "Trying to frighten me?"

"Free advice. That's all."

Paulsen's laughter died. "Save it for your clients in Washington."

I opened my eyes in time to see the man named Hurst step forward and hand Paulsen something the size of a plum. Paulsen quickly pulled away the dark fabric, uncovering a stone. The men stared at the stone, not speaking. Then Paulsen slipped it into his trench coat.

"If you live long enough, you might see me again," Hurst drawled, turning to go.

"I'm hoping for something else," Paulsen said. "And I usually get what I want."

Hurst walked away, but Paulsen stood alone in the courtyard, his eyes fixed on the stone beasts guarding the gate. He seemed to be waiting for something.

Without thinking, I slipped out of the bathroom and grabbed my bag as I headed for the door. A painful sensation was gnawing its way through my chest cavity, and when I reached the open staircase above the lobby, I realized it was either fear or hope.

Paulsen knows what's wrong with me, I thought. *He knows.* No one else does.

I hurried down the stairs into the deserted lobby, wondering what the hell I was doing, stalking a pathologist in downtown La Paz. Pushing open the glass doors, I walked out into the night. There were no cars in sight, but the street noises from the nearby Prado resonated bluntly around me. The hotel and museum were at the end of a quiet cul-de-sac, a cobblestone walkway connecting them to the busy Prado. Paulsen was moving swiftly up the walkway, his pale coat billowing out behind him. His companion was nowhere in sight.

"Paulsen!" I called, stepping out onto the cobblestones. He kept going.

"Paulsen!"

I looked back at the stone beasts guarding the museum.

Phantasma, he'd called me. A ghost.

I followed Paulsen's trail up to the Prado. Buses and cabs moved in spurts on each side of the tree-lined central boulevard. It was still dark, but women in skirts with long braids under their bowler hats stood sweeping the sidewalks. Shopkeepers were unfastening the bars on a few isolated windows. No sign of Paulsen.

I paused on the entrance to the Prado, realizing that I had somehow arrived at the threshold of a new world. I'd spent almost half my life in the company of adults, wearing girlish dresses that made me look even younger than I really was. I'd given recitals on three continents, soloed with sixty orchestras, whipped off diabolical cascades of fingered octaves on live television. But I'd never been alone in a city after dark.

I took a deep breath, gripped the strap of my bag, and walked out onto the Prado.

A group of boys lounged against the stucco walls, all of them wearing balaclavas or ski masks. They looked like a team of bank robbers. I swerved anxiously out of their way, then realized they were just shoe-shine boys. *Lustrabotas*, Lucia had called them. One of them pursued me with his shoe-shining kit, pointing at my flats and offering to polish them. I shook my head and turned away, almost tripping over a man crouched on a blanket near the corner.

"Excuse me," I blurted out. "*Lo siento.*"

The old man stared a thousand yards straight ahead, his eyes covered with a rheumy white film. I glimpsed a jarful of coins in his withered hands, and then something urgent and hopeless twisted in my gut: a sharp, sickening desire to commit those hands to memory, to hold onto every veiny, gnarled knuckle. My dad's hands had been ravaged by arthritis. Had they looked that way in the end? I couldn't remember.

I unzipped the outer compartment of my bag and found a handful of bolivianos. The old man lifted his head in thanks as the coins hit the jar, his sightless gaze wandering upward. But when they reached my face, his gummy eyes abruptly focused, filling with horror and comprehension. With a harsh cry he dropped the jar and flung up his arm to protect his face.

I hurried away, quickly and purposefully, trying to look like someone who had a reason to be on the streets of La Paz at 5:00 A.M. Two shops ahead of me, I could make out a refuge of sorts, an ATM embedded into the wall. But all I could think about was the old man.

How could a blind man see? What had he seen?

Willing myself to be calm, I walked on, my eyes on the ground, a fist pressed against the center of my chest. But here's the strange thing: my heart wasn't racing at all. It pulsed steadily at exactly 60 beats per minute, the same fluid tempo as a Viennese waltz.

Arriving at the cash machine, I breathed slowly and forced my limbs to relax. My fingers opened like a pair of stiff fans, then dropped to my sides. Much better.

I glanced over my shoulder to see if the boys had followed. They were still at the corner. With them, a tall shape in a long coat. *Paulsen.*

For a moment I just stared. Then I took a cautious step in Paulsen's direction, abandoning the ATM. Almost immediately, a hand seized my arm, pulling me backward.

The raspy voice was low and ingratiating. "Careful, miss."

Short and solid, his jowls ice-picked with scars, the man gripping my arm was entirely familiar. It was Hurst, the man Paulsen met outside the museum.

I tried to slip out of his grasp, but his grip tightened, and another beefy hand seized my other arm.

"It isn't safe here for a girl like you," he murmured. "Not with the old ones so close."

"Let me go," I snarled, twisting my face away. I shifted my feet, trying to calculate where his kneecap might be.

He leaned over my shoulder, and his eyes dropped to the slight contours of my torso. "You're going to need protection."

Sick with disgust, I tried to breathe, tried to come up with a plan. I should have stayed in my bubble, in my glass-walled hotel. I should never have come here.

Forty feet away, Paulsen had dropped to his knees, reaching for something lying on the ground. Would he hear me if I screamed? Would he even care?

"You're very energetic," Hurst whispered in my ear, his breath greasy and foul. "*Impressive.* The old ones—they can feel it, too."

"We're done here." I stomped hard on his insole.

With a grunt of pain, Hurst released me and staggered

backwards, and I twisted out of his grasp. He grimaced, his eyes disappearing into folds of pitted skin, but he wasn't hurt nearly enough to satisfy me.

"Go on, little girl," he called as I ran away. "I'm sure we'll meet again."

I clutched my leather bag and ran toward Paulsen. I needed to get away from Hurst. But I was still seething with white-hot fury, and I desperately wanted to hurt someone. Paulsen would do just fine.

What the hell was he doing, acting helpful and pretending he liked music, only to end up conspiring in the alleyway with a creepy pervert who—

My thoughts came to a sudden stop. Paulsen was kneeling on the ground, his long hair falling across his cheeks. His hand rested on the neck of an old man with crippled hands and blind, milky eyes. A dead man. The glass jar lay nearby, spilling coins across the coarse woolen blanket.

The street boys hovered a respectable distance away. Their eyes shone brightly in their black ski masks. One of them, the boy who had offered to polish my ballet flats, looked up blankly as I approached, his face empty of recognition.

"Dr. Paulsen," I whispered.

Paulsen started almost imperceptibly. Then he turned his head, the rest of his body still. "You. Of course."

He abruptly got to his feet, as if he'd made some kind of decision. Stepping away from the body, he drew closer and closer, until I could smell the cotton fabric of his weathered raincoat.

"You shouldn't be here," he said, a terrible coldness in his voice.

Was he blaming me for what happened?

"I'm not a kid," I snapped. "I have as much right to be here as you do."

"That's not what I meant."

Paulsen's eyes seemed to be lit from within, their color approaching silver. I stared up at him, almost hypnotized, and for the first time that night, I experienced complete, heart-pounding terror. Just for an instant, I was on the edge of a ravine, struggling to keep my balance and knowing it was already too late.

Then the awful moment passed, and I realized I was cold and exhausted and standing over the body of a dead man. Sirens were pounding, an ambulance approaching.

Paulsen had not looked away. "You shouldn't be here, but you are. How is that possible?"

A DEAL WITH THE DEVIL

"Where's Mikhail?" Lucia peered out the window of our publicist Raysa's apartment, as if hoping to see our second violinist twenty-eight stories below. "Why isn't he here?"

"Maybe we shouldn't have scheduled rehearsal so early," I said, taking off my jacket and struggling to appear engaged. But all I could think about was Paulsen.

"Early? It's eleven fifteen." Lucia gave me a look that said: *I'll deal with you later.* As if she hadn't dealt with me enough already.

I shouldn't be here, I thought, remembering Paulsen's accusation. But I am.

What gave him the right to say that?

Lucia turned to David Weiss, who was positioning the endpin of his cello into a tiny groove in the hardwood floor. "Well? Is he sick or hung-over? Which is it?"

David furrowed his dark eyebrows, briefly resembling a Hollywood terrorist. "When I left, Mikhail was moving very slowly in the direction of the shower. Guess he's no longer on *gringo* time."

Lucia's lips were not naturally thin. But for a few seconds, she achieved it: the tight, grim look of an irritable schoolmarm. "Was he ever on *gringo* time?"

She had been angry since 5:00 AM, when she woke to find the window open, the viola on the counter, and me gone. She called the police, of course, who arrived just as Paulsen brought me home. Paulsen smoothed everything over, saying I had acute mountain sickness. But why had he done that?

"And you," she snarled, turning on me again. "I missed my interview with the TV station because I thought you'd been kidnapped and killed. You do realize that David and I are responsible for your safety? If Paulsen hadn't found you . . ."

I tried to make eye contact with Lucia and ended up looking at her chin. I wanted to tell her I was an emancipated minor, working to support my disabled mother. I wanted to tell her I'd been touring the world longer than she'd been out of college. I wanted to tell her I didn't need a control freak in stilettos, who was less than half the musician I was, to boss me around.

But I couldn't say any of those things, because I couldn't tour alone anymore, and I needed Lucia and the quartet even more than they needed me. A string quartet is like a four-person marriage. With just one person off balance, the entire house of cards could tumble to the ground. I still wasn't used to that.

David set down his bow and tapped the screen of his phone. "Text from Mikhail. He's on his way."

Lucia steepled her fingers together. "Tell him to head downhill on the Prado. Remind him it's the tall building with the big Sony sign on the roof."

David looked at her in disgust. "You wanna call him yourself?"

This was hardly the first time Mikhail was late. David and Lucia recruited him three years ago, when his drinking was still under control. When I met them in February, their violist Rachel had just been indicted on felony charges, leaving them with one rock-star cellist, one high-strung diva, and one disastrous alcoholic.

Lucia noticed the edge in David's voice and redirected her venom. "He's fifteen minutes late. And Isobel's delusional with hypoxia, and sleepwalking on the Prado. And what's your problem? Don't you even care?"

There was a brief silence as her question spread through the room and settled into the cracks in the floor. The swinging door between the kitchen and the dining room was slightly open, and I could just glimpse Raysa's maid peering in from the kitchen.

David gave up, as if Lucia had said something unforgivable, and began paging through his Popper etudes.

Lucia sucked in a hissing breath. "What's wrong with him?"

I blinked, unsettled by the faint music seeping into my ears. "Steroids, maybe."

She rewarded me with a crooked smile.

I felt a strange, unspecific dread, wanting urgently to play my viola, to find refuge in the music. I took a breath, my lungs as shallow as a cluttered ashtray. Surely Mikhail would come soon, the rehearsal would begin, and the voices in my head would go away.

I should have been listening to those voices, asking myself what they meant. But I didn't want to hear them. I didn't want to face what I'd done, what I couldn't undo.

It was painful enough trying to think about last night. I'd wanted so badly to remember that old beggar's hands, and now I'd gotten my wish. Those twisted dead fingers were like wallpaper in my mind, and I couldn't get free of them.

But why didn't anyone seem to remember me? The shoeshine boys were there. They were there when I gave the old man the coins. They saw me. Didn't they?

It was almost as if I'd been erased.

I opened my case and lifted up the flame-colored Stahler. As always, its strings were perfectly in tune.

"Isobel! Did you even hear a word I just said?"

"Sorry?" I turned from my viola case.

"We're having our tea early," Lucia said, pulling out a chair, "which you would know by now if you weren't staring off into space, clinging to your viola as if your life depended on it. Sit down."

With a pang of queasiness, I placed the instrument back in its velvet-lined case. As the case snapped shut, I flashed back to the pale man on the ambassador's staircase, and the dead thing in his hand. Where had I seen him before?

"I don't think I'm hungry," I said, and then a fragment of memory came back: a shadow over my mother's face, the day they took her away.

He was there, I thought with sudden conviction. He was there in the kitchen when we found my dad.

"You need to eat, Isobel. You're a skeleton." Lucia directed her scowl at David. "And you. Are you coming?"

"Nope." David tapped his book of etudes.

Raysa called for her maid. "*Esperanza, mate y salteñas, por favor.*"

"Give me a minute," I told them. "I need to call my mom."

The buttery tenor of David's cello began to soar through the apartment, and I stepped into the quiet kitchen and dialed the family line at Prairie St. James. The phone rang and rang. When the nursing assistant finally picked up the phone, I could hear a woman screaming in the background. *My mom.*

A harried voice came on the line. "Prairie St. James."

I took a deep breath. "This is Isobel Linden."

"Could you please call back? This isn't a good time."

"I just want—" I began, but the line was already dead.

I focused on the blue and white kitchen tiles and tried to collect myself, but a pulsing drone battered at the edges of my mind.

I've lost her. What if she's lost forever?

Lucia shook out her linen napkin as I joined her at the table. "Everything okay?"

"Just fine," I said, and pocketed the phone. "Everything's fine."

Lucia glanced at the ornate clock resting on the cabinet. "Mikhail ought to be here. We need to work on the Schubert."

The hard plastic phone pressed against my hipbone. "Why aren't we playing the Dvorak here, like we will in Buenos Aires?"

"Enrique Rodriguez insisted on *Death and the Maiden*. He basically said, 'No Schubert, no tour dates.' Which I think is absolutely ridiculous."

"Enrique Rodriguez?" I asked, surprised.

"He's our Bolivian sponsor. Did you even *read* the contract?"

"I just thought the ambassador—" I broke off. "I mean, Enrique's my age."

Why was Enrique sponsoring our tour? And why would he insist on *Death and the Maiden*?

Raysa's maid Esperanza came in with pastries and *salteñas* she'd bought on the street, and Raysa set down the silver coffee service and a teapot.

"Enrique's certainly very young to be a major sponsor." Raysa handed me a cup of coca tea. "He's only eighteen, but extremely rich. His family made a fortune in the tin mines."

"So is he single?" Lucia asked, getting right to the point. Abandoned by her father in Argentina when she was six, she was all business when it came to men.

"Of course." Raysa's voice dropped. "People say he'll never marry, but I think—"

"Never marry?" I asked. "Why not?"

She shrugged. "They claim that his family is cursed, that his grandfather made a deal with the devil. People tell stories, you know."

"People in small ponds are jealous," Lucia stated flatly. She stirred her coffee and poked at the various sugar substitutes on the table. "That's what it is. They don't want anyone to succeed in the real world. It's even worse in Minnesota."

She asked for honey, and Esperanza hurried away, long braids and pleated dress swaying.

I took a sip of the bitter coca tea. Unlike the tea Enrique brought me last night, this cup had large pieces of dried coca leaf clinging to the sides. I nudged a leaf out of my way, remembering the sadness on Enrique's face as he'd named the broken statue.

"*Tio* would never curse the innocent," he'd said.

Did he actually believe the devil was real?

"*Hola!* Good to see English-speaking faces." We all looked

up. Esperanza had returned almost immediately, Mikhail Leiberov in tow. He came in smiling, his glasses smudged, his nose a little red. The broken blood vessel forking across his left eye was gone.

Raysa swept her highlighted hair behind her shoulders and reached for the pastries. "Mikhail, we're so glad you're here. Would you care for *salteñas*?"

Mikhail took a seat and stretched his arms. "Sure. Got some coffee?"

Lucia picked up her own coffee cup, her expression deliberately flat. "Are you sober enough to rehearse?" The acid in her voice could have eaten its way through a metal door.

"I'm here, aren't I?"

"Do you realize—" Lucia began, but David cut her off.

"Lucy. Let it go."

David and Lucia stared at each other, like gunslingers. Mikhail's eyes flitted between them, a slight frown on his face.

The four of us, I thought with amused disgust. *We're like a family.*

But I didn't need the three of them. I still had a mother, no matter what the doctors said. Caught between hope and dread, I slipped the phone out of my pocket. Maybe she'd talk to me this time.

I ducked into the refuge of Raysa's kitchen and glimpsed sunlight coming in from the laundry room. Inching past the old-fashioned turquoise washing machine, I made my way out to the narrow balcony. The cold air filled my lungs.

I surveyed the sprawling city, trying not to remember the sound of my mother screaming. A million people lived in this canyon, their stucco homes clinging to steep hills, surrounded by a saw-toothed mountain range. My mom would have loved this place. If we'd come to La Paz when I was a soloist, she would have filled her notebooks with poetry. But now it would always be too late.

I opened my phone and hit redial.

The nurses at Prairie St. James weren't happy to hear from me again. "Your mother's very calm right now. We don't want her getting agitated."

"Could you at least tell her I called?"

"Would you hold, please?"

I gripped my phone, feeling a perverse urge to jump into the wind. Cutting through the heart of the city was a steep ravine, the jagged strip of darkness we'd seen on the way back from the party.

Finally, one of the hospital psychiatrists came on the line. "Miss Linden, I'm very sorry, but your mother doesn't wish to speak with you. It's symptomatic of her illness. She covers her ears when she hears your voice."

I turned my back on the city and pressed my forehead to the cold doorframe.

"Why?" I asked, knowing the question was futile.

"She says it isn't you, that you aren't her daughter."

THE PALE MAN

I'm not unfeeling. I'm not a heartless person. But when I hung up the phone, I did what any performer would do: I went back to the dining room, finished my tea, and then rehearsed the Schubert quartet for an hour and a half.

When you spend your life onstage, without an understudy or a backup, you learn to put away the things you can't handle. You close all your pain into a little box, and you promise you'll come back to it later. You promise.

After quartet practice, David and I accompanied Lucia to the *Teatro Municipal* for her solo rehearsal with the National Orchestra. The *Municipal* was a gorgeous old concert hall, with ornate gold balconies draped in red velvet. But the sound didn't resonate at all.

David crept over to my side of the theater, disgust written across his face. "This place is dead," he whispered. "Why aren't we playing at the new concert hall?"

"Enrique Rodriguez," I told him. "Lucia says he insisted on the *Municipal*."

Enrique was a puzzle. When we met, I simply assumed he was a guest of the ambassador. Instead, he was running the show, insisting on hearing *Death and the Maiden*. But why did our concerts have to be here?

David nudged my viola case away from his foot. "He can

have his way, but this hall is going to swallow us up."

The sound in the hall was horribly muffled, and Lucia wasn't getting any help onstage. Maestro Balcones, the conductor, wore a sweaty black turtleneck and resembled a cruel bird of prey. He flitted aimlessly through each movement of the Sibelius violin concerto and stopped only when something disastrous happened. Even worse, he was cueing the orchestra early, cutting short Lucia's solo parts.

Next to me, David bristled with hostility. "Good thing she knows it cold." He closed his copy of the score.

"Lucia sounds beautiful anyway." I whispered back, grateful to be to be in the same room as music so magical. I'd played the Sibelius concerto countless times, and I'd never grown tired of it. Every passage resonated with loneliness or sorrow: all of it transformed, as if by alchemy, into brief flashes of transcendent beauty.

If I were telling myself the truth, I would have admitted that I wanted to be onstage playing the Sibelius myself. My performance would have been more controlled and less bombastic than Lucia's. In the *danse macabre* section at the end, I would have—but that life was over. I was in the quartet now.

People said it was a step down, playing the viola instead of the violin. And maybe it was. But they hadn't heard my Stahler.

David was quiet, listening. He really did look like a rock star, which meant that most of the fans coming backstage after our quartet concerts were female.

"Lucy played this concerto at the Tchaikovsky Competition," he said. "Five years ago, in Moscow. It was fantastic."

"Were you there?" I asked, surprised.

He ran a hand along the canvas spine of his score, watching the stage, where Lucia had paused to pull a broken strand of horsehair from her bow. "I was there."

David's face was raw with an emotion I belatedly recognized as longing. I turned away, embarrassed to be witnessing something so private. Why hadn't I seen what was between them? How could I have missed it?

Three rows ahead of us, at orchestra right, I saw that someone else was watching the rehearsal, a woman in her thirties with long brown hair. A soft alpaca shawl draped across her body. She was staring up at Lucia, her face as raw as David's had been. But her expression wasn't longing. It looked more like dread.

"Isobel," David whispered. "Your nose is bleeding."

"Is it?" I touched my hand to my face, and it came away red. A drop trickled across my creased palm, reminding me of something I couldn't name, something I needed to remember. "It's the dry air."

"Tell me about it. My cello's nearly cracking. You need a tissue?" He began to stand up.

"I've got stuff here." I reached for my case and found a packet of tissues. Then I unzipped the compartment holding my viola. The air was desert-dry, and the humidifier I'd filled yesterday was already empty. I lifted the viola and flipped it over, checking for cracks. Nothing was wrong. And yet . . .

I looked up. The woman in the theater was still staring at Lucia, her shawl-covered body now hunched as if in pain. Standing directly behind her was a pale man dressed in black. He had no eyebrows, and his skin stretched tightly across his skull.

The man from the ambassador's staircase.

As I watched, he reached forward with a bony finger to touch the woman. He swept aside a few fine strands of dark hair, his bloodless fingertip just grazing her left ear. She convulsed, and then a sound caused them both to freeze.

My fingers burned, and beneath them, my viola trembled with the brief, dissonant chord I'd drawn from its strings. Why had I done that?

The pale man slowly turned my way, his empty eyes seeking mine. I saw then that there was something wrong, something irreparably wrong, with his face. He was young, but his flesh pulled tightly over his cheekbones, like the skin of a fading movie star with an aggressive facelift. His eyes were flat and dead. I dropped my gaze to my viola, determined not to face him. I knew those eyes. I was sure of it now.

He's the one. I felt my heart pound. *He took my dad.*

"Shhh," said David, still watching the stage. "They're starting the third movement."

He nudged my hand. "And your nose is still bleeding."

THE PULSE

"Lean forward a little," David said, grabbing the tissue and pressing it to my upper lip. "Don't tip your head back."

He pinched the soft parts of my nose together, and I struggled to breathe through my mouth. Blood drained into the back of my throat, salty and wet.

As the orchestra launched into the *danse macabre*, I glimpsed a gaunt figure dressed in black, silently exiting the theater. He might have been smiling.

"Sorry, David," I whispered. "I know you wanted to watch."

"Don't apologize. It's not your fault."

But he didn't know that. He didn't know anything.

A few hours later, we met Mikhail and the orchestra patrons at the *Club de La Paz*. A tall obelisk guarded the front entrance, like a sentinel protecting the mummies in a tomb.

What had Paulsen said about himself? *I'm one of those who interrogate the dead.*

I tried to imagine Paulsen in his laboratory, asking questions of the dead. But I couldn't see him in a laboratory. I could only see him on the streets of La Paz, his hard face filled with accusation.

There were walls I'd built in my mind, stacked high with immovable stones. But Paulsen kept finding the tight spaces between the stones, kept forcing his way in. I needed to keep him out.

Circulating with drinks before gathering in the dining hall, we met the *Auspiciadores*, the patrons sponsoring Lucia's solo performances in La Paz. Many of them spoke English, much to Mikhail's relief. And most crowded around Lucia, much to my relief. I just wanted the evening to be over, so I could go back to my hotel and play my viola.

There was security there, and something else.

Mikhail befriended a handsome bartender, who obligingly made him drinks two at a time.

"Have a *chuflay*," he said, holding one of his glasses out towards me. "It's basically *singani* and Sprite."

"No way. If I'm not going to be carded, I'm choosing my own drink." I turned to the bartender. "*Vino tinto, por favor.*"

"Did you hear what that Paulsen guy was saying about wine?" Mikhail asked.

I didn't want to be reminded of Paulsen again, but Mikhail looked beaten-down and lonely. Lucia had been hard on him. "Something about tannins?"

"Right. Those Anglo-Saxon mummies got turned into leather by the tannic acid in the bogs. It completely tanned their hides." He snickered, finding his little joke much funnier than any normal person ever would.

"That's *so* funny, Mikhail."

"But you see, tannins are good for you. They're in green tea. And wine."

"So?"

"So, here's the really big question," Mikhail lowered his voice and took a step closer, the patchy skin on his nose practically brushing my temple. "If we drink enough wine, will we be preserved?"

"Preserved from what?" came a voice from behind us.

I turned and found myself facing our sponsor. Enrique Rodriguez was leaning against the entrance to the ballroom, dressed in black and holding a goblet in one slender hand. As he stepped across the floor, he projected a mesmerizing grace and ease, as if he were casually restraining himself from floating through the air. Framed against the Art Deco windows, he seemed to belong to an older age or a newer world.

"Isobel." Enrique surprised me by kissing my cheek. "I hope you're feeling better."

"Much better," I said, not sure whether I should call him Enrique or not. "It's nice to see you again."

Enrique's eyes sparkled. "I understand you've met our esteemed director."

"Esteemed?" Mikhail snorted into his *chuflay*. I sent him a warning look, but Enrique just laughed.

"Fair enough," he admitted, his tone confiding and amused. "I keep arguing we need to replace Balcones, but no one listens to me. They think I'm just an upstart." He spoke softly, casting a glance over his shoulder.

"They?" I asked, taking in the inhabitants of room, most of them lighter-skinned than Enrique, all at least twice our age.

"The *Auspiciadores*. Orchestras are terrible investments, you know, and this one's always a single step from bankruptcy. Balcones brings in the audiences, so he stays."

An elderly woman in a cobalt gown approached, reaching for Enrique's hand.

"*Buenas noches,* Paloma," he said, taking her hand and kissing her cheek. She held tightly to Enrique's hand, and I noticed her other hand had a slight tremor.

She twisted her wrinkled neck to see over her shoulder, and I saw she was looking at someone who'd just joined Ambassador Melton and Lucia at the bar. It was Hurst.

I took a shallow breath, felt my chest burn. I remembered Hurst's fingers sinking into my arms. He said we'd see each other again.

Enrique stiffened, his eyes on Hurst's brick-shaped body. "We have a party-crasher."

I swallowed, too horrified to speak. But there was no reason to be so frightened. Hurst was just a pervert from the dollar store.

"Why is he allowed to stay?" I finally managed to ask.

Enrique ran a finger over the rim of his goblet. "Some people find him useful, I suppose."

Hurst inched closer to Lucia, extending his hand to touch the dark curls resting on her shoulder. But she turned her head, raised one magnificent eyebrow, and gave him her most terrifying look, the one that said: "And Now You Shall Die."

Hurst's hand retreated like a scurrying rodent, his pockmarked face stretching into an earnest, appeasing smile.

Next to me, Paloma scowled. "*Quitagusto*," she muttered, the furrowed lines between her eyebrows deepening. Mikhail watched curiously, sipping his *chuflay*.

"Would you excuse me?" Enrique reached out to touch my shoulder, his voice sinking to a whisper. "I think it's time for Mr. Hurst to leave."

He took Paloma's arm and crossed the broad Art Deco hall. Paloma introduced herself to Lucia, and the two women began chatting like old friends, their heads tilting from side to side. Enrique stepped close to Hurst and whispered in his ear.

Hurst backed away from Enrique, bristling, and shot a glance at the ambassador. But Ambassador Melton simply sighed, almost as if disappointed, his broad shoulders rippling in a dismissive shrug. And then, just like that, Hurst and Enrique were gone.

Mikhail caught my eye. "Way to go, Enrique!"

I lifted my chin, felt my lungs fill with clean air.

"So you're the resident bouncer," Mikhail smirked when Enrique returned, "and one of the *Auspicious* people who keeps this orchestra afloat."

Enrique smiled politely at Mikhail's mistranslation. "Me? Auspicious? I don't know about that."

I remembered Raysa's matter-of-fact tone as she'd served me the tea. *They claim that his family is cursed, that his grandfather made a deal with the devil.*

We soon found ourselves in the dining hall, at a long table set with an astonishing amount of silver. Enrique handed a crisp bill to the headwaiter and gave him my name. Returning, the waiter held up a place card with my name on it.

Enrique smiled. "*Muchísimas gracias, señor.*"

We took our seats and I poked at the folds of my pretty napkin, stealing a glance at Enrique. He caught my eye and grinned. "I hope you don't mind sitting with me instead of the ambassador."

It occurred to me that this was almost like a date. With someone my own age. With someone who actually knew what it was like to be the only teenager in the room.

I found myself smiling back. "I don't mind at all."

Sooner or later, I was going to have to learn to eat snails. I only wish I'd been a little higher on the learning curve before attempting to consume them in front of Enrique. I suspect he knew I was facing my worst culinary nightmare, for he spent much of the first course chatting with Ana-Maria, the pretty debutante across the table.

I pushed a slimy snail to the side of my plate, feeling guilty. They couldn't be easy to find in La Paz.

"You shouldn't be here," I whispered to the snail. "But you are. How is that possible?"

What had Paulsen meant when he said that? And why had the old beggar looked at me with such horror?

I haven't done anything, I told myself. But part of my mind, the part I didn't want to visit or even know about, wondered if that was really true. The old man was dead, and so was my father.

Enrique returned his attention to me as a waiter brought us new plates, and a pair of men in ankle-length aprons approached with a huge platter of meats. "How are you liking La Paz so far, Isobel?"

"Very well. But I'm feeling guilty because I'm not eating much of this wonderful food." Three glistening slices of steak now rested on my plate.

"Of course. The altitude sickness." An odd look flitted across Enrique's face: a strange combination of hunger and concern, quickly replaced by a warm smile.

Across the table, Ana-Maria was quizzing Mikhail about our concert. Her wide, expressive eyes reminded me of a certain tabloid queen: a former child star with a crazy stage mother, who'd fallen from her Disney glory into scandal and public drunkenness.

I never bought those trashy tabloids. I never made fun of those lost girls. It would have been too easy for me to become one.

"Mr. Leiberov," Ana-Maria's voice was unusually high and light. "Enrique says you will play a quartet called *Death and the Maiden*. Do all quartets have names?"

"No." Mikhail spoke slowly, having reached the point in his drunkenness where he had to concentrate on his words. "Schubert wrote a vocal piece called *Death and the Maiden*. Then he recycled the melody for the string quartet."

"The singer was Death?"

"Yeah. He sings stuff like, 'Give me your hand, and you'll sleep in my arms.' That kind of thing."

"Who plays Death in the quartet?"

Mikhail hesitated, unused to thinking of a quartet as playing a character.

"The first violin has the melody, mostly," I put in. "But also the cello."

Ana-Maria had one more question. "But what do you do? Are you the maiden?"

Mikhail sniffed impatiently. People who didn't understand chamber music always asked questions like that. "We're the pulse. We keep things going."

The dessert was a perfect tiramisu. As the bittersweet liqueur dissolved on my tongue, I felt strangely at peace. The pale man was nowhere in sight, the altitude sickness under control. There were no voices. No creepy perverts selling mysterious stones. No scornful pathologists obsessed with the dead. Nothing could touch me here.

At that moment, Enrique reached out with a finely boned hand and touched my arm. "I have to tell you this. I heard you play in April, when I was in Washington."

"You did?"

"I knew right away I had to invite you to La Paz. I've never heard that kind of phrasing. There was a moment during the Schubert, when it felt like nothing in the world existed, except your music. It was magical."

I stared at him, shocked. I felt that way every time we performed that quartet.

He understands, I thought. He understands how a few minutes of music can transform the entire world.

"You're very generous," I managed to say. "*Death and the Maiden* is becoming our signature piece. We'll be recording it for Naxos in July, when we get back."

Enrique leaned closer, his dark eyes becoming softer, more luminous. "But it's the strangest thing. I didn't realize it was *you* playing viola. I read your name on the program, and I saw you on stage, and I heard the amazing performance, but I didn't make the connection. I didn't *see* you. It was only afterward, when I was back in La Paz, that I realized you were the same Isobel Linden who won the Menuhin competition."

He hesitated. "I mean: I have all your albums. You'd think I would have recognized you."

Yet another person who didn't see me, didn't remember me. It shouldn't have mattered at all, but for a moment I tasted bile. Something was happening. I was fading.

"Well, I've changed," I said, trying to sound indifferent. "I'm not a kid anymore, not a violinist. I'm playing the viola now, and I'm almost eighteen. Everyone thinks of me as an adult." Then I remembered my mom's nurses at Prairie St. James. "Well, almost everyone."

"I know how you feel," Enrique said with a gentle smile, misunderstanding my last comment. "There are people in this room who've been on the symphony board since before I was born. And they won't ever let me forget that."

"So you pay all the bills and they still treat you like a kid?" Mikhail butted in.

Enrique shrugged. "Pretty much."

Mikhail rolled his eyes, and I couldn't suppress a laugh. "That's gotta suck."

Lucia came to join us then, having extricated herself from Maestro Balcones.

"My God," she whispered, and slid into Ana-Maria's empty chair. "Free at last."

Enrique nodded in the direction of Balcones. "The Maestro seemed to be having an animated conversation—"

"With my balcony." Lucia finished his sentence for him, with an amused glance at her impressive cleavage.

Enrique sighed. "I *am* sorry."

"I'm a big girl," Lucia said breezily. "It's nothing I can't handle."

"I was just telling Isobel that I heard you perform in Washington. I was wondering how you met, how you formed the quartet?"

"We've been in residency in Minneapolis for four years now. But in February," Lucia flung out a careless hand, as if dismissing the whole ugly police drama with the previous violist, "we suddenly needed a new violist, and Isobel had just switched."

"So you recruited Isobel?"

She shook her head. "We met at a violin shop in Minneapolis. The soundpost had collapsed on my Vuillaume, so I rushed it in to Claire's for repairs. And there was this black door next to the ladies room."

"The door's made of lead," I told Enrique, "and it opens to a room-sized safe. The environment's completely controlled, so the luthiers use it to store instruments and wood."

"So anyhow," Lucia said, grabbing back the reins of her story, "I'm coming out of the ladies room, and I swear to God, I hear the most beautiful music in the world."

"I'm pretty sure it was just a Kreutzer etude."

"It was *not* Kreutzer. It was haunting, uncanny. It had these eerie shifting harmonies and *bariolage* effects, as if two instruments were playing instead of one. Like it was a forgotten Ysaÿe sonata no one had ever heard before."

"Kreutzer," I repeated. "I'm pretty sure."

Lucia ignored me. "So I stepped into the safe, and there

was all this priceless lumber. Blocks of ebony, maple dug up from shipwrecks, perfect sheets of spruce. And these old, old instruments hanging on the racks. And Isobel was playing this ancient melody, and her hair was in this blonde ponytail, and I remember fixating on the rubber band holding her hair together, because it was the only thing in the room that wasn't hundreds of years old. It was the only thing I knew for sure was real."

Lucia swallowed, a vein pulsing in her throat. Enrique and I stared.

Then Mikhail broke the spell. "That doesn't sound like Kreutzer to me."

THE STAHLER

"Why does Enrique speak such perfect English?" Lucia wanted to know. We were in the *Club de La Paz* limo, making the short trip back to the hotel. Normally, we would have walked, but Mikhail was close to passing out.

"His dad sent him to Washington every summer, to stay with friends."

"Interesting," Lucia said, with the air of a stock analyst evaluating market conditions. "And useful. So tell us: what else did he talk about?"

"Well," I began, aware that I was gossiping about a boy, like one of those girls on TV. Or like a normal girl, if normal girls really did that. "Enrique loves classical music, but he's also a big supporter of Bolivian folk music. He's promised to take me to a *peña*."

Enrique was perfection itself, I thought, remembering how he looked at me, how he talked about music. My mind began to construct a ski chalet in the mountains.

"That sounds like a contradiction." David nudged Mikhail's drooping head off his shoulder, already sick of the girl talk. "How can this guy support the indigenous tradition if he's listening to Bartok all the time? You need to forget him."

"Thank you, David." Lucia sighed, not bothering to restrain her sarcasm. "We'd be lost without your insights."

"I'm just saying—"

"And why do you just *assume* that anyone who appreciates classical music is giving up their cultural heritage?"

David raised his voice, startling the driver. "I do not think that. I never said that."

"This Ana-Maria. Do you think she's Enrique's girlfriend?" I asked, ignoring the cold looks Lucia and David were sending back and forth.

"I wouldn't think so," Lucia said, settling down. "Enrique doesn't have a chance with a girl like that. Even if her father does launder money for the *narcos*."

"What do you mean?"

"I mean he's completely unsuitable to her family. Raysa told me the whole story. Everyone was shocked when Enrique's father made him his heir. To this day, people still don't believe he's legit."

"So her family won't let him date her? They're afraid his money will go away?"

Lucia gripped the door handle as we made a sharp left onto Tiwanaku Street and approached the archeology museum.

"His money's not going anywhere. It's because of who and what he is."

"What do you mean? That story about the curse?"

Lucia sighed. "Of course not. Do you even know anything about anything, Isobel? Of course you don't. You're pale and thin and blonde and no one—not even you—gives your appearance a second thought. You've never once looked in a mirror and wondered if you were light enough to be accepted.

"Enrique's father was a terrible old man. He treated his servants like animals. And when his wife died, he started messing with the kitchen maids, with his daughter's nannies. He'd get them pregnant, pay for one illegal abortion after another, and throw them out. Enrique's mother was a 16-year old girl from the country, with a sixth grade education. She wouldn't abort her baby."

"So what happened? Did he marry her?"

Lucia gave me one of her pitying looks, reaching for her shawl as the car came to a stop. "Are you kidding me? A simple country girl? He didn't even pay for her funeral."

We got out of the car, and David and Lucia hobbled up to the Hotel Miranda, half-dragging Mikhail between them. I hung back, feeling left out and forgotten. I'd thought things would be different if I could just join a quartet and be part of an ensemble. But I was still alone in the world. I still didn't belong.

Enrique didn't seem to belong either, but that didn't mean that he and I had anything in common, apart from not having parents anymore, and not fitting in.

The gates to the archeology museum were closed, and I saw that the stone beasts guarding the gates weren't just single animals. They were mountain lions perched on top of grinning, disembodied human heads. I stared at the fierce, snarling creatures, suddenly sick with guilt and fear.

They stared back. It was almost as if they could see me.

I'll call the hospital again tomorrow. And I'll just listen. Even if she's crazy, she's still my mom.

Back in the hotel room, Lucia was waiting. "You will *never* guess who wants to have coffee with me." With an air of triumph, she held out a memo card with a phone number on it. The logo on the gray paper looked like three interlocking shields, followed by a name and title: Henrik Paulsen, M.D., Mayo Clinic School of Medicine.

"He's from the Mayo Clinic," she said, preening a little. "Just an hour's drive from Minneapolis."

"Awesome," I said, not meaning it.

"Jealous?" she asked hopefully.

"Not even close." I took out my earrings and set them on the teak tray. The black pearls gleamed in the lamplight, like a tiny pair of malignant eyeballs. "He's older than you are. And he digs up dead people."

"I just thought you had a thing for him," she said over her shoulder, heading for the bathroom.

"I don't have a thing for Paulsen," I began to say, but she was already gone. Or for Enrique, I told myself.

I knew what men were like, and I wasn't in any danger of having a 'thing' for anyone. The sum total of my sexual experience included only unwanted attention from creepy older men—most recently, being grabbed on the Prado by that asshole Hurst. I could do without any more of that.

I brought out my viola while Lucia took a shower. After clamping the heavy chrome mute onto the bridge, I began to play. Or rather, the Stahler began to play itself.

I kept drawing the bow across the strings, and the past kept unfolding before my eyes, like a sped-up scratchy newsreel, complete with tinny music. It all came back: Claire's varnish-scented violin shop. The long struggle to find a new violin. My father's voice saying, "We'll try Chicago. Bein & Fushi may connect us with a new sponsor."

Then, finally, the glossy black surface of a thick metal door.

"You're playing it again," I heard Lucia say.

"What?"

"That music." She came out of the bathroom, toweling her hair. "It's not Kreutzer. It's something I've never heard before. It sounds like Ysaÿe. *La Malinconia.* But it's not that, either." She hummed a single note, as if still hearing fragments of a melody.

"You know more about it than I do."

"Are you okay?" Lucia asked, beginning to frown.

I looked away. "I need to take a shower."

I placed the Stahler on my bed and closed the bathroom door. Then I turned on the shower and stepped out of my black dress. The steam fogged the mirror as I stared at my pale reflection, and after awhile, the reflection asked, "You think maybe you're being punished for your sins?"

I might have wanted to answer that question, but a sound burst from the bedroom: a woman screaming.

I threw open the door and rushed into the room. Lucia had collapsed onto the floor between the beds, the orange varnish of the Stahler blazing like fire against her pale blue robe. Her fingers gripped the viola, and her eyes stared straight ahead.

She wasn't breathing.

HOSPITAL OBRERO

Anyone who thinks CPR is sexy has seen too many TV shows. It's an ugly, wrenching, brutal business, and that's when it works.

The human brain can survive for only five minutes without oxygen. Henrik Paulsen was at our door in two minutes. He had Lucia breathing on her own in four.

"Get your friends," he snapped when it was over, wiping vomit from Lucia's neck and chin. "And put some clothes on."

Hospital Obrero's lobby was quiet and stagnant. But as Paulsen followed David and the paramedics in, barking something to the orderly, hospital staff appeared from nowhere. The doors of the ER opened wide and swallowed them up.

I rushed to the registration desk with Lucia's passport and insurance cards. The air was strong with chemicals, and a faint metallic taste pricked my tongue.

Punishment, I thought. This is what it tastes like.

Eventually, I sank into a chair, conscious of the eerie silence in the waiting room. Two little boys stared at me, their mother pacing with a baby in her shawl. A subtitled American comedy played soundlessly on TV.

Trying to not to think about Lucia, I examined the tiny ridges on my thumbnails. I tried to remember when I'd last trimmed my nails. In May. Over a month ago.

David returned from the ER and took the papers, his face grim. "Did you reach Mikhail?"

I shook my head. "Left a message."

"Huh." He sank into a chair, dark hair falling into anguished eyes.

"He's probably someplace where he can't hear his phone," I said, wanting to sound consoling but sounding pointless instead.

"Of course he is," David muttered, not consoled. A rectangular clock marked time above his head, its hands close to midnight.

When Paulsen finally returned, he was curt. "She's stable. Come with me."

But what was wrong with her? I hurried after Paulsen, about to burst with questions when I realized he wasn't paying attention to us. He was staring at the front of the elevator, his eyes focused on the seam between the doors.

We arrived in Lucia's room to find her propped up on a hospital bed, whimpering and batting feebly at the IV stuck into her hand. The doctors had put an oxygen tube in her nose, making her delicate face seem sinister and distorted. Seeing the tube and Lucia's sunken eyes, I began to feel a smothering, irrational sense of guilt.

I shouldn't be here, I told myself. And now Lucia was suffering. And if the viola was causing it . . . but I couldn't even think about that.

Lucia's brown eyes stared, completely unfocused, into the space in front of her.

David pulled up a chair and reached for Lucia's hand. "Is it altitude sickness?"

"Possibly." Paulsen folded a small piece of paper he was holding, running his fingers along the crease. "They're running some tests. But her body's severely dehydrated, which isn't entirely consistent with *soroche*."

He paused, as if considering what to say next. "What was she doing when you found her, Isobel?"

I swallowed hard, decided to lie. "I heard a scream, and when I came out of the bathroom, she was just lying there."

I couldn't bear to look at Lucia anymore. I focused on the darkness outside the window. Our figures reflected dimly in the glass: the white bulk of the bed with David stooped beside it; Paulsen's tall form in his long tan coat; and my own body, small and pale, features blurred and distorted by the darkness. I couldn't see my face. It was probably for the best.

Lucia soon lapsed into a drug-fueled sleep. Seeing her lying motionless on the hospital bed, David twisted his hands and made a sound like a creaking door.

"Is she going to be okay?"

"Probably." Paulsen's face was neutral. "We'll hope there's no organ damage, and that her kidneys don't fail."

I sucked in my breath and looked away. The man was so appallingly calm. How could he be unmoved while saying something so dreadful, so obscenely wrong? No wonder he spent his time with dead people. He didn't know how to deal with the living.

Mikhail finally called an hour later, and David crept out of the room, whispering into the phone. Paulsen stood in the doorway, watching David go. Then he returned to Lucia's bedside and leaned over to check the flow meter on the oxygen tube. Lucia stirred a little and fell back asleep.

Paulsen shrugged out of his coat and settled back into the cushioned gray chair beside me. He wore jeans and a dull green thermal shirt, and he needed to shave.

The hospital was oppressively quiet, and it occurred to me that it might be a long night. I didn't want to talk about Lucia. Paulsen would probably make another tactless, unforgivable remark. As for his business with Hurst, I didn't want to know about it.

I hazarded another glance at him. He was gazing steadily at me. With his long gold hair and his silver-gray eyes, he was definitely striking. But he was also watching me intently, as if I were an interesting specimen for analysis.

I shuddered, remembering Hurst's ugly promise to find me again. What if Paulsen were thinking about me in the same way? What if his cold eyes were hiding a monster every bit as ugly as his horrible friend?

"She was with you." It was a statement, not a question.

"Yes." What if *I* was the monster?

As if he could hear the question in my heart, Paulsen reached over and seized my left hand, turning it so he could see the faded scar that crossed the pale skin of my wrist.

He examined it silently, and I sat frozen, afraid to breathe or move. No one had ever noticed my scar before.

"You're lucky," he finally said, "that you can still use your hand."

"I had surgery," I whispered. "For carpal tunnel. I'd been playing too much."

This was met with excruciating silence. Paulsen ran his thumb along the scar.

"I see." He abruptly let go of my wrist. "Four or five months ago."

"Yes," I said, and remembered to breathe. "Four or five months ago."

Paulsen's voice chilled the entire room. "You've had a lucky break, Isobel. Don't let it happen again."

I looked away, sick with fear. Did he know what I'd done? Or was he talking about Lucia? There was nothing I could say.

But I wasn't going to let him have the last word. Not without turning the tables.

"How'd you get *your* scar?" I sneered. "A lucky break?"

His eyes dropped to the white diagonal line crossing his knuckles.

"I tried to save someone," he said quietly. "Someone who couldn't be saved."

Paulsen's gaze flicked to Lucia, his expression so unforgivingly cold that I knew at once it must have been a woman he'd tried to save. A woman he'd lost forever.

A hoarse moan came from the bed, and Lucia stirred. Her voice cracked. "Where am I? What's happening?"

Paulsen got to his feet and touched her shoulder. "You're in the hospital, Miss Baigorria."

Lucia recoiled. "The hospital? Where's David?"

"David's here. I'll let him know you're awake."

Paulsen left the room, and I leaned closer to Lucia. "You're fine. You just got a little dehydrated."

"I was playing music," she said, her eyes strangely bright. "I was playing the most beautiful music in the world."

"Where? Where were you playing?"

"In my dream." Lucia shook her head, confused, and caught sight of the IV stuck into her right hand. She choked back a sob. It sounded like the death rattle of a giant bird.

A single tear streaked down her cheek. "I was playing your viola, wasn't I?"

I exhaled, unable to speak.

"I got so curious," she went on, in a breathless, forced staccato, "Because you always sound so beautiful. And I picked it up, and then I realized I was touching your viola. And how would I like it if somebody were using my Vuillaume? And then I felt so awful. So awful."

She pressed her dry lips together, no longer the Lucia I knew. It was almost as if she'd become someone else.

"It's okay," I repeated mechanically. "You're okay."

She blinked several times, and her face crumpled. "I don't know how you can play it. Your hands are so small, and the neck is so thick. It doesn't speak easily at all."

My eyes fell to my hands, to the faded scar inside my wrist. "It *is* hard to play," I said, mostly to myself. "It takes a lot out of you. But it gives a lot back."

"I had to dig in with the bow, and then it sounded so harsh, as if . . ." Lucia's voice trailed off and she began to cry.

"But Lucia," I said, looking up. "I heard you. You weren't playing. You were screaming."

THE REPLACEMENT

The next day brought consequences. Our publicist Raysa arrived at the hospital in a shiny red suit, equipped with a Toshiba laptop and a full-blown nervous breakdown. Enrique Rodriguez showed up in jeans and polished leather shoes, accompanied by an old indigenous woman carrying a large basket.

"This is Arminda," Enrique told us. "She brought coffee and breakfast."

Arminda smiled warmly, showing an uneven set of teeth. She wore an apron and a faded cardigan over her pleated blue dress, her gray-streaked braids parted in the middle. She produced a set of dainty white cups and began pouring coffee from a thermos, her bright eyes flitting between Lucia and the coffee cups.

"*Mate de coca*," she said, offering Lucia a murky green, pungent-smelling variation on coca tea. Lucia took a single sip and soon drifted back into sleep.

"*Gracias*, Arminda." Enrique handed her the rest of Lucia's tea, and she took it, nodding silently.

Raysa declined the spicy empanadas and paced around the room. "The doctor says Lucia's too weak to leave the hospital. How will she play her solo with the orchestra?"

"She won't," David said flatly, not looking up from Lucia. "We'll cancel."

"Cancel?" Raysa spun on her heels and appealed to Enrique. "Both solo concerts are sold out. They might as well cancel the rest of their tour."

Enrique opened his hands, indicating helplessness. "What else can we do, Raysa? There's no other way. We'll have to refund the tickets."

I watched the numbers crunching inside Raysa's impeccably groomed head. Orchestra musicians, rehearsal time, hall rental, publicity—it would cost a fortune.

"I'm sure you can afford that," Raysa said to Enrique, her voice biting. "It's only money to you. But what about the disappointed audiences?"

"We have cancellation insurance," Mikhail said, not realizing he was fueling Raysa's fire. He still wore last night's clothes, and he stank of whiskey and stale sweat. "It would cover the solo concerts, and the quartet concert in Cochabamba."

Raysa barely managed to avoid wrinkling her nose. "This will affect your quartet's reputation," she said dismissively. "And your insurance rates."

Mikhail's lanky form seemed to shrink. "Okay. Whatever."

"The important thing," Enrique said, cutting through the discussion without raising his voice, "is that Lucia has a chance to recover. She *has* to get better."

"Exactly," said David coldly, still watching Lucia. "What good is our reputation if we're only a trio?"

"We don't have to cancel the solo concerts." All eyes turned to me, and David raised an expectant eyebrow. I paused, mentally debating whether I actually wanted a pair of solo concerts resting on my shoulders, whether I wanted to go back to my old life.

I took a breath. "I can play the Sibelius concerto in my sleep. I recorded it with the Detroit Symphony when I was fifteen. I just need a violin."

My old life was gone. But I could still do the job.

David set down his coffee. "Are you sure? Because there's no going back."

"I'm sure."

He looked at Mikhail, then Enrique. "Okay, then. Isobel can replace Lucia this weekend. We'll cancel the quartet concert in Cochabamba."

Instead of responding, Mikhail scowled, reached for a cold chicken *salteña*, and stuffed the pastry into his mouth.

"We have a plan," Enrique told Raysa, with surprising authority. "I'll call Gualberto in Cochabamba. You manage the announcements."

Raysa exhaled with relief. "Perfect. Instead of a sensational Argentine soloist, we'll have an amazing prodigy from the States." She bounced out of the room, her heels clacking on the linoleum.

Enrique's eyes met mine in gratitude. "Thank you, Isobel." He whispered something to Arminda, and the old woman shuffled slowly over to me, carrying a cup and saucer.

"*Bueno,*" she said, simply. "*Bueno.*"

"Why me?" Three hours later, Mikhail was still refusing to loan me his violin. "Why do I have to give up my instrument?"

We were in *Heladería Dumbo*, a cafe on the Prado with cartoonish art, ice cream specialties, and classic rock on the sound system. A friendly neon elephant flapped its giant ears above the door.

"I'm a professional," I told him, digging the large brown seeds out of my cherimoya ice cream. "And I will do a good job, no matter what instrument I'm playing. It's bad enough for Lucia that she's in the hospital and can't play. She doesn't need to be hearing people say how well I played her concerto on her own violin."

"Listen to reason, Mikhail." David's voice grew edgy. He tugged a straw from its wrapper and shoved it into his Coke. "Just give Isobel your violin. For 36 hours."

Mikhail pulled his glasses off his face and began rubbing them with a napkin. "So everyone's worried about Lucia, about how she'll feel if Izzy plays her Vuillaume. What about me? I performed the Sibelius at Curtis! I can play that concerto too."

David gave him a hard stare. "Do you have it memorized right now? Do you have it under control? If you don't, then shut up and give Isobel your violin."

"No fucking way." Mikhail grabbed his Cuban sandwich and stormed out.

David shook his head and squeezed lime into his Coke, and I listened to the sounds of the cafe. Children laughing, lovers whispering, and a man's voice singing of heartbreak and loneliness.

Outside, a group of men in green-grey uniforms trotted in pairs across the promenade. I watched them pass. "Enrique says the miners are protesting near the cathedral. Something about the politicians exploiting the natural resources."

David shrugged. "Government-sponsored looting. It's no different in the States." He reached into his leather coat and pulled out his phone, his face weary and drawn.

"It's okay, you know." I told him. "I can play the Vuillaume. I just thought it would be better if we asked Mikhail." I took a bite of ice cream, and the cherimoya melted slowly on my tongue.

He was quiet for a moment. "I know."

"I just . . ." I drew a ragged breath. "I don't want to mess things up. This quartet is so important to me, and I'm trying so hard to get things right, but sometimes I feel like everything I do is wrong."

I remembered suddenly that I still hadn't called the nurses at Prairie St. James. I still hadn't spoken to my mother.

"You aren't ever going to get things right with Mikhail," David said reluctantly. "He hasn't been happy since you joined the quartet."

I focused on my green paper placemat. "Is it because I'm too young?"

David snorted and sipped his Coke. "It's because you're too good. We all know you could play circles around Mikhail, even Lucy, if you wanted to. I've heard your recordings, Isobel. You've got no business, playing viola in a chamber group. Lucy heard you play, and she was obsessed. She couldn't imagine choosing anyone else. I wanted her to be happy, and I knew I could work with you. I knew you could adapt to playing chamber music. But Mikhail—"

"What?"

"When we had Rachel, Mikhail always knew where he stood. She was a great player, but we all knew she was the weak link in the quartet. Like a lot of viola players."

"No offense," he added quickly. "But now Mikhail's the weak link. And he hates it."

"I'm sorry," I whispered. "I didn't know."

All my life, the answer to every problem had always been 'Work harder.' That was my strength. I simply practiced harder than anyone else. But I wasn't good at dealing with problems that involved people. I'd never had to learn how.

David nudged my frosted ice cream bowl. "How's the cherimoya?"

"It tastes like apple juice. But it's got seeds in it."

He leaned over to examine the brown seeds. "You think you're supposed to eat them?"

"I don't know," I began, and then I realized he was teasing me.

The rest of the day was a blur. I arrived at *Teatro Municipal* for rehearsal, listened to Balcones sputter and complain, and managed to run through the entire Sibelius concerto on Lucia's beautiful French violin.

Back at the hotel, I rifled through the evening gowns in my trunk, finally pulling out a leftover dress from my soloist days, a tea-length peach gown with a demure neckline and tiny ruffles.

I put it on, stepped into my ballet flats, and consulted the mirror. With my hair in pigtails and my freckles on display, I could pass for fourteen again.

It wasn't really that hard, slipping back into the role of the precocious child star. I knew the whole routine. I simply had to show up and conquer one of the great warhorses of the violin repertoire, looking as young and innocent as possible. The audience would marvel at my talent, fawn condescendingly over my youth, and mutter afterwards that they were pretty sure I'd never had a life.

What was difficult—or maybe even impossible—was knowing how to move on, how to build an identity as an adult musician. I remembered turning seventeen last fall and buying a new, low-cut red dress to wear for a recital in New York. After my Franck sonata ended, I sensed something different in the air. Something voyeuristic, possessive.

I put that dress away afterward.

At 6:00 P.M., I called the family line at Prairie St. James. The head nurse, Carissa Jones, sounded angry and defensive. "I'm sure Dr. Himmelman told you: your mother doesn't want to hear your voice. It's interfering with her treatment."

"I understand," I said, tears welling up in my eyes. I paced in front of the bed and gripped the satin fabric of my skirt. By force of will, I tried to make the tears go away. "I won't say anything, I promise. I just want to hear her."

And then I couldn't help myself, and I was crying like a child, my chest heaving painfully with each ugly sob. "I'm sorry," I said, gulping for air. "I only want to listen. Please. She's my mom."

"Just a minute, Isobel." Carissa's voice softened. She placed her phone on mute.

I forced myself to stop crying and carried the Stahler over to the door, setting it beside Lucia's Vuillaume. Then I heard music coming through the phone, fragments of a beautiful, achingly familiar melody. The phrasing was unmistakable.

Carissa Jones was back on the line. "Are you there?"

"That's my recording," I insisted. "That's my Tchaikovsky concerto. That's me."

"I know. I'm going to put this on speakerphone so you can hear."

The sound shifted abruptly as she switched the phone to speaker. Through the static I could hear the second movement of the Tchaikovsky violin concerto. I could hear my violin soaring above the orchestra. Clear, perfect, impossibly sweet.

Then I heard my mother's voice, desolate as an abandoned puppy.

"My baby," she cried as the orchestra swelled. "My poor little girl."

THE ENCORE

Enrique and Ambassador Melton met me backstage at *Teatro Municipal.* The green room felt like a walk-in freezer, and I'd resorted to playing imaginary cadenzas with my left hand and wearing a bulky fleece glove on my right. Raysa Veizaga was acting as my unwelcome wingman.

Not that there was anything wrong with Raysa, but she wasn't my mom, and no one else had ever waited backstage with me before a solo performance. Whether it was Houston, Chicago, or Vienna, my mom would have found a ripe banana for me to eat, and she would have kept the chatter to a minimum.

My mom would have done a lot of things, but I knew she wasn't ever going to be that person or do those things again. She was gone, and I was finally beginning to understand what had taken her.

It was a relief when Raysa took a break and I saw Enrique and Ambassador Melton peering through the door of the green room. The ambassador held out an elegantly minimalist box of pralines.

"Our lovely soloist!" he declared. Pompous older men used the word 'lovely' to refer to anything female, which wasn't exactly a distinctive compliment.

I accepted the chocolates with a professional smile, acutely aware that my ruffled peach dress and pigtails had taken half a decade off my age. I was back in the circus freak-show again.

The ambassador was straining the seams of his too-tight tuxedo, but Enrique looked devastatingly handsome in a custom charcoal suit.

"We're so grateful—" Enrique began, but I cut him short.

"Please, Enrique. Don't thank me." I rustled the fingers of my fleece glove and looked around for my water bottle. "I'm just glad I can help."

Ambassador Melton approached the coffee table, where the Stahler and the Vuillaume were resting in their cases. "And this is Lucia's famous violin!"

Enrique lifted a restraining hand, but Melton was already picking up the violin.

"Ambassador! I really need to tune that," I snapped, rushing forward and reaching for the violin. Lucia's Vuillaume was worth a half a million dollars.

"So sorry," the ambassador said, relinquishing the violin. "You'll forgive me. But may I—could I please see the crest?"

I turned it over so he could see the coat of arms painted on the flame-colored maple back. Vuillaume's best instruments were illustrated with the heraldry of whatever nineteenth-century prince commissioned them, and Lucia's violin featured a golden shield with a black phoenix *affronté,* surrounded by flames.

"Extraordinary," he breathed, his stubby fingers reaching to touch the outspread raven wings. "The black phoenix."

I straightened the cloth I'd been using to cover the chinrest and exchanged an anxious glance with Enrique.

"We'd better let Isobel get ready," Enrique said briskly. "She needs to keep her fingers warm."

"Of course," the ambassador whispered, his eyes still on the phoenix. Then, as if sensing he'd made a social error, he took note of my Stahler.

"And this is your viola!" he exclaimed, rubbing his hands together. "Such a unique shade of orange. And the carvings on the f-holes are so ornate. How very nice."

"Enough, Jack," Enrique said, interrupting the

ambassador's rhapsodies. "Isobel needs to get ready."

"My apologies," Ambassador Melton said, his gaze returning to the Vuillaume. His watery blue eyes looked eager, almost greedy.

Enrique leaned close. "Ready, Isobel?"

I took a breath, feeling the princess seams of my silky dress pressing into my ribcage. "I'm ready."

"Then break a leg." Enrique left to find his seat, first brushing my cheek with an unexpected kiss. He turned in the doorway just for a moment.

"You'll be perfect," he said, and then he was gone.

I watched Enrique go, my cheek tingling, not sure what I was feeling. Nerves, maybe. Or something else.

"Ah! Josefina," said the ambassador, who still hadn't left. A woman came in with Raysa, and I realized I knew her face.

Her long brown hair was pulled back, revealing sensitive features and luminous, melancholy brown eyes. *The woman from the rehearsal.*

She reached for the ambassador's arm, and under her dark shawl, I could see she was heavily pregnant.

"May I present my wife," said Ambassador Melton, with the smug air of a man who knows he's gotten lucky. "Darling, this is Isobel Linden."

"It's a pleasure to meet you," I said, awkwardly holding out my gloved right hand. She smiled for just a moment, lightly squeezed my glove, and then seemed to wilt.

"I'm so eager to hear you play," she said in lightly accented English. But her eyes displayed no eagerness at all, only dread. Her face was strangely familiar to me, like a sepia-tinted photograph of a long-dead ancestor, taken from a dusty old album.

I watched her and the ambassador walk away. Then I wrenched my mind back to the opening notes of the Sibelius concerto. I had work to do.

During the rollicking Brahms overture, I peeked through the curtains to see the audience. I couldn't spot Enrique anywhere, but Ambassador Melton was in a private balcony nearest the stage, his large pink face and reddish blonde hair clearly visible in the sea of dark hair. Sitting next to him was Josefina, her body huddled under her alpaca shawl.

I stepped back from the curtain, unexpectedly disquieted, and went to find Raysa.

"I'll leave this with you," I said, brushing rosin dust from the Stahler. "If I need an encore, I might use the viola."

"Sure," Raysa said, not looking up from her text message. Then I heard applause.

Jean Sibelius was a tormented, alcoholic man, and his pitch-dark personality is written into every note of his violin concerto. One early critic called the concerto "boring Nordic dreariness." It's full of gloom, even the mock-military *danse macabre* at the end. But it's not boring at all. It's electrifying.

I led Balcones out onto the stage and took a bow. The lights were so bright I couldn't see any of the audience, except in the private balconies near the stage. Ambassador Melton and his wife were applauding politely. Behind them, his long fingers caressing the red velvet curtain, stood a gaunt, pale man without eyebrows.

My ankles buckled and I nearly lost my balance, suddenly wrenched apart by a vision so potent it must have been a memory: a dark stain on a white surface, the stench of something burning. *He's come back.*

I wanted to cry out, to stop what I knew was about to happen. But it was already too late. Like water bubbling in a tiny fountain, the violins in the orchestra had already begun their soft, shimmering entrance.

I lifted my bow, and I began to play.

The Allegro gave way to the Adagio without a moment to breathe, and my fingers danced through one virtuoso passage after another, while my mind struggled to stay focused, to keep my blinders on. The only thing that mattered was the music.

But when we finally reached the break before the third movement, I let the blinders slip, and I saw the pale man drift closer to Josefina. Her head rested on her hand, her face drained, sick, and desperate. Unseen, he was stroking her fine hair with his long, bony fingers. Ignoring me.

Maestro Balcones whipped the cellos and basses into the frenzied drum-like beat of the *danse macabre*. The third movement had begun, and I'd finally grasped what was happening. Josefina was in danger, and I had no power to stop it. Not with my power as a musician, not with Lucia's violin. Yesterday, I'd been able to draw the pale man's attention, using the same viola that had landed Lucia in the hospital.

It was the Stahler that was setting him on fire.

At the end of the Sibelius, Balcones pulled out all the stops, giving the horns and the trombones a chance to bellow and surge before the entire concerto came crashing to a halt. Applause thundered through the hall, with an immediate ovation.

I took a bow, but my thoughts were with the pale man. I had to stop him.

I came out for my curtain call holding the Stahler, knowing what I had to do. But Enrique was waiting below the stage, his dark eyes shining. He held up a bouquet of salmon-colored roses. He'd matched them to my dress.

"Thank you, Enrique." As I accepted the roses, our hands touched, and his broad face sparked with a sudden smile.

I quickly handed the roses to the concertmaster. Then, without giving the audience a chance to quiet down, I immediately began to play, my eyes fixed on the pale man. I didn't know what I was playing, and I knew I would never be able to remember. But it didn't matter. I had his attention, and that of everyone else in the hall.

His tight, stretched features took on a look of wonderment, and he moved away from Josefina, resting his long arms on the velvet-covered railing before him.

I kept playing, and the eerie haunting music filled the darkened hall. It filled my heart, opening heavy doors that led to cold rooms deep underground. I played on.

Then I made a mistake: I allowed myself to gaze into those hollow eyes. There was nothing there.

My fingers clenched, and the viola bow slipped from my hands, hitting the floor with a sickening snap. I stooped down to pick up my fallen bow and realized something was terribly wrong.

Behind me, the National Orchestra was motionless. Before me, the audience was transfixed. The ambassador and Josefina were immobile. In the front row, an old woman was frozen in the act of adjusting her glasses. No one was moving at all.

Then I heard footsteps. Henrik Paulsen came striding down the center aisle, his long hair gleaming in the dim light. As he approached the stage, I could make out the expression on his face: absolute fury.

"What have you done?" he hissed, reaching up and grabbing at the broken bow. I snatched it up and pulled it out of his reach.

"I'm trying to help!" I looked from Paulsen to the pale man, who still watched, unblinking.

"I'm no musician," Paulsen spat out, "but I recognize a summoning spell when I hear one. Do you even know what you've awakened?"

"I haven't awakened anyone," I said, pointing at the pale man, who was now striking his hands together, in slow, ironic applause. "He was already here."

Paulsen turned to face the pale man, something terrible in his eyes.

"Him?" he said contemptuously. "He's the least of your problems."

THE PEÑA

The encore ended abruptly, leaving the audience in waking confusion. Everyone agreed it was beautiful, and the next day the critic from *La Razón* would describe it as a "strikingly original composition, sadly interrupted when the soloist broke her bow."

No one was certain what caused me to drop the bow. Some said a white bird had swiftly flown across the theater, flashing its wings in front of me as I played. Others claimed the disruption was a bouquet of pale roses someone tossed onto the stage. Enrique thought he'd glimpsed a tall man at the base of the stage, and the bright flash of a forbidden camera. I couldn't tell him what I saw.

"Please, Isobel. Just say something." Sitting with me in the green room while the orchestra plodded through the Mahler symphony, Enrique tried to bring me back from the edge. "Talk to me. Tell me what I can do."

But I was sick with horror and despair, and a black shroud was slowly constricting my vision, canceling out everything on the periphery, leaving only a narrow circle of images in the space before me. I couldn't see. A blunt, prickling numbness spurred my fingertips and needled my upper lip.

Enrique tried again, taking hold of my hands. "It can be repaired. Or replaced. Give me your insurance card, and I'll call them right now, so you can file a claim."

I looked into his kind, worried eyes, wondering what he was talking about. Then I got it: he thought I was worried about the bow.

"It's a Sartory," I managed to say, clinging to the name of the bow-maker as if it were a lifeline. "It's worth more than a new car."

Enrique nodded, his face somber. "I know."

But he didn't know. He didn't know that I didn't give a damn about a few shreds of horsehair and a piece of wood, no matter how valuable. I didn't give a damn about scrapping an encore in front of 1,200 people.

What mattered, the only thing that mattered, was the huge, terrifying gulf between us. Whatever his grandfather had done, whatever curse lay upon him and his family, Enrique still lived in the world as a normal human being. Could I say the same?

Cringing, I remembered the coffin-like silence of the ornate concert hall, and the stale rush of warm air as the gears of time began to turn once more. Paulsen had stared at the pale man, his face as grim as a duelist with a sword. Then he'd headed for the nearest exit, as the audience began to murmur and stir.

If I was right, then Paulsen was some kind of monster who could challenge death and stop time. But what did that make me?

When the Mahler symphony finally ended, I realized that Raysa Veizaga was nowhere to be found. Her wool coat rested on the sofa in the green room, its embroidered lapels strangely faded. I hadn't seen her since I changed instruments for the encore.

Apprehensive, I peered into the hallway, wondering why she hadn't been watching Lucia's precious violin.

"Raysa left her coat," I told Enrique, not wanting to alarm him, not wanting to alarm myself. Surely, she was fine.

"She's probably in the lobby, chatting with patrons," Enrique said with a shrug, and offered to drive me home.

"Unless you're hungry," he added, looking hopeful. "Have you had dinner?" It was after ten o'clock.

"I never eat much before a concert," I said, realizing

belatedly that he was asking me out on a date. It was finally happening: I'd finally met someone I actually wanted to spend time with, on a day when it didn't matter anymore.

"You must be starving. Let me take you to a *peña*, and we'll get a late dinner, maybe some *chairo*."

I lifted my chin, determined to see things through. People were counting on me. "Deal. But only if you promise not to mention the bow."

"Deal," Enrique said. "But may I tell you how brilliant your Sibelius was?"

"God, no. I've heard that. *Ad nauseam.*"

"Then let me tell you something else instead."

I watched him warily. "What?"

Enrique leaned close, his voice barely more than a whisper. "It's going to be okay."

Exhausted, I closed my eyes. "Thank you."

When I opened them again, Enrique was reaching for the strap of my viola case. I tugged it out of his reach.

"Could you carry the Vuillaume instead?" I held out Lucia's leather case. "It's worth a fortune, and I'm not trusting myself anymore."

I slung the Stahler over my shoulder. I almost expected the case to be vibrating with inhuman malice, but I felt nothing. Nothing at all.

The *peña* was in a colonial building near the old plaza. The air smelled like grilled meat and cumin, and the musicians were setting up on a cramped stage in the back.

"Raysa told us you're a pianist," I said as we found our table. "Do you ever play with a group?"

Enrique shook his head, black hair shining under the tavern lights. "I don't get many chances to perform." He sounded almost regretful.

"But anyway," he produced a sudden, lopsided grin, "I'm a patron, not a player."

"You're a wonderful patron," I said gently, wondering if there was more to the story. I'd given up so much, to be who I was. I'd given up my entire childhood. But I never could have given up my music. Not for anything.

We sat down near the front of the old tavern, and Enrique turned his chair so he could see both the musicians and me. A wave of hair had escaped one of my pigtails, and he reached forward to brush it from my face, looking as if a curtain had just been raised. Feeling his fingers grazing my skin, I nervously examined the red tablecloth.

Enrique tucked the wayward lock behind my ear, saying, "Much better," as he smoothed it into place. I glanced up to see him smiling at me.

"Those are beautiful earrings."

"Thanks. I can't wear anything too shiny on stage, so it's usually just the same black pearls, all the time." I felt a familiar twist of pain in my chest, but I went on. "They were a gift from my dad."

"Do your parents worry, when you travel without them? Or are they used to it by now?"

I shook my head. "My dad died four months ago. And my mom—that's complicated. She's in the hospital."

I caught myself in the middle of a sigh, and managed to smile instead. I was not going to collapse into a ball of self-pity on my first, and probably only, date.

"God." Enrique reached for my hand and took a breath, searching for words. "I'm sorry. I do know what it's like, being on your own like that. It gets better."

"Thank you." I looked at his hand covering mine, feeling relieved, somehow.

The musicians were still setting up as we ordered our *chairo*, which was apparently a traditional La Paz stew made from meat and *chuños*.

"*Chuños*. Are those the dehydrated potatoes we had at the *Club de La Paz*?"

Enrique nodded. "They're crushed under the feet of barefoot farmers, to get all the moisture out. Then frozen until they're black. They've been a staple here since the days of the Tiwanaku Empire."

"I'm going to trust that you know what you're doing, ordering this *chairo* stew. Because the *chuños* we had at the *Club de La Paz* tasted like Styrofoam."

Enrique held my gaze and smiled. "I do know what I'm doing."

He murmured with approval as a short woman in a colorful folk costume stepped onto the stage. "Maria Halas is here. This will be different."

"Different?"

"The Potosi style. It's like a Chinese opera singer. Or a patient in a dentist's chair. You'll see."

"I'm lucky to be here with an expert," I said, and sipped some Diet Coke. Enrique had ordered a tall amber glass of *Paceña* beer, which surprised me somehow.

"I'm an enthusiast, not an expert," he said with a shrug.

I nudged his glass. "So a *Paceña* is a girl from La Paz?"

"Exactly." Enrique raised his glass, and his eyes met mine. "Here's our very traditional, somewhat sexist toast: 'To *Paceña*, the blonde who never betrays you.'" He looked so ludicrous with his foamy beer and his custom charcoal suit, that in spite of everything, I burst out laughing.

"To *Paceña*," I echoed, clinking his glass. My whole life was in ruins, and I was in a bar, drinking and laughing with a cursed boy. I'd have to chalk that one up to denial.

For a moment I felt immune, as if the cold anger in Paulsen's eyes could never touch me again. It was such a relief to be with someone normal, someone who couldn't see the pale man, who didn't know I was a monster. Everything with Enrique was so easy.

He seemed so gentle, so untroubled, not at all like someone whose family was cursed. I wished I knew him better. I wished I had the courage to ask.

"So the singer's from Potosi?" I asked. "Where the famous silver mines are."

"Where the silver mines *were*. It's mostly zinc and other metals now. In my grandfather's day it was tin. Potosi is one of the highest cities in the world, over fourteen thousand feet. But it's not too far from Sucre, or from the place where Paulsen's team is working."

I swirled my drink with a straw, trying to remember whether I'd discussed Paulsen's dig with Enrique.

Then I decided to plunge in. "Mikhail wants to see Paulsen's mummies when we get to Sucre, and he really wants to visit a mine. He likes to say I got myself cursed, when I broke the ambassador's statue."

For a moment, I saw Mikhail's smug grin as his fingers traced a clumsy cross over the porous clay of *Tio's* forehead. I saw myself grabbing his arm, only to watch a crack spread across the statue, only to feel something dry and intangible pass through us, as if . . .

Enrique raised an eyebrow. "Does Mikhail really believe you've been cursed?"

"Probably not. But can I tell you something?" I asked, my chest tightening.

"Of course."

I looked into his dark, fathomless eyes. "I didn't touch that statue. Mikhail did. He doesn't remember."

Enrique frowned, confused. "But you took the blame."

"Somebody had to. Mikhail may have a master's degree, but he doesn't really do that whole responsibility thing, you know?"

"Believe me, I do know." Enrique looked weary, and I thought about the weight he was carrying: sponsoring a national concert series, helping us with Lucia's illness. Most guys his age were starting college, taking calculus, drinking beer.

Granted, Enrique was drinking beer.

"I don't think Mikhail needs to worry about being cursed." Enrique spoke slowly, as if choosing his words with care. "But mines are dangerous, so if he wants to see another statue of *Tio*, he should probably just come over to my house."

"You have a statue of *Tio*?" I asked, disbelieving.

Enrique smiled. "I do."

"But why?" I asked, and immediately realized how rude that sounded. "I mean, where did you get it?"

"It belonged to my father, from my grandfather's mine. It's

to make sure I don't forget."

"Forget?"

"My responsibilities. To my family, to the mining cooperative." Enrique started to say something more, and stopped.

"But isn't *Tio* evil? The ambassador was telling us—"

"The ambassador is an American. He doesn't really understand *ch'alla*—the ritual of exchange. He imagines that *Tio* is a demon sent to punish the wicked, exactly the same as the devil of Christianity. But *Tio* is far more than that."

I ran a calloused finger along the top of my glass, trying to process this. "So, these miners. Do they think that if God can't help them, then maybe the devil will?"

"Something like that."

"What do *you* think?" Raysa had said that Enrique was Catholic.

Enrique shrugged, his eyes far away. "I think if you believe in the devil, then you've given him power. And then you'll have to contend with that power."

My throat constricted, and I remembered the pale man's slow, ironic applause in the frozen concert hall. Paulsen didn't fear him, despite knowing what he was, despite seeing him with his own eyes. But Paulsen did fear something else, something he said I'd awakened. Whatever it was, I would have to contend with it.

A microphone crackled on my left. I turned my attention to the stage, which had a painted mural behind the musicians. The center of the mural featured a mustachioed Spanish man, with stylized flames and a ribbon of faded words above his head. The sides of the mural depicted native workers with baskets and shovels and hoes.

"Who's that man in the painting? What's he saying?"

"Murillo, one of the first rebels against the crown," Enrique said, as if it were obvious. Seeing my embarrassed look, he added, "This restaurant is close to the spot where he was lynched, in 1810. When he died, he said, *Yo muero, pero la tea que he encendido ya no podrán extinguirla los tiranos.*"

I liked the hushed way he recited those words, as if they had some secret meaning that few understood. *I will die, but the fire I've ignited no tyrant can extinguish.*

"Do you believe that? That Murillo's fire is still burning?"

Enrique set down his *Paceña* glass, his expression remote. "Bolivia has had over 150 attempted coups in its history, probably a world record. No dictator can stifle freedom in our country for long."

The musicians began to play a *cueca*, with strong binary rhythms and pentatonic harmonies. The bandleader struck an insistent beat on his tiny armadillo-backed guitar. The music spun like a kaleidoscope, and Enrique focused on the stage, where the singers circled each other, waving their handkerchiefs in a flirtatious dance.

Then Enrique reached over and briefly touched my arm, and my skin flared as if I'd been scorched. Shocked, I lifted my hands from the table.

"Listen," he whispered, his eyes still on the stage.

My gaze followed the elegant line of his hand, and my throat grew parched. His fingers circled the *Paceña* glass. He brought the glass to his lips.

How strange, I thought, and watched him drink. How very strange.

"Have you noticed?" Enrique set down his glass. "Most of these songs begin and end on the minor third."

The piece concluded just then on the minor third, leaving the song both open and complete. As the final chord resonated through the room, I sensed an unfamiliar emotion, right before it was spirited away. I began to applaud, and I wondered if the emotion had been joy.

I turned to Enrique, hoping to see something in his eyes, some kind of awareness or recognition. Had he felt it too? But his sharply angled chin was lowered, his hand reaching into the inner pocket of his dusky suit. He pulled out a thin black phone. It buzzed faintly in his hand.

He looked at the number and answered, just as the musicians began another *cueca*. The soprano shook a rattle made of sheep's hooves, and Enrique turned pale and touched his upper lip.

"I'll be right there," he said in Spanish and pushed back his chair.

"What is it?"

His face was like stone. "They've found Raysa Veizaga. She's dead."

THE MORGUE

How could an evening change so quickly?

Enrique's black Audi snaked through darkened, narrow streets on the way to *Hospital Obrero*. The cumin-laced scent of the smoky restaurant still lingered in my nostrils, but the musicians and their haunting panpipes were already taking on the quality of a dream. I felt as if I were again trapped with Paulsen in the oppressive silence of the concert hall, while my precious date with Enrique was fading from memory, slipping from my grasp, as if it had never been anything more than a momentary reprieve.

Enrique stared at the road, and I tried to ignore the scene that stubbornly played over and over in my mind. Raysa Veizaga was waiting for me backstage. She was reaching for the Stahler as I slipped the Vuillaume into its case, and then she was handing me the Stahler for the encore. I hit replay, and again she handed me the Stahler.

What happened to Raysa after that? Was I the last person to see her alive? When I returned from the disastrous encore, she was already gone.

The lobby of the hospital was surprisingly crowded. Unlike Thursday night, when we brought Lucia in, every seat in the waiting room was occupied. Old and young, whole families waited together, and the chatter of adults and the wailing of children ricocheted off the dull green walls.

The noises of the crowd felt sharp and unnatural, as if I'd suddenly become an old woman who couldn't manage the controls on her hearing aid. I stared mutely at the waiting families, letting their unreal voices pierce through me, while Enrique leaned over the desk and spoke with the tired-looking orderly. She picked up her phone and made a call.

Enrique turned to face me, his jaw set. "They need me to formally identify the body. Raysa's family lives in Santa Cruz, and I'm the one here in La Paz who knew her best."

His eyes dropped to my collarbone. "You don't have to come in, you know. You can wait here. I'll take you back to the hotel as soon as I can."

"I'm going with you."

"I already know you're brave, Isobel. You don't have to prove anything to me."

"I don't have to prove anything to anybody. But Raysa was our publicist here, and she was our friend. And I may have been the last person to see her alive."

"That doesn't mean—"

"Enrique, I'm going to see her."

He pressed his lips together and sighed. "We'll go together then."

The Bolivian police were waiting for us in the morgue. The officer in charge took one look at my blonde pigtails and silky peach dress and decided I was unfit to view Raysa's body.

"*No se admiten niños,*" he said, blocking our way. He gestured to a sofa in a nearby waiting room.

Enrique stepped between us, his voice low. They turned away. During their brief discussion, Enrique said my name, and the officer looked past Enrique's shoulder, eyeing me suspiciously. I stared coolly back. Then Enrique handed him Lucia's violin case, several folded bills curled against the leather strap. The officer walked over to me, his expression thick with disdain, and tugged at the Stahler hanging from my shoulder.

"Let's go in," Enrique said.

It's possible that all autopsy rooms look the same. Clean tile walls, gurneys with sturdy locking casters, and banks of refrigerated metal boxes, stacked three shelves high. Occupying the center of the room was a large illuminated island with a stainless steel sink attached to one end, which reminded me, inexplicably, of an expensive hair salon.

What a photograph could never capture or convey was the alarming scrape of metal against metal, the astringent odor, or the chilly, oppressive sense of time. A tense urgency filled the room, as if it held deep secrets and was accustomed to keeping them.

A stunted orderly in green scrubs met us at the threshold and led us to a gurney covered with a white sheet, where a dry, dusty scent rose into the air, like a parched plot of land in the desert sun. The orderly turned his back, standing watch while the policeman lifted the sheet.

What I'd feared couldn't have prepared me for the reality of seeing Raysa lying there on the gurney. Somehow, I'd imagined that she would look as though she were asleep. I'd visualized her arched eyebrows, precise lipstick, and smooth, highlighted hair, and tried to imagine those features on a dead Raysa, peacefully asleep.

But the tortured body on the gurney wasn't sleeping, and she hadn't died in peace.

Raysa's brown and leathery lips were pulled back from her teeth, exposing dried, blackened gums and a wild grimace of a smile. Her hair stood out in clumps like stiff straw. Her hands clawed the air with bony, desiccated fingers, and whole sections of her papery skin were peeling away from her knotted muscles and pulling free from the bony smoothness of her skull.

She died in pain, I thought, forcing myself to look. She died in terrible pain.

I fought against a surge of nausea. Enrique stared at Raysa's mummified body and covered his mouth with his hand. Then Paulsen's voice sounded in my memory, so fierce and so clear that my knees buckled and I went down.

Do you even know what you've awakened?

With quick efficiency, the policeman lifted me to my feet

and marched me out of the room.

"No," I cried, trying to regain my footing, trying to turn myself around.

Obviously experienced with shell-shocked visitors to the morgue, the police officer half-dragged me to the sofa outside, rotated my body to face him, and nudged me into a sitting position on the burgundy fabric. Then he returned to the morgue, leaving me with the musical instruments and the stacks of magazines.

I watched the door swing shut and swore aloud. I wasn't a little child who had to be protected from the truth. I'd seen the dead before. I'd stood soaking wet in the kitchen of my own home, watching the life drain from my father's body. I'd seen the dead, and I'd seen the pale man who took them for his own.

The tension in my body surged, and a sharp pain compressed my forehead. I wanted more than anything to cry, but my eyes felt parched and scratchy. I tipped my head back and tried to fill my lungs with air.

Then the door connecting the morgue to the rest of the hospital opened, revealing a tall man with high cheekbones and long, sun-bleached hair.

"Miss Linden," Henrik Paulsen said. "This is a surprise."

I bit my lip, surprised to find that I was not at all surprised. "You," I said accusingly. "Of course."

"What are you doing here?" Paulsen asked, stepping aside as a pair of orderlies wheeled in a body. His voice sounded rough, and his hair looked limp and tangled.

I ignored him and began paging through a Bolivian women's magazine.

Paulsen picked up a side chair and placed it next to the sofa, facing me. "Are you going to answer my question?"

I curled the magazine into a stiff roll. "I'm getting my kicks, obviously. What are you doing here?"

He glanced down, touched the white scar that crossed the knuckles of his right hand, its stitch marks jutting out like fish-bones. "David called. He said Raysa was dead."

"Then you already know why I'm here."

Paulsen leaned back in his chair, and for a moment the room was silent. "You've got that backwards, Isobel. I already know why Raysa's dead. It's because you're here. But why? What are you doing in La Paz?"

"You think this is my fault?" I tossed the magazine aside and threw up my hands, disbelieving. "I haven't done anything, Paulsen. We're on tour here. The concerts, the master classes—this is what we do for a living."

"Why Bolivia? Why now?"

"Enrique Rodriguez. He sponsored our tour. Now answer my question. Is this really my fault?"

Paulsen's faded eyes held mine. "It is. I know it."

I stared at him, stricken. All at once, I was back at the ambassador's party, meeting him for the first time, seeing myself fixed under his microscope. I couldn't speak, and the tongue in my mouth didn't seem to belong to me.

Before I could find my voice, a slender woman in a white coat entered, flicking through a chart. Paulsen shrugged out of his coat and extracted a card from his wallet.

He presented the doctor with his card. "Raysa Veizaga?"

The doctor nodded, her voice hushed. Perhaps she told him then what I already knew: that something hotter and crueler than a desert sun had turned Raysa into leather.

I felt a slight chill, and for a moment I heard the sound of a distant radio. Paulsen looked across the room at me, cold and aloof as a tree in winter. The fury he'd shown in the concert hall was gone. Raysa was dead, and no amount of anger would change that.

He tried next to retrieve his coat, but the interruption from the doctor had given me time to overcome my shock, and I wasn't about to let him walk away.

"You hateful bastard," I snarled, sliding over to sit on his coat and clutching the edges in my fists. "There isn't enough pain in the world already? You want to add to mine? You belong here in the morgue, where no one has to listen to your bullshit accusations. And you're *not* getting your coat back."

"I can live with that," Paulsen said dispassionately. "People can live with anything. But only if they keep their blood circulating."

I tried not to look at him.

He leaned closer. "How do you keep your blood circulating?"

"I breathe, Paulsen. You should try it sometime."

He blinked once. "Fine. You don't have to tell me the truth. Just be sure you tell yourself the truth."

I faltered, sick with a sudden fear. "What's that supposed to mean?"

He looked past me to the morgue, where Enrique and the police officer were exiting the cold room in silence. Enrique's face was bloodless and gray.

I got to my feet. "Enrique?"

Paulsen retrieved his coat and headed for the door. "The truth, Isobel," he said under his breath. "When you're done playing games, give me a call."

A MESSAGE

I woke the next day surrounded by light. I'd been too exhausted to close the drapes when I got home, and now the morning sun was spilling through the hotel windows.

The Stahler and the Vuillaume rested silently on Lucia's untouched bed, the room as empty as a deserted theater. I tipped my head back and stared at the ceiling, and soon the white plaster surface became a screen for the dancing threads of shadow that moved across the surface of my eyes. 'Floaters,' my father had called them.

It's like looking at snow, I thought, remembering the many times I'd trudged through winter cold with insubstantial shadows flickering across my gaze. I could see those spots of darkness, but only when surrounded by emptiness and light. Yet they had always been there, right before my eyes.

At 10:00 AM, Enrique met Mikhail and me at the hotel, and we drove back to the hospital, not speaking of Raysa. Enrique gave Mikhail an appraising look as he crawled into the back seat, then turned to me as if to say, *It stays between us.*

I respected that. I had secrets of my own, even from myself.

Uncomfortable with any amount of silence, Mikhail carried the conversation.

"I picked up our mail in the lobby," he gloated, "And look

what I got. Henrik gave me a copy of his new book, *The Natural History of Mummies*. See? Cambridge University Press. He gave it to me."

He leaned forward between the leather seats and held out a glossy paperback, which had a grisly photo of a bog mummy on the cover. The mummy was curled into a fetal position, her leathery skin the shade of moldy hazelnuts.

Enrique's hand twitched on the steering wheel, and the car wavered for an instant on the crowded exchange in front of the Americas Bridge.

"God, that's disgusting," I said, trying not to recoil. "Was there any other mail?"

Mikhail diminished a few sizes and scowled. "Just a card from the ambassador. And this thing for you." He shoved a small envelope into my hand.

I saw the jagged handwriting on the envelope and slipped it into my jacket. Beside me, Enrique was focused on the traffic, following a crowded *Trufi* sedan across the long, slanting bridge into the *Miraflores* district.

I glanced into the back seat and saw the sullen droop of Mikhail's shoulders. He stared back at me, something dark and angular reflected in the lenses of his dirty glasses, something that never should have been there. I caught my breath and turned away, a bead of sweat prickling my upper lip. When I looked again, the apparition was gone.

"So, Paulsen's a world expert on mummies," I said, my voice neutral. "He probably wants to show us his burial site."

Mikhail lifted his narrow chin. "Last time I checked, he was just taking me. He knows you guys don't care." He glared pointedly out the window.

When we arrived at *Hospital Obrero*, Enrique reached for my hand, his fingers curling around mine. "I need to make some arrangements for Raysa's family. I'll pick you up before your concert. You have my number, Isobel."

I looked at him wordlessly, wanting to say something grateful, something comforting, something true. But there was nothing I could say.

"About the quartet," Enrique went on. "I know you can't practice anymore at Raysa's apartment. But I have a rehearsal space in my house, near the Witches' Market. Let the others know."

"Thank you." I squeezed his hand and got out of the car.

David stood waiting in the lobby, unwashed and unshaven, a bundle of newspapers tucked under one arm. He'd stuffed his black hair into a knitted cap.

"You okay, Isobel?" he asked, looking me over.

I took in the circles under his eyes. "I'm okay. You?"

He nodded, lips pressed like a clamp.

"We've all had a shock," he said, turning to Mikhail, "but we need to move forward. We're not going to talk about Raysa, okay? Not in front of Lucia."

Lucia was feeling better. We found her propped up in her adjustable hospital bed, her lips gleaming with fresh burgundy gloss, her chestnut hair swept into a sleek chignon. Her eyes were less hollow than the day before, as if she'd patted some extra skin around them during the night.

"The doctor says I can go home tomorrow morning," she said with brittle, forced cheer. "I'm almost fully rehydrated. Which is about time, because I am sick to death of these IVs, and I am sick to death of this hospital food. If Ambassador Melton hadn't brought the coffee and the fruit tray, I don't even know what I would have done."

"Hey," said Mikhail, approaching the breakfast platter. "They've got those green fruits that look like hand grenades." He picked one up and gave it an experimental toss.

"His wife Josefina helped me do my hair," Lucia went on, turning her head to show a profile view. "She really is very kind."

"The ambassador has a wife?" asked Mikhail. "Is he hiding her, like Bluebeard or something? Why haven't we seen her at any of the parties?"

Lucia sighed. "Do you have to be so melodramatic?"

David slid a few coral slices of mango onto a napkin and handed them to me. "She didn't say, but I think she's having a difficult pregnancy."

"Preeclampsia." Lucia said. "She's not allowed to spend much time on her feet. And now she's had such a terrible shock."

Was Raysa's death really such a shock to Josefina? I remembered the despair I'd seen in Josefina's eyes, the hopeless sense of dread. She had the face of a woman who expected tragedy to strike at any time.

Lucia's voice quavered and broke. "She and Raysa were working together on a charity project. They were raising money for a shelter in El Alto, to help women who were displaced by the coca eradication campaigns. Raysa was really committed."

We fell silent, thinking of Raysa Veizaga. It was all I could do to keep from screaming aloud.

It's my fault, I thought, and Paulsen knows it. But if that's true, then it's *all* my fault. Raysa. Lucia. The old man. My father.

Mikhail asked, "Is it true that Raysa was burned alive right behind the theater?"

Lucia's mouth opened in shock.

"Enough!" David said, with one of his blackest looks.

Mikhail set his jaw. "I'm just saying, it could have been Isobel instead. And if the guy who did it is still on the loose—"

David drew himself up to his full impressive height. "Nothing's going to happen to Isobel. We're going to look out for each other. End of story."

He shifted into his role as authoritative concert manager. "Let's read some reviews and see where we stand. The quartet concerts are selling out."

He opened his copies of *El Diario* and *La Razón* and insisted that Lucia translate the concert reviews. All the reviews were good, and none contained any negative speculations about whether our quartet concerts next week would actually happen.

Then Lucia found the article in *La Paz Perspective*, the English language weekend paper. The reviewer apparently served as both a food critic and a music critic, and his descriptions were saturated with ludicrous food imagery.

Lucia read aloud, using a lofty, highbrow tone of voice. "Mahler's first symphony, aptly known as 'The Titan,' is a weighty meal to which the Sibelius violin concerto makes a delicious pre-prandial aperitif." She grimaced with disgust. "The Sibelius violin concerto? A pre-prandial aperitif? Is he kidding?"

"What a joke," muttered David.

I shrugged. "Let's just hope that doesn't end up online."

"And listen to this," Lucia went on. "'Ms. Linden's tone is full-bodied and rich, with pleasing hints of smoke and honey.'"

"Full-bodied, huh?" Mikhail was incorrigible. "Did he even *look* at her?"

"Do you mind?" I snarled, completely losing my temper. "I didn't put my entire reputation on the line, with no advance notice and less than four hours of sleep, just so you could stand around and make jokes about the size of my chest."

Mikhail smirked. "I'm just saying—"

"The ambassador had more intelligent things to say," David said, cutting Mikhail off. "He said the audience was spellbound. He said the second movement was the most beautiful thing he's ever heard in La Paz."

Lucia brightened. "Yes. He was so glad you played my Vuillaume. He kept talking about what a magnificent, legendary instrument it is. He knew the names of *all* the previous owners, and he was so excited that you showed him the black phoenix on the back. It's like he's obsessed or something. Oh, and he's going to make some calls, so you can get a new viola bow."

I felt a flicker of dismay. The Stahler: it would need to be played again, and soon. We had quartet rehearsals, concerts. I had almost allowed myself to forget.

We were all quiet for a moment. Then Mikhail tossed his grenade fruit and caught it again. "Well, at least the Sibelius went okay," he said, surprising us all.

"Yes," Lucia straightened up. "Thank you, Isobel."

"I'm glad I can help," I said mechanically. As if lured off-course by an irresistible siren, my mind slipped back to the soaring notes of the Sibelius concerto, then struggled to block the horrible truth that followed: Paulsen's fury, the frozen silence of the encore. It couldn't have been real. But it was, and Raysa was gone.

"I'll be playing again soon." Lucia raised her fists like a prizefighter, boxing a few shadows. "I'm feeling better all the time."

"That's what we want to hear," David said, his voice tight. He bent his head suddenly over the breakfast tray, pouring everyone coffee.

Then Mikhail brought out his book of mummies, bragging about his close personal friendship with Henrik Paulsen, and he and David began to groan and shudder their way through the ghastly photographs.

I sat down by the window with my coffee and opened the envelope Mikhail had given me in the car. Inside was a gray sheet of stationery, with Paulsen's phone number at the top. Paulsen had written three sentences in a jagged, sprawling, cursive hand.

Do you remember what you said when we first met? Maybe the girl on the mountain was innocent. Maybe she even thought she was lucky.

I stared at the note, not sure I understood.

CODA

Mikhail reluctantly agreed to stay with Lucia for a few hours, so David and I shared a cab back to the hotel.

"Please take a shower," I begged as we entered the Hotel Miranda's lobby. "You've been at the hospital for two days, and you're disgusting."

"I will," David said, acknowledging the young receptionist with a practiced twitch of his eyebrows. "But we need to get started right away. Ambassador Melton said he'd help you find a bow."

I came to an abrupt stop, and the awful memory played itself again: *Raysa handed me the Stahler.*

"I can't."

"What?" David took my elbow and pulled me toward the elevator. "Isobel. You can't play Schubert—and certainly not Shostakovich—using one of Lucia's bows. We need to start looking."

"What's wrong with her old Hill bow?" I asked, stalling for time. "It's got to be better than anything we'll find in La Paz." I couldn't play the Stahler anymore. I had to stop.

"It weighs less than 60 grams. She told me." David steered me into the elevator and pushed the button for the third floor. "It won't project on a viola, and you'll never get a clear sound. Give me ten minutes to clean up, I'll call the ambassador, and we'll—"

"No!" I gripped the elevator rail beside me, holding on as if the elevator were about to plummet. David stared, struck speechless by my vehemence. He reached out to touch my shoulder, and I flinched.

"Please," I whispered, backing into the corner of the elevator. "I still have a concerto to play. On a violin that I don't even know very well. I can't be handling any viola bows. Not today."

David let his hands fall to his side. "You're right. I wasn't thinking. That would totally mess you up." The doors opened, and he followed me to my room. "I'll get something set up for Sunday, okay? And some fresh clothes for Lucia."

I inserted my card into the door, queasy with resignation. I would have to play the Stahler on Sunday. There wasn't a choice anymore. Perhaps there never had been.

"I can help you with the clothes," I muttered.

"No, you can't," David said, unslinging his backpack from his shoulder. "She doesn't trust either of us. I mean, what if we chose the wrong shoes?"

I snorted, and pointed to the dresser. "Her entire world would come to an end."

David consulted his list and began sorting through Lucia's designer lingerie. "She trusts you with the Sibelius, though. She never doubted you could just step in at the last minute and play."

I gave him a quick smile. "Really? What kind of pain meds do they have her on?"

"For what it's worth, I never doubted it either."

"Thanks." In the mirror above the dresser, I caught a glimpse of my face. There was a freckle above my right eyebrow that seemed darker than before.

You've had a lucky break, Paulsen told me when Lucia collapsed. *Don't let it happen again.* But there was no escape. There was nothing I could do.

I opened the safe and pulled out Lucia's jewelry roll, then slipped into the chair beside the dresser, trying not to look at the Stahler lying on the bed.

I hadn't touched it since the encore.

Resting on the dresser was Lucia's zippered calfskin portfolio, stuffed with sheet music and a Sibelius score. An omnibus edition of Tartini's "Devil's Trill" lay on top.

"Was Lucia going to use the Tartini cadenza for an encore?" I hadn't remembered her practicing it.

"Probably. She has before."

I remembered the moment in the ambassador's foyer, just before Mikhail touched the statue of *Tio*, just before he made the sign of a cross. What had he said to me?

"There's a long history of violinists who sell their soul to the devil. Tartini. Paganini. Dude down in Georgia. But never any stories about a little viola player."

I picked up the heavy vellum. A facsimile of Tartini's famous letter to Lalande was printed on the top. But I didn't need to read the letter. I knew the translation by heart.

One night, I dreamt I made a pact with the devil.

David lifted a stack of sweaters from the dresser. "Can I ask you something?"

"Sure."

"Why did you switch to viola in the first place? I mean, don't get me wrong. It's not that I think every violist is a failed violinist. But you're an incredible violinist. And playing the viola is so—" He paused, searching for something tactful to say.

"Limiting?" I'd heard that line of reasoning before. My father had said that.

"Exactly." He began stuffing a red cashmere V-neck into his backpack. "No offense."

I set down the Tartini music, reaching for the sweater. "Let me fold that. If you get it wrinkled, she'll kill you. And then we'll be without a cellist."

I rolled the sweater into a tube. "I never wanted to play the viola. I mean, my parents had their hearts set on my being a violinist. I just wanted to play that viola."

"The Stahler?" He handed me Lucia's black knitted skirt and I rolled it up.

"The Stahler."

"And your parents were cool with that?"

"They weren't." I held out the rolled-up skirt. "My dad wanted me to take it back. But after he died, it really didn't matter anymore."

David grew still. "Wow. You want to talk about that?"

I picked up a bottle of water and unscrewed the top. "Maybe some other time." *When hell freezes over.*

David picked up Lucia's velvet jewelry roll. "Your viola looks different, you know. Like the f-holes are too close to the bridge. Fantastic sound, though."

The sound wasn't the problem: it was the price. I imagined my beautiful mother, locked away in a sterile hospital room, her glossy brown hair turning file-cabinet gray. I would give anything to make her well. I would give everything.

I raised my chin, aware of my slump into self-pity. "That fantastic sound you've been hearing? That's not the Stahler. It's my technique."

"I'm sure you're right about that. I've never heard of Stahler before."

I shrugged. "Nobody has. He made only three instruments, and mine was the last one, before he cashed in his chips."

David paused unexpectedly over the jewelry roll, holding a glistening opal necklace I'd never seen Lucia wear. His expression was unreadable. "He gave up?"

"Not exactly," I said, and for some perverse reason, I started to laugh. "He killed himself instead."

After David left, I turned on my metronome and went through section after section of the Sibelius concerto, skipping the parts I knew I could manage without rehearsing. Even with a heavy chrome mute clamped onto the bridge, the Vuillaume resonated with clear, sweet beauty. But a faint, pulsing drone was seeping through the plaster walls, sabotaging my concentration.

I knew that music: I knew what it was now. It was the Stahler, demanding to be played. It was the pale man's voice, announcing his grisly place in the world.

I rested the Vuillaume in its case and reached for my water bottle. It was empty, all the bottles were empty. And I was so thirsty. I wondered if I should just drink a glass of tap water and risk a raging case of dysentery. What difference could it possibly make?

I unfolded Paulsen's note, reading it one more time. The dull gray paper fluttered in my hand. Why had Paulsen sent me that? There was nothing lucky about me.

Across the room, a brown canvas case rested on Lucia's bed. The Stahler.

I'm not going to play it, I told myself, approaching the case with dread. I'm just going to look.

The pulsing music droned on, pulling me closer.

With trembling hands, I opened the case and looked inside. The viola rested on the crushed velvet lining, its garish orange varnish gleaming in the afternoon light.

David had said the Stahler's f-holes were too close to the bridge. They were, and rather than forming simple curlicues at the ends, they bifurcated into ornate pairs of tendrils. I drew near the light of the window and lifted the Stahler to inspect the interior. A nondescript paper label was glued inside: *Georg Stahler. Dresden 1909.*

I tilted the instrument, peering inside. On the left side of the viola, below the tip of the f-hole, I could make out a faint mark on the maple back: a symbol like a target caught in the crosshairs. Above the symbol, a few smudged graphite letters.

My hands suddenly cold, I set the Stahler down.

I'd been reading music since I was three years old. I knew a coda mark when I saw one. A coda was a tail, the part of the song that came after the end.

"Oh, God," I said aloud.

It was true, then. I was the thing that came after the end.

I fled to the bathroom and peered anxiously into the mirror. Apart from the darkened freckle above my eyebrow, there were no surprises.

Lucia's expensive Swiss skin cream was sitting on the

counter. Inexplicably frantic, I unsnapped the cover and squeezed a dollop of rosemary-scented cream into my hand. I rubbed it into my face. I looked into the mirror, and a pale, freckled face stared back.

So many freckles. Lucia didn't have freckles. But my face was splattered with them, and in my shallower moments, I'd often worried they would turn into cancerous blights, or the kind of ugly age spots found on retired golfers in Florida.

At the hospital, I'd noticed that Paulsen's skin looked darker than it really was. His high cheekbones were covered with sun damage, and his faint freckles merged together with his tan. Every day, the sun and the wind were scarring his face and stripping the color from his hair.

Maybe I could trust him, even talk to him. Maybe he would understand.

I realized what I was thinking and snapped the lid back onto Lucia's skin cream. I would not be talking to Paulsen. He seemed to think I was some kind of zombie.

But he's wrong about that, I thought with disgust, and went to buy some bottled water. Whoever heard of a zombie with freckles?

On the way back from the Prado with my bottled water, I realized that I hadn't played the Stahler in nearly 20 hours. I was paying for it now. The long shadows of the afternoon sun were sucking me downward into the cold pavement. My chest felt hollow, and the droning voices of the dead thudded against my eardrums.

Somehow I made it back to the narrow deserted walkway between the Prado and the hotel. Then I watched my black shoes moving in slow motion and realized that taking another step would be impossible. I could barely hold up my head, let alone carry a bagful of water bottles. Simply breathing the thin air felt like a tenuous, heroic act.

I slumped against the wall and struggled to catch my breath. One of the Viscachani bottles tipped out of my canvas bag and rolled down the cobblestoned path. Detached, I watched as a polished pair of wingtip shoes approached the water bottle. Then the wingtips slowly rotated to face me.

I lifted my drooping head, just in time to see the smirking face of a brick-shaped man, whose pockmarked features were all too familiar. *Hurst.*

Before I could react, his right shoulder moved back. A fist suddenly appeared where his shoulder had been, exploding against my jaw. I felt the back of my head strike the brick wall, and I heard a dull, sickening thud. Everything went dark.

Then prisms of color and light gave way to a blurry wall, a hint of sky. Hurst was gripping my neck in a vice, his heavy forearm pressed hard against my throat.

Oh God, I thought, racked with pain. This can't be happening. Not to me.

Frantic, I grabbed at his arm, trying to pull it away from my neck, but Hurst tightened his bruising grip, almost crushing my airway.

I tried to scream, but only a dry rattling sound emerged from the back of my burning throat. I felt my legs giving way, felt myself sinking. Then I heard a crisp snapping sound and glimpsed the metal flash of a knife.

"No!" I struggled to get free, but Hurst held me tight in his grasp. I felt the knife rough against the back of my neck, and suddenly the pressure on my throat relaxed as the knife cut through my ponytail.

Hurst held a thick coil of blonde hair triumphantly in front of my eyes, his ragged breath hot against my cheek.

"We've established that you can feel pain," he whispered in my ear. "But what else can you feel?"

THE VISITOR

Hurst was standing over me, grinning, a clump of blonde hair gripped like a trophy in his beefy hand.

"Such pretty hair," he rasped. "Soft as a baby's. But you're not as young and innocent as you look, are you? I've seen your kind before, and I've brought them down."

Something fierce and unrecognizable surged inside me when he said that: a wild source of energy, an endless capacity for cruelty. It was an absolute mistake for him to stand around gloating, because I wasn't a nice girl anymore. If I ever had been.

With a harsh cry, I lunged forward and clawed at his sneering face, gaining traction when my fingers found one of his eyes.

"You won't need both of these," I hissed, driving my fingers inward and twisting hard. Hurst howled and tried to yank his head away, but he was standing too close. I heard him scream, and then I felt a sickening release of tension, as if a grape skin had given way in a wine press.

Hurst fled, screaming. I sank exhausted to the ground. My throat burned, and my entire jaw pulsed with fire. Bracing myself against the cool brick wall, I gradually became aware of something sticky pooling inside my cheek.

I don't know how much time passed after that. When the world started moving again, a little boy materialized before me, a tray of candies harnessed to his neck.

"*Dulces, señorita?*" he asked, looking curiously at me. The boy's face was smudged, his clothes the color of mud and clay. His feet were sandal-shod with old automobile tires. But on his tray, the yellow triangles of chocolate were pristine.

"Toblerone," I mumbled mechanically, digging in my purse for some coins.

He handed me a yellow Toblerone bar and hesitated, his eyes fixed on my forehead. Then he hurried away.

I gripped the chocolate in my hand, swallowing blood and then swallowing it again. I reached for my purse and tried to find my phone. In Bolivia, 911 was 011. But what else was I supposed to dial? Wasn't there a country code? I couldn't remember.

The low, droning voices of the dead weren't tormenting me anymore. They had been replaced by a loud creaking noise that seemed to be swelling upward from the sewers of the city, grinding like the gears of an ancient, horrific machine.

"Isobel." Henrik Paulsen was crouching beside me, his face aghast. His long hair was pulled back, and a gray canvas satchel hung from the shoulder of his faded coat. "What's happened to you?"

"Hurst." Disoriented, I held out the Toblerone like a peace offering.

He accepted the chocolate without a word, still staring at my face.

"Take me back," I mumbled. "To the hotel. I have a concert."

Paulsen tried to pull me to my feet. He managed to get my body halfway upright before I veered to the left and crumpled onto the cobblestones, vomiting fiercely against the brick wall. "Sorry," I gasped, my nostrils stinging. "Oh, God."

I coughed and retched and wiped my mouth on my sleeve. Paulsen put his arm over my shoulder and held back what was left of my hair.

Exhausted, I stared at the vile-looking puddle of watery blood. My skin was sweaty and prickling, and I couldn't control my shivering.

"He found you alone, didn't he?" Paulsen said with a disturbing calm, opening his phone. "And he took your hair."

I gaped at him and realized that bloody drool was threatening to spill from the corner of my mouth. I spat onto the ground, then found a tissue and wedged it into my cheek.

"I thought he was your friend." I swallowed, tasting bile.

For a long time, Paulsen said nothing. Then he dialed the number for the police.

The two police officers couldn't have been much older than I was, and their grey-green uniforms made them look less like police officers than underage soldiers. They seemed visibly excited about starting a manhunt for a violent, hair-stealing American pervert.

They talked almost exclusively to Paulsen, while I rested in the back of their police car. When they did look at me, their conversation flagged. They stared at my forehead, just as the boy had done, then glanced swiftly at each other and looked away.

Experimentally, I touched my fingers to the freckle above my eyebrow. It felt different: tight and slick, like a scorched patch of skin recovering from a burn.

I withdrew my hand from my forehead and nudged my chin. My jaw throbbed rhythmically, each pulse crushing me with pain. I had no idea how it would feel to clamp down on the chinrest of Lucia's Vuillaume, but I was going to have to find out. Soon.

Paulsen approached the car carrying my purse and canvas shopping bag, darting a glance at the archeology museum across the street. "We're done."

"Good." I swung my legs around and planted them unsteadily on the cobblestones. "I've got a concert in less than two hours."

Paulsen narrowed his eyes in disbelief. "You really think that's going to happen?"

"I know it is," I said. "Now get me back to my room."

"Why is it so important?"

I clamped my teeth together, feeling the tight pull of my inflamed gums, puffing and swelling against my teeth. What was wrong with him that he couldn't understand?

"It's my job, Paulsen. It's what I do."

"It's Lucia's job. You don't have to torture yourself to play her concerto. Why don't you let this one go?"

I drew a shaky breath and pulled myself to my feet. "Why don't you tell me why you and Hurst are such great friends?"

Paulsen's gaze shifted past my ear, as if he were assessing the stone lions guarding the museum. "He's not my friend. He just knows people."

"What kind of people?"

"The kind who can find things that aren't easy to find."

"Things like my hair, I suppose." My voice broke, and I took a wobbly step forward, falling against the door of the police car.

Paulsen reacted swiftly, catching me in his arms. "I can help you, Isobel. If you'll let me." He said it so softly, he might have been whispering.

I stared at him, shocked. I wanted so desperately to be touched, to be able to feel something more than loneliness and pain. But it was pointless to want anything from anyone.

"No, you can't," I said, pulling back. "You're just a voyeur and a pervert, like Hurst."

I expected him to protest or defend himself, but instead, almost reluctantly, he let me go. "Will you be okay?"

I turned away, my fingers sticky with vomit. "I'll be okay."

I made a fist around my bundle of nasty, sodden tissues and headed for the hotel entrance. My steps were steady, but I felt myself slipping, losing my balance, as if I were fighting to keep my footing on a tightrope. Waiting for me at the bottom, more awful than any death, was the future. I couldn't think about any of it. I just had to keep going.

Halfway to the hotel, I spotted a trashcan placed outside the archeology museum. Stuffing the dirty tissues into the metal bin, I saw the museum courtyard was empty.

"Good riddance," I muttered, rubbing my hands together.

Paulsen followed my gaze to the rectangular stone statues bordering the gate. The mountain lions perched atop the human heads, snarling.

"When you feel better," he said, his tone deliberately casual, "I can take you and Mikhail around the museum. I know the curator very well."

"Do they have any mummies in there?" I asked, bitterly. "I'm trying to make new friends."

Paulsen searched my face, then smiled. "They do."

He picked up the canvas bag holding my water bottles and threw his satchel over his shoulder. "Come on," he said, and held out his arm. "I'll take you back home."

I wavered for a moment and finally took Paulsen's arm. Then I froze.

A tall, bearded man was sitting on a bench inside the museum courtyard, tossing crumbs to the pigeons. He wore black pants and a ragged sweater, and under his grizzled beard was a face I knew better than my own.

"Dad!" Tearing myself away from Paulsen, I hobbled over to the fence, seized the wrought-iron bars, and peered through. "Dad!"

My father looked up from the pigeons, and crumbs fell through his outstretched fingers. I thought I saw him smile.

Why now? Why had my father waited all this time, only to haunt me now?

Then the sleeve of Paulsen's weathered coat abruptly blocked my view of the courtyard. When I could see again, my father was gone.

"That wasn't your father!" Paulsen hissed, pulling me away from the fence and dragging me back to the pavement. "There's no one there."

A tense crackling sound agitated the air, as if we were standing too close to a giant power line. Above the gate, the stone lions gleamed like gold in the afternoon light.

I slumped to the ground, felt my heart empty itself of hope. Flattening my palms against the pavement, I looked again at the empty courtyard. Of course he was gone. He had never been there.

"That wasn't my father," I said, my mouth thick with blood. "It couldn't have been. I killed him."

PRELUDE TO A FUNERAL

My mother was the great beauty of her family, a dark-haired poet with the poise of a 1950's film star. When my father died, leaving us comfortably provided for, my great-aunt Gladys was less than sympathetic.

"You and your mother won't have to worry about anything," she said as we collected the flowers and cards after the funeral. "Eleanor was lucky to meet a man like your father. She did very well for herself."

Standing in the sanctuary with a vase of lilies in my hands, I felt my numb, bewildered grief ignite into a blistering rage. I knew Gladys never liked my dad. But he was my father, and I loved him.

Did Gladys think he was nothing more than an investment that paid off nicely for my mom? Was she really that heartless? Couldn't she see how devastated, how utterly unhinged, my mom was?

I weighed the vase in my hand, trying to calm my desire to heap lilies and damnation on my great-aunt's poodle-white head. Then I realized that Gladys was watching her own daughter, Susan, help my mother out of her church pew. My mom's thin shoulders were shaking, and Susan was holding her close.

The taste of bitterness left my throat. Susan was my mom's favorite cousin: a sweet, gentle woman whose marriage had imprisoned her in poverty and violence. She'd been pretty once, too.

"Dad always took good care of us," I said, not letting Gladys see I was hurt.

Gladys stuffed a handful of sympathy cards into a flowery yellow tote bag. "Yes, he did."

Five days earlier, my father had still been alive, and Gladys had used that same yellow tote bag to bring rippled potato chips and a can of processed cheese to my parents' 25th wedding anniversary. Open-faced sandwiches are a Scandinavian-American tradition, but it's doubtful that any café in Minneapolis sells open-faced spray cheese sandwiches topped with broken rippled potato chips and thin slices of green olive.

"Not again!" my father groaned as Gladys marched into our kitchen, her maroon pantsuit neatly accessorized, a bag of Wonder Bread dangling from one plump hand.

"You know it's Auntie's little tradition, Dad." I knew my mother would graciously serve the cheesy sandwiches on the same platter as her prosciutto-wrapped dates and my father's favorite chutney.

"Tradition is for people who can't evolve," he muttered through his beard, and he picked up his wine glass and exited the kitchen.

The guests at the party were mostly members of my father's law firm or friends and relatives of my mom. My dad didn't have a lot of friends, just grateful clients and powerful enemies. He was a notoriously tenacious litigator, known for the dogged ruthlessness with which he went after big companies with big money. My mom was a poet, known for the dreamy innocence with which she asked those same big companies to support the local youth symphony.

After eight years of homeschooling, my parents had given up pretending I had friends of my own, so at parties I had to fend for myself. I spent the first ten minutes of the party trapped beside the grand piano, listening politely while my mother's cousin Dorothy described the beneficial impact of a low sugar diet on her tilted uterus problem.

Then my old violin teacher, Mrs. Mary Kean, rolled up in her wheelchair to rescue me, pinching my cheek and telling me I looked "beautiful, darling."

Over ninety years old, but still speaking in the superbly plummy accent of her British childhood, Mrs. Kean began telling everyone her favorite story about my father.

"Twelve inches of snow," she warbled, "and I thought for certain I would have my Saturday off. No wretched little students coming to my house. I had just put on a nice pot of tea and brought out my favorite Lord Peter Wimsey, when I heard pounding at my door. It was that confounded Robert Linden, saying 'Hullo, Mary! I've shoveled your drive. Isobel's here for her lesson.'"

Mrs. Kean waved her gnarled hands. "And I thought to myself, 'Blast the man!'"

Everyone laughed, and I looked around the room and smiled. There were so many stories she could have told about me. Playing Lalo's *Symphonie Espagnole* with the Minnesota Orchestra when I was ten. Winning the Yehudi Menuhin competition when I was eleven. Getting my first recording contract when I was twelve. But Mrs. Kean always chose the story about my dad, how he wouldn't give up a single lesson.

In his profession, my father played the long game, meticulously managing complex lawsuits that dragged on for up to a decade. He was playing the long game with my career as well, already planning my future.

When I turned seventeen, he hired a New York image consultant named Georgia Lamb to help me launch my adult career. Isobel 2.0, he called it. Georgia's plan was for a big makeover. Saucy retro clothes, a sharp pixie haircut, and whatever else old people with lots of money considered smart and sexy.

My father was pursuing Georgia's concept with all the determination of a bulldog. But I wasn't having any of that. I didn't need to hire someone to tell me how to grow up.

I offered Mrs. Kean a currant scone with clotted cream,

which we'd ordered specially for her from a pastry shop in St. Paul.

She rested the gilded plate on her lap, saying, "Beautiful, darling."

Then I heard the sound I was dreading: my father's voice.

"Isobel," he said. "Aren't you going to play your Stradivarius for us?"

I dug my toes into the Turkish rug. "It's not my Strad anymore. It's going back to BMK Verlag on Valentine's Day, so they can loan it to some other girl. Somebody younger and shinier than I am. Happy Valentine's Day to me."

My father sucked in his breath. "Isobel—"

"I got a new viola yesterday," I told Mrs. Kean, with a fierce, deliberate smile.

"Excellent, darling," she mumbled through her crumbly scone. "Always good to have a viola."

"I'm going to play that instead."

My father lowered his voice. "Please don't start that viola nonsense again."

"Why not? You're always saying how competitive everything is for concert violinists. You're always saying I need to distinguish myself, set myself apart. Why shouldn't I play the viola instead?"

My father smiled at the guests and seized my elbow, steering me into the kitchen. "There's no market for viola soloists. None. Do you want to spend the rest of your life in a bankrupt orchestra, going oompa, loompa with the tuba section? Because if you play the viola, that's what your life is going to be like. That, and playing *The Nutcracker Suite* every single year for Christmas. For the rest of your life."

"That's not going to happen." I said, shaking my arm loose. "I'm going to play chamber music."

"And how long do you think that quartet option will last? You want to play second fiddle to that prima donna we met at Claire's, Lucia what's-her-name? I didn't spend a fortune on your education so you could—"

"Robert," my mother's voice cut in. She was holding an

aromatic platter of warm cheeses, drizzled with a brown butter glaze. "Would you please take this out to our guests?"

My parents exchanged a quiet look, one that I knew well but had never managed to translate, and then my father nodded and took the cheeses to the living room.

I grabbed a chocolate-covered strawberry and yanked off the stem. "How the hell did you stay married for 25 years? *Why* do you put up with him?"

"Your father has very strong opinions," my mom began.

"About controlling my life."

My mom wiped her hands with a dishtowel and began filling a stainless steel carafe with coffee. A tiny vertical line creased the skin above her coral lips, something I'd never noticed before. "He isn't trying to control you, Isobel. He's just trying to help you build your career, in an industry that doesn't allow mistakes."

"It might be nice to make my own mistakes. Or at the very least, choose my own clothes. I feel like I've spent the last eight years on a tiny little stage built for puppets. I feel like I'm never going to have anything of my own." I threw down the mangled strawberry, aware that I was close to tears.

She adjusted the black plastic spout on the carafe. "Your father believes in me, you know. I don't make any money, but in all these years, he has never once told me how to write a poem. He trusts in my art."

I watched her lips move, wondering what that had to do with me.

She set down the carafe. "And he trusts in your art. Has he ever told you how to phrase a passage, how to play a cadenza?"

"No," I admitted. "He hasn't."

"He believes in you, Isobel. And he doesn't want you to throw away your future."

Something twisted in my chest, something that felt like remorse. I thought about my shiny new Stahler viola, about the freedom I'd thought it would offer. I couldn't remember why I'd wanted it so badly.

"I'll take it back," I whispered, relenting. "And we'll keep looking for a violin. I'll take it back in the morning."

But I didn't take the viola back in the morning. After the gifts had been opened and the guests had all gone home, I went upstairs and retreated to my bedroom. I pulled open the doors of my closet, seeing the long row of pretty dresses my father had chosen for my performances, each one perfectly suited to an oversized flower girl at a lavish Southern wedding.

I was seventeen. I couldn't be that innocent child prodigy anymore. But what was I going to be instead?

I went over to my dresser and picked up the fashion sketches Georgia Lamb had sent my father. Short pixie-like hair. Dark eye makeup. Vibrant 1960's colors.

I flipped my ponytail over the top of my head and peered into the mirror, trying to imagine myself with short hair and bangs.

Would it really be so bad? It was only packaging and personal branding, designed to attract concert promoters and the few people who still bought classical CDs. It wasn't as if they were taking away my music. And it wasn't as if there was anyone in my life who actually cared what I looked like, or who loved me when I wasn't performing.

All I want is to play music, I thought, my eyes falling on the new viola. *That's all I will ever want.*

When I opened the case and picked up the Stahler, the loneliness and frustration inside me swelled up so fiercely, I was sure my heart would burst open and spill its contents onto the rug.

I brushed my thumb across the strings, surprised to find the Stahler perfectly in tune. Then I rosined the bow and began to play a melody I didn't know. The viola sounded so warm and comforting at first, as if its voice, deep and clear as a summer rainstorm, was calling out to me, telling me to play forever.

And for a while, dizzy with longing, I kept playing, kept listening to that voice, only half-aware that it had grown darker and more urgent.

Don't stop, it echoed every time I paused. *You are playing the most beautiful music in the world.*

My ears were burning, and I knew it was true, and I knew I could never give it up. This was where I belonged.

At some point, my arms aching, I must have set the viola down. At some point, I must have made my way to the bathroom and found my father's razor blades. At some point, I must have filled the claw-footed bathtub and stepped into the water.

In the morning, the water was icy cold and dense with blood, and the music was forgotten. Downstairs in the kitchen, I could hear my mother screaming.

THE MIRROR

Henrik Paulsen was the sort of man who could hear you'd killed your father and not even flutter an eyelash. He didn't need to know about the bathtub, the razor blades, my father dead of a heart attack on the hard kitchen floor. It was all the same to him.

"Let's get back to your room," he said, cool and indifferent as an overworked assassin. He gathered up my bags and headed for the hotel, and he didn't look back. Heartsick, I limped after him, stealing a final desperate look at the museum courtyard. There was no one there.

We hurried silently through the Hotel Miranda's lobby, nodding to the receptionist, ignoring the curious stares of the German tourists. But when we got to my room, Paulsen's behavior changed.

"Now tell me the truth," he ordered, his voice taut with accusation. His eyes swept the contents of the room, and he dumped my bag of water bottles onto Lucia's bed. "Under normal circumstances, no one could play a violin concerto after being mugged. But I'm going to assume you have a plan. How do you expect to hold a violin under your fractured jaw?"

"I'll manage," I muttered, tugging off my bloodstained jacket. "You don't need to worry about me."

Paulsen stepped closer, two spots of color flaring just below his cheekbones. "I know you can manage. What I don't know is how."

I pressed my tongue against my aching molars and backed away from Paulsen, avoiding the hard stare in his pale eyes. The Stahler was lying on the bed, beckoning me. I imagined holding its varnished warmth in my hands, drawing Lucia's bow across its trembling strings. All I had to do was play it, and I would be strong again. But what would it cost me?

"The viola," Paulsen said from across the room, watching my hungry eyes on the Stahler. His face was on fire, as if he'd finally glimpsed the armies of his enemy. "It's keeping you going."

Strange, I thought. He didn't say it was keeping me alive.

I turned away from the Stahler and approached the mirror hanging over Lucia's dresser, fear and dread gnawing at my chest. An apparition awaited me in the glass.

My blonde hair was short and ragged, falling just past my chin on the right, barely covering my ear on the left. My bandaged jaw bloomed like a purple flower, and the left side of my face had bloated and swelled. Suspended over this ruin was something that took my breath away. The freckle above my eyebrow was gone.

In its place was a shiny patch of grayish-brown skin, leathery and wrinkled as an old saddle. I raised a fingertip to touch the thick, rubbery surface.

"You see," said Paulsen. "It's failing."

One of the problems with being only provisionally alive is that you can't really hyperventilate. I knew I was panicking. I could feel the entire contents of my brain beginning to boil, but my heart wasn't racing at all. It kept thumping along like a perfectly timed Viennese waltz. I could almost hear the cheery refrain of "The Blue Danube."

It's the stroke of midnight, I thought incoherently, remembering the old beggar I'd helped to his death. *But there's no new year.*

I leaned closer to the mirror and fingered the dark leathery spot on my forehead, and a tiny patch of freckled skin peeled away from the edge, flaking off like a pale speck of dandruff.

Underneath, more leather.

"Oh, God," I choked out, and rushed into the bathroom to throw up. I heaved, and a long thread of scarlet stained the white porcelain sink.

"God isn't going to help you," said Paulsen, following me into the bathroom. "The old gods have power here."

I crouched over the sink, queasy with horror and sickened by my own blood. Outside the bathroom, I could hear a faint pounding. Someone was knocking at the door.

"Get rid of them," I snarled and yanked a towel off the rack.

Paulsen moved swiftly out of the bathroom, and I slammed the door behind him.

Illuminated by the bright vanity fixture above the sink, the elliptical patch of grayish brown leather looked even darker, more pronounced. Under stage lights, the audience would see it from the third balcony. There was no pretending it wasn't there.

"Isobel," I heard a voice call. "It's Enrique."

I clutched the towel to my bloodstained mouth and looked around for something to cover the spot. There wasn't anything. Then I remembered Lucia's first-aid kit. I unzipped her leopard-print pouch and found a sleek metal case filled with Band-Aids. With trembling hands, I tore off a paper wrapper and pasted a beige rectangle above my eyebrow.

"Enrique," I said, struggling to open the door. "Guess you heard the news."

Enrique was standing with Paulsen in the middle of my hotel room, dressed in black and clasping his hands together like a priest.

I took one look at the fear and concern carved across his face, and all my resolve splintered into a thousand useless pieces. I made a harsh sound in my throat, like wounded raptor, and immediately Enrique's lean arms were around me, and he was telling me it would be okay. I buried my bandaged forehead in his shoulder, something hot and caustic guttering in the sockets of my eyes.

Enrique tightened his arms around my shoulders. "I can't believe Hurst did this to you, in broad daylight."

"He's crazy, Enrique." I clutched the smooth wool of his coat, not wanting to let go. "He's obsessed."

Enrique stepped back, and I could see the fury darkening his features.

"He'll be arrested right away," he said, with cold resolve. "There's nowhere in this city that man can hide."

"The police will probably find him," Paulsen agreed, his eyes glittering, his tone almost amused.

I glared at Paulsen, but he simply opened a bottle of mineral water and poured some into a glass. "Drink this, Isobel."

"I don't want it."

"You need it."

"He's right, Isobel." Enrique stepped between us. "Please drink something."

I brought the glass to my lips and struggled to swallow, and Enrique watched me with a sick, angry look on his face.

Behind him, Paulsen set the water bottle back on the bed. Then he reached for the Stahler with a steady hand. I paused, water pooling on my tongue, watching in horror as Paulsen's fingers brushed the strings. But nothing happened.

"Ayesha," he murmured, as if saying the name of a lover. The viola made a faint, dying sound.

Enrique dug into his coat for his phone. "We need to call Ricardo Balcones. We need to contact the *Municipal*."

"You needn't bother," I told him, snaking my neck back and forth and straightening my aching shoulders. "I'll be ready for the concert in an hour."

Enrique froze, the phone halfway from his pocket to his ear.

"Please tell me you don't mean that." His voice was flat, disbelieving.

I glanced at Paulsen, who shrugged as if to say, *The concert is your problem.* Then I looked at the viola beside him. If I continued to play the Stahler, the pale man might choose to take another life. Or, maybe he wouldn't, since his actions followed no pattern I could understand. But if I didn't play the Stahler, he would certainly take mine.

There's no escape, I thought. And I'm damned no matter what I do.

"I'll be fine." Like a criminal condemned by her own testimony, I walked over to Lucia's bed and picked up the Stahler. "I just need to warm up first."

THE SACRED MOUNTAIN

When the Sibelius concerto was finally over, Enrique Rodriguez met me in the green room.

"Isobel," he said, "you can't go back to your hotel."

Gathering up my bouquets in their rustling cellophane wrappers, he pulled open the warped wooden door. "Hurst is still out there, and you'll be a prisoner in your room."

I brushed the flecks of rosin from the Vuillaume and sighed, my joints creaking like a broken wind-up toy. Playing the Stahler for an hour had restored most of my strength, and somehow I'd managed to paint up my face and trudge through the Sibelius violin concerto. But it was a clumsy, trudging performance, and Enrique knew it.

The audience at *Teatro Municipal,* of course, was in paroxysms of delight. But they had only been hearing the notes.

"But where can I go?" I asked. "I can't stay at the hospital with David and Lucia." I eased my body out of the lumpy sofa and closed Lucia's violin case with a snap.

Enrique thought for a moment. "You could always share a room with Mikhail."

"Are you kidding? He hates me," I burst out, then realized Enrique was joking. I gritted my teeth, wishing I hadn't said a word.

Unperturbed, Enrique handed me his long black coat. "You wouldn't be in a string quartet if you didn't hate each other.

Didn't the *Quartetto Italiano* insist on taking separate flights to every concert? Didn't they stay in separate hotels?"

"They had money," I told him, slipping gingerly into his coat. "And some serious romantic problems."

But so do we, I thought, remembering the anguish on David's face as he paced all night in Lucia's hospital room. We have nothing but problems.

"You can stay with me," Enrique said softly. "You'll be safe at my house."

I hesitated. "But I don't—"

"Have a toothbrush?" He picked up Lucia's Vuillaume and slung it over his shoulder. "That's not a problem."

By the time we left the theater, Maestro Balcones had already begun the Mahler symphony, and we could hear the sound of staccato trumpets filtering through the doors to the lobby. Floodlights illuminated the *Municipal*'s red and white stucco walls. The historic Murillo Plaza was nearly empty, and Enrique's car was nowhere to be found.

I paused at the top of the stone steps, alarmed by the empty parking spot. But Enrique shifted the bouquets to his left arm and began strolling, his movements almost leisurely. I followed, and we passed the various citizens of the night: indigenous women in flat shoes and pleated dresses, Spanish women in fitted skirts and high heels, men with black hair in dark jackets and dusty trousers.

"What happened to the boys?" I asked. "The ones you bribed to guard your car?"

"Joyride." Enrique shrugged, the broad angles of his cheekbones inflecting upwards in a smile. "They'll be back. They probably thought we'd stay for the Mahler."

We stopped in front of an elegant colonial hotel, just across from the spot where the patriot Murillo was hanged. I looked around the plaza, half-afraid that Hurst was waiting for me in the darkness. Enrique was right about one thing, at least. In La Paz, a man like Hurst could be spotted from a mile away.

"How do you know they'll be back?"

Enrique raised a casual hand as his shiny black Audi approached, its seats crammed with guilty-looking boys in yellow soccer shirts.

"Because," he said calmly, "they know who I am."

He drove in silence for a while, the street lamps tattooing his skin with moving patterns of shadow and light. In the intermittent darkness, I couldn't quite see his face, but I thought he might be smiling.

"What's so funny?"

"Do you remember when we met?" he asked, his voice both amused and sincere. "You were collapsed on that sofa after Mikhail broke the statue, and Jack was terrified you wouldn't be able to play the quartet concerts."

"Ambassador Melton? He was terrified?"

"Lucia was so eager to reassure him. She said you were made of iron."

"That's me," I said, and remembered to smile. My fractured jaw throbbed in time with my pulse. "Tough as nails."

I locked my fingers together, determined not to touch the Band-Aid on my forehead. I wondered if the leathery patch was growing.

"Lucia didn't know the half of it." Enrique's characteristic ease gave way, and I sensed a hint of something dark, almost fierce. "Playing that concerto, after what you've been through. There's no one like you, Isobel. You're nothing less than a miracle."

I searched his face, my mouth dry. What did he mean, a miracle?

We pulled up into an alleyway, and I realized that we'd arrived in an old residential part of the city. A stooped man in a cardigan tugged open a tall gate.

"Where are we?"

Enrique steered through the gate. "Near the Witches' Market. At my house."

Enrique's home was a colonial mansion, inherited from his father and in the family for over 80 years. The house itself was much older than that, and set into a hill. Breezeways encircled the inner courtyard on both floors, and thick walls of stone protected the interlocking rooms from the noises of the street. A fountain bubbled peacefully, guarded by lichen-encrusted angels.

We went up the courtyard stairs to the second floor. The devil was waiting for us in the entrance hall.

El Tio sat cross-legged on a gilt-edged sideboard, which was trimmed with marble panels so blue they reminded me of lapis lazuli. Enrique's statue was smaller and more battered than the ambassador's, with red paint peeling from its broken clay horns, and crudely shaped feet drawn close to its giant phallus.

I had thought that *Tio's* presence would bring back visions of the pale man, or churn up the voices of the dead. But the room was utterly silent and empty. Fingers trembling, I reached out to touch the rough clay on the devil's forehead, and a strange sensation came over me, something completely unexpected. *Peace.*

"You'll be safe here," Enrique said, setting down the flowers and throwing open the doors to the drawing room. "Completely safe."

Above the statue of *Tio* hung a faded charcoal drawing of a mountain, a cone-shaped peak with a sprawling colonial city at its base.

"This mountain," I said, my eyes following the outline of the peak. "Is this where *Tio* came from?"

Enrique returned, almost reluctantly, and looked up at the drawing. "The *Cerro Rico*. The mountain was sacred to the Inca, and to the Tiwanaku who came before them."

He took my hand. "They call it the mountain that swallows men."

"It swallows men?" On the table before me, *Tio* seemed to be smiling.

Enrique began tracing an intricate diagram onto the top of my hand. "For three hundred years, *Cerro Rico* produced legendary amounts of silver. People say the silver from that single mountain could have built a bridge all the way to Spain. They also say you could have built another bridge back to

Bolivia, using only the bones of the men who died in its mines. There were millions of them.

"At one point the Spanish government enacted the *Ley de la Mita*, which forced all the men in the territory to work in the mines. Enslaved miners stayed deep in the mountain for weeks at a time, eating and sleeping underground."

Enrique held my ghost-patterned hand out before him, inspecting his handiwork. "They didn't live very long."

Appalled, I tugged my hand away. "They were forced to sleep in the mines?"

Somehow, sleeping underground seemed more monstrous than being forced to work there. I looked up at the drawing of *Cerro Rico*, seeing a brutal empire of imperishable stone.

Enrique nodded. "When they came out after a shift, they had to bandage their eyes against the sun."

I remembered then the smudged face of the little boy who'd sold me chocolates after Hurst's attack, and I saw what his future might once have been. Endless darkness and a blistering sun.

No wonder, I thought. No wonder they turned to *Tio*. He offered them protection.

I stepped back from the painting as Enrique ran a single tapered finger along the frame.

"Dusty," he murmured. He turned slightly, looking about the room. "Let me show you my piano."

The elegant drawing room was arranged around a Steinway grand, its top scattered with sheet music. Enrique stepped into the dining room, calling for a maid, and I peeked at the front of the piano. A copy of "Pictures at an Exhibition" rested on the stand. The keys were faintly yellow, but the rest of the piano gleamed as if just taken from the showroom.

I clasped my hands together behind my back, telling myself not to touch any of Enrique's bronze sculptures. Pausing in front of a glowing Turner-like landscape painting, I heard a light chord coming from the piano.

"Our dinner's almost ready," Enrique said with a smile, swiveling on the piano stool. "But first, listen to this."

He began to play a Beethoven sonata, with all the cultured assurance of a concert soloist. I slipped into a carved wooden chair and listened, and the music swept through the beautiful old room like a blessing.

He should have been a musician, I thought, with a sudden, aching sadness. He has the power of enchantment.

A hushed flurry of voices abruptly punctuated Enrique's sonata, and the oak doors to the dining room creaked and slid apart.

Enrique lifted his hands from the keyboard. "Arminda?"

The old housekeeper stood in the doorway, her arms clasped tightly around a trembling girl in a bright shawl. It was Esperanza, Raysa Veizaga's maid. Enrique stepped forward and took hold of the girl's hands, and she burst into hysterical tears.

I got to my feet and listened helplessly, straining to derive meaning from the stream of Aymara words pouring from Esperanza's lips.

Enrique looked back over his shoulder, his face tight. "The police are outside. They found Hurst in the Witches' Market."

My hands flew to my cropped hair, and a dull terror punched me in the chest. "They've arrested him?"

"He's dead, Isobel. He's been torn apart."

MERCADO DE LAS BRUJAS

Enrique and I followed the police officers along a dark street to the Witches' Market, rushing past wooden stands filled with dried reptiles, carved Inca crosses, and potent-smelling herbs. The large shops in the *Mercado de las Brujas* were all closed, and most of the women at the booths were silently packing their wares. We passed a gruesome display of shriveled creatures, their stiff gray bodies dangling from hooks above an old Aymara woman in a black shawl. Enrique slowed his pace long enough for me to take a look.

"What are those?" I had seen one before. I knew it.

The vision came back to me at once: the ambassador's staircase, and the dead thing withering in the pale man's hand.

"Dried llama fetuses." Seeing my horror, Enrique added, "Not for eating."

The women packing up the stands reminded me of Enrique's housekeeper, who'd intercepted us in the courtyard with a tray of tea and hard rolls. Arminda's lined, sad face had barely moved as Enrique and the officers declined the tea. She'd simply tightened her grip on the silver tray and slowly climbed the stairs back to the kitchen.

I was unbearably thirsty, I realized with surprise. I could have used that cup of tea.

My tongue felt thick in my mouth, as if it were wrapped in strips of cotton. We walked past a display of skinned sheep's heads, each one exactly the right size for a pot of soup. I tried to swallow and kept on walking.

The sparse rays of distant streetlights filtered through the narrow cobblestone streets. We approached a store displaying rows of wooden coffins. A group of men in gray-green uniforms stood with flashlights around a tarp. One of them lifted a corner of the tarp, and in the bright glare of the flashlight, I glimpsed a torn fragment of a brown coat, something that had once been an arm.

"Hurst," I whispered aloud, my lungs burning as I remembered his shiny wingtip shoes, his sneering, pockmarked face.

The detective in charge approached, the yellow beam of his flashlight illuminating a clear plastic bag. Inside were a few strands of blonde hair and a glossy black tube of Chanel lipstick.

"*Esto es tuyo?*" he asked, eyeing my butchered hair and my bandaged face.

I hesitated, then nodded. "*Si, mi cabello.*"

Uneasy, I remembered something: Lucia used Chanel lipstick. I wished I could see the color. But the detective was already moving on, asking me to identify my attacker.

For the second time in twenty-four hours, I stood numbly and watched as a curtain was lifted, revealing the unnatural death of someone I had known. Hurst's head had almost been ripped from his torso, and a long red scar tore diagonally across his pitted face. His left eye was missing.

The detective asked questions. I mumbled affirmatives and took refuge in Enrique's arms. My jaw throbbed, and when I tried to swallow, there was something in the way, blocking the back of my throat.

Behind the detective, a young officer wearing latex gloves emptied a thick wad of crisp $100 bills into a plastic evidence bag and sealed it shut.

"That's a lot of American cash," Enrique muttered, his face pinched with disgust.

The gloved officer picked up the last of Hurst's effects: a

plastic shopping bag distorted into sharp angles by whatever stiff object was inside. I took a step forward and glimpsed the shriveled heads of two dried llamas poking out above the fabric.

What did Hurst want with those horrible things? They were like mummies.

I remembered Henrik Paulsen's message about the mummified Inca girl. *Maybe the girl on the mountain was innocent. Maybe she even thought she was lucky.*

I still didn't understand why Paulsen wanted to remind me of that, and part of me feared that something terrible would happen, if I ever did understand.

But that was a crazy thing to be afraid of. After all, I was standing over the remains of my attacker, inhabiting a body that shouldn't be here. What could possibly be more terrible than that?

The police detective dismissed us, but Enrique didn't respond. He was staring straight ahead, his eyes fixed on an old movie poster peeling from the wall. He seemed impossibly remote, a thousand years away.

"Enrique, let's get out of here. They say we can go now."

Enrique started and looked around, as if he'd stumbled while sleepwalking.

"Of course." His eyes found mine. "Of course."

We walked quietly in the dark street, under the spires of the great stone cathedral. Then we turned a corner and arrived in an entirely different market. The women selling herbs were gone, replaced by laughter, recorded music, and the greasy smell of street food.

Enrique surveyed the new market with relief. "Here," he said, reaching into the pocket of his leather coat. "Let's get something to drink."

"Is this still the Witches' Market?" I huddled in Enrique's wool coat and my thin black dress. The grilled aroma of *anticuchos* filled the cold air. Through the bars of the shop windows, I could see bright ethnic dresses, woven blankets, buckets of flowers.

Enrique shook his head. "People like us aren't welcome to shop there."

"Then what was Hurst doing there? And what did he do with my hair?"

"I don't know, Isobel. Paulsen told me Hurst dealt in antiques."

I remembered the thick wad of $100 bills, and I knew with an utter certainty that Hurst had sold my hair. But who would pay that kind of money for my ponytail?

I tried to massage the back of my neck with my hand, but my muscles felt like long swollen cords radiating from my spine. I thought of Paulsen, standing with Hurst in the lamplight below my hotel, and again I heard his cold, impatient question: *Do you have the Mother's Stone?*

"Enrique, did the ambassador invite Hurst to the *Club de La Paz?*"

Enrique frowned, as if recalling something. "I don't think he could have. The political situation is so volatile, the president is threatening to sever diplomatic relations. Jack has to restrict the guest lists at all his parties, even if they're just for cultural events."

We stopped in front of a rustic wooden stand balanced with large vats of liquid. The air smelled like a jelly doughnut factory. A plump girl in a green shawl was filling glasses with a hot, sweet-smelling drink the color of plum juice.

Enrique inspected the grainy liquid. "That's *api*, made from creamed corn."

"Is it safe for me to drink?" My tongue felt like it had tripled in size.

"Maybe not, but I can get you a Coke."

He began to order, and I found a seat on a long wooden bench that stretched out beneath a brown canvas tarp. I peered up at the huge grommets punched through the edges of the tarp, fragments of light flaring above me like bloated stars. Then the lights gave way to memory, and again I saw the plastic tarp covering what was left of Hurst. He had died a terrible, gruesome death.

I waited to feel relief, but none came. Instead, a sudden, poisonous terror flooded through me. *He took my hair. And then he died.*

The Stahler turned Raysa into a mummy. It nearly killed Lucia as well. But Hurst never touched the damned thing. He touched me instead, and he paid with his life.

Enrique dropped a handful of coins into the vendor's open hand and reached for a pair of Coke bottles. "Here you are," he said, sitting down and handing me a drink.

"Enrique?"

"Yes?"

"Those dried llamas. You said they're not for eating."

"God, no." He made a face and sipped some Coke.

"Then what are they for?"

Enrique set down his bottle, a tiny line forming between his eyebrows.

"Offerings," he said slowly. "Sacrifice."

THE VIRGIN

Sacrifice? The word made me sick inside. It was always the innocent who were being sacrificed. Like that mummified Inca girl left to die on the mountaintop, her head compressed into a cone to please some vengeful god.

I knew I wasn't innocent. I'd made terrible choices, choices that could never be undone. After months of denial and confusion, I'd finally accepted the truth: my father had died so the Stahler could own me forever. The Stahler might be moving blood through my veins, having claimed my father's life instead of my own, but I was a freak, an abomination, and what I'd become had broken my mother's mind. And now, someone or something in this city of old gods wanted every trace of me gone.

We walked back to Enrique's house in the darkness. As we passed the market stands on Linares Street, I saw a woman locking up her stall. A wind had picked up in the city, ruffling her plastic bags of coca leaves. I could see the dried llamas stacked in a heap behind her, each one as gaunt and rigid as a blundering taxidermist's first cat.

"Those llamas. What kind of sacrifice are they?"

Enrique pulled up the collar of his leather coat. "They're for Pachamama, the goddess of the earth. Most Bolivians have a llama fetus buried under the foundations of their house, a payment to the earth mother for cutting into the ground. But some people also burn the llamas, as offerings."

"What kind of person would burn a mummified baby llama?" I asked, appalled.

Enrique glanced at me and reached into his coat for a small flashlight. His eyes were hooded, as if in pain.

"People do strange things, Isobel. When they think they have to."

I lowered my head, aware that I'd hurt him in some way. I just didn't know how.

We continued walking, not speaking, and moved up through the old residential neighborhood above the market. The stone mansions seemed to have been there forever, but I knew that wasn't true. They'd been built by colonial wealth and exploitation, by men like Enrique's grandfather. I wondered what kind of man that grandfather was, a man strong or ruthless enough to wrest an empire from the devil's mountain. I wondered what price he'd been willing to pay.

Enrique and I must have been taking the long way back to his house, because we arrived abruptly at a small pavilion, high above the lights of the Prado.

"Where are we?" I asked as we stepped up to a railing and looked out at the city.

"On higher ground." Enrique drew closer, his voice infinitely expressive. "You have to see La Paz from above, to understand how beautiful it is. When you get back from Sucre, I'll take you up to the *altiplano*, and we'll drive to the ruins of Tiwanaku, to the home of the old gods. I'll take you everywhere, Isobel."

I managed a nervous smile, suddenly realizing how close his body was to mine.

La Paz was beautiful at midnight, its glittering patterns of light disrupted by the dark gorge that cut through the city. From our chilly vantage point on the hillside, I could really see the huge night sky, as well. An entire field of constellations stretched out before us: many new, and some familiar, but far from their expected homes.

"Do you know how to find the Southern Cross?" Enrique

placed an arm over my shoulders, and the weight of his arm felt so easy, so light.

I followed the line of his other arm to a point on the horizon, climbing up. There they were: four bright stars, so symmetrically arranged as to be an unchanging guide. They had always been there, but I had never seen them.

That night, I slept in an unfamiliar bed. Enrique guided me past the kitchens to a small bedroom on the second floor of his house.

"You'll be safe here," he said, standing on the breezeway outside my bedroom, his back to the fountain in the courtyard. "There's an alarm protecting the entire house, and old Pablo sleeps in the next room."

"Thank you, Enrique." Across the courtyard, I could see the stooped body of his housekeeper Arminda at the top of the stairs. She opened the door to the main entrance hall, revealing the illuminated statue of *Tio*.

Enrique followed my gaze and turned to watch as Arminda placed something small at the base of the statue.

"An offering," he whispered, as my questioning eyes found his. "Arminda is a *yatiri*, a spiritual healer. She follows the old ways."

I wanted to respond, but I couldn't find the right words, and I couldn't look away. Enrique's dark eyes looked back, unblinking.

"And you?" I finally asked. "Do you follow the old ways?"

Instead of answering, Enrique took a step forward, and his lips briefly brushed mine. "Good night, Isobel."

My heart pounding, I watched him go. How easy it had been, just to close my eyes and let his lips touch mine. I'd been alone for so long, sleepwalking through my life. I'd forgotten how much I'd once wanted to live in the world. But it wasn't too late, was it? I could change, really change. I could do things differently from now on.

I latched the heavy wooden door and looked around my bedroom. The old stone building had no central heating, and the gleaming red filament of a space heater warmed the simple room. Hanging over the wrought iron bed was a large oil painting of the Virgin Mary. It was very old, with a deep crack in its ornately carved frame.

I remembered Ambassador Melton's words at the party: "Many conflate the earth mother Pachamama with the Virgin Mary, and some even find room in their worship for the devil." He had seemed so skeptical of the old traditions, so frankly condescending.

Enrique wasn't like that. He knew what it meant to be caught by the past, held in one place forever.

I took off my dress and crawled under the cold blankets, the metallic scent of the space heater stinging my nostrils, and I wondered again what price Enrique's grandfather had paid for his wealth and power. What terrible curse had trapped his family?

Then I realized that Raysa Veizaga must have known.

"People tell stories," she'd said. She must have told Lucia.

At dawn, I heard voices. The second hand on the old electric clock ticked faintly, and I lay in bed, listening as each distant click coincided with a throbbing jolt of pain through my fractured jaw. My pulse was 60 beats per minute. Exactly.

I heard the voices again, louder this time, and I got up, mechanically touching the Band-Aid on my forehead. I could feel the rubber-like patch of gray skin firmly fixed under the latex rectangle, its outline unchanged, at least for now. Relieved, I stepped into my flats and wrapped my naked body in the warmth of Enrique's long black coat.

Outside in the courtyard, the winter wind was blowing dead leaves in random elliptical patterns, and a woman was calling Enrique's name, her voice desperate and afraid. I hid behind a stone pillar and peered over the edge of the balcony.

It was Josefina, Ambassador Melton's wife.

"Enrique!" she called, tugging at the tall iron gates behind the fountain, an old copper lantern illuminating her pregnant body. "Enrique!"

A door screeched on its hinges, and Enrique bolted down the stairs in his leather jacket, followed by Arminda. He threw open the gate, and the old housekeeper rushed forward and enclosed Josefina in her arms.

"Arminda!" Josefina clung to the old woman and sobbed. "*Ayudame!*"

Then I heard a man's voice shouting in English. "I won't allow this," Ambassador Melton yelled, his red face glowering as he pushed his way through the gate. "You belong with me, Josefina. Not here with this useless witchdoctor."

"*Ayudame!*" Josefina cried, clinging to Arminda's bent shoulders. "*Ayudame!*"

"I've had enough of your hysteria," the ambassador announced, marching into the courtyard and reaching for Josefina's arm. "You're coming home."

"Let her go, Jack," Enrique said coldly, stepping between them. "And get out."

The ambassador's face darkened to purple. "How dare you!"

Enrique stood his ground. "I dare. She's my sister, and this is my home."

DEATH AND THE MAIDEN

Josefina and Arminda disappeared into the house, and Enrique slammed the gate shut as Ambassador Melton shouted and cursed.

"You'll regret this," he howled at Enrique's departing figure.

Enrique turned with sudden, vicious anger. In five quick steps, he was back at the gate, only inches from the ambassador's florid face. "What are you going to do, Jack? Send the CIA to my house? Because your wife wants to be in her childhood home?"

"You think your *Tio* can save her? You can't protect her, Enrique."

Enrique didn't flinch. "You're wrong about that."

"You're giving her false hope. You and that old witch."

"*You're* trespassing. I'm offering sanctuary."

The ambassador stepped back from the gate, his eyes hard. "You don't know what you're doing, boy. And you're a fool if you think you can handle this on your own."

I bent over the balcony, straining to hear, as Enrique's voice dropped to a whisper. "You should look out for yourself. Word on the street says the president wants you gone."

An eerie silence filled the stone courtyard. I slipped back into my room, overcome. What was going on? Josefina had come here seeking refuge, but what kind of protection could

Enrique offer, that the ambassador couldn't? Even if he was her brother.

I fell backward onto the bed and looked up at the oil painting of the Virgin Mary. She gazed down upon me, benevolent and kind.

I remembered the strange, unexpected sensation I'd felt when I touched Enrique's statue of *Tio*: a feeling of peace.

"You'll be safe here," Enrique had said. "Completely safe."

Was I so lost, so damned, that the devil himself had decided to protect me? Was Enrique?

He kissed me, I thought with sudden, reckless wonder. And he wanted more. We both wanted more.

I brought my fingers to my lips, a dull ache gathering inside me. Naked under Enrique's black coat, I rolled to my side, rubbing my head against the pillow.

Then I heard a faint crackling sound, like a cellophane wrapper being crumpled and discarded. My heart drummed against my ribs in panic. I sat up at once and lifted my hand to the side of my head. Under the fine strands of hair covering the top of my ear, I could feel a tiny, jagged spur of cartilage. I grabbed my purse from the bedpost, rummaged around for my compact mirror, and looked.

The narrow rim at the top of my ear had splintered off in a clean, sharp break.

The mirror fell from my hand, clattering against the floor, and my gaze dropped to the pillow, where an elliptical curve of fine gray powder rested on the soft white fabric.

If you're wondering what it means to die, you should probably know this: you're going to leave something behind. A final cadence, you could say. A coda. You won't be around to see the form it will take. But everyone you love will be caught up in its wake.

Huddled under Enrique's coat, I sat cross-legged on my bed, waiting for the sun to finish rising. David and Lucia and Mikhail were coming for rehearsal in the morning. The show would go on. The Stahler would be played. But what would it do to me? What would it do to my friends?

David and Lucia arrived at 9:00 AM. They looked surprisingly well as Arminda showed them in: Lucia neatly dressed in her black skirt and lush red sweater, David clean and mostly free of stubble. They both looked so ordinary, so healthy, and so perfect, I wanted to cry with relief. They were safe, for now. But where was Mikhail?

As he placed his cello in the entrance hall, I saw that David had brought me the Stahler. I watched him set down the viola, and desire and self-loathing immediately began gnawing at me, like a dual form of cancer. I needed to touch those resonant strings, to feel it come alive in my hands, and I needed it soon, before another part of my body splintered into dust.

David paused to examine the statue of *Tío*, his brow furrowed. Then he lifted his head and saw me standing in the drawing room. "Isobel! What the hell?"

"Oh my God!" Lucia shrieked, seeing my bandaged face and my mangled hair. She rushed past David. "I knew you were hurt, but I had no idea."

I closed the distance between us and gave her a hug.

"Trust me," I lied, "it isn't as bad as it looks."

"Shouldn't you go to the hospital?" Lucia cringed away from my hug, as if she were being forced to hold a dead kitten. "Your cheek is all puffy. And it's almost green!"

I guided her past the Steinway, pulled open the heavy doors to the dining room. "You're one to talk. You're fresh from the hospital yourself. Really, I'm fine."

"But you look hideous." Lucia's horror deepened. "And you went out on stage like that? In front of 1,200 people?"

I made a show of nonchalance. "I had makeup, and most of them weren't close enough to see my face." I didn't want to remember what lay under the latex Band-Aid or the fringe of short blonde hair, but there was no way not to remember.

"Where's Mikhail?" I asked, deflecting further inquiries about my appearance.

Lucia made a dismissive gesture. "He's gone. Out. Whatever. Where's Enrique?"

I hesitated, not sure what I should tell her about Josefina.

David's eyes darted around the elegantly furnished dining room. "After what happened to Hurst, Enrique has got to be worried about security."

Arminda offered David a cup of Bolivian coffee. He took his cup and saucer to the stone-mullioned window and scanned the empty street below. When Enrique came in a moment later, the two men exchanged a brief look, as if conveying a message in code.

"What about Hurst, then?" David asked.

"He's dead." Enrique's voice was cold.

Exasperated, David stole another glance at the empty street. "Yes, we heard. But who killed him? And who killed Raysa Veizaga? What did the police say?"

Enrique glanced at Lucia and shook his head.

Hearing Raysa's name, Lucia bent over her coffee and mumbled a prayer. "We need to go to the cathedral," she said when she was done. "To pray for Raysa's soul."

"You're not going anywhere without an escort," David began haughtily, trailing off as Josefina Melton entered the dining room. Her body moved slowly, her luminous eyes haunted with pain.

"You've met my sister, Josefina?" Enrique asked, in the awkward silence that followed.

"Of course," David set down his coffee and politely kissed Josefina's cheek, but I saw Lucia's eyes widen with shock.

"It's so good to see you again," David said to Josefina, pulling out a chair for her beside Lucia's. "You didn't tell us Enrique was your brother."

"My half-brother," Josefina told him in her lightly accented English. "I was away at school when Enrique was born. I married my first husband a few months later. It's been a long time since I was Josefina Rodriguez."

Enrique poured his sister a cup of coffee, his face a cipher. "In the late 70's and early '80's, when Josefina was a girl, our country went through a succession of bloody military coups. Our father openly supported a brutal dictator. It's to Josefina's advantage that few people know she's a Rodriguez."

"And Ambassador Melton?" I asked, feigning ignorance. "Does he know?"

Enrique and Josefina exchanged a glance.

"He knows," Enrique said. "He's always known."

Josefina sighed. "I have no secrets from him. He's my husband."

"What's Josefina doing here?" Lucia whispered a few minutes later, when I showed her where to find the bathroom.

I pushed open the door and found the old-fashioned pearl light switch. "She ran away from the ambassador, and Enrique threw him out."

Lucia dragged me into the bathroom and shut the door, her eyebrows a taut line.

"It's the curse." She paced in front of the toilet, which had a brass chain hanging from a tank near the ceiling. "She must be afraid she'll die when her baby is born. That's what happened to Enrique's mother. That's what happened to her own mother. Raysa told me: their family can only sustain itself through death."

I thought of the coca leaves I'd seen at the base of Enrique's statue, and the quiet reverence Arminda had shown to *Tío* during the night. They were trying to appease the devil, to gain protection from Death. And the ambassador didn't think they could succeed.

I blotted my face with a damp cloth and struggled to remember what had happened at the ambassador's party, only four days ago. Mikhail had reached out to touch the devil, making a sign of the cross, just as I grabbed his arm. Why had the statue broken at that moment? And why had the pale man appeared on the staircase?

"Josefina kept a statue of *Tío* in the ambassador's house," I told Lucia. "The one that Mikhail and I broke. Enrique says the miners have one in every mine. They think if they're too far underground for God to help, they can appeal to *Tío* instead."

Lucia shook her head, indignant. "But they're not out of

God's reach. They can't be. No one is." She turned to face the crackled mirror above the old pedestal sink, and our eyes met in the glass.

"Oh Isobel," she sighed, her gaze falling. "I can't imagine what you've been through. I can't even bear to look at you. I'm so sorry we came here. We should have gone straight to Buenos Aires."

My mother's worn, faded features took shape in my mind. She couldn't bear to look at me either, not even to hear my voice. In her madness, she had always known the truth, which only my encounter with *Tío* had forced me see. I had come to this city for a reason, already dead. But why?

"Lucia," I said quietly, folding the white towel. "Everything's going to be okay."

We returned to the dining room, where David and Josefina were sitting together at the long mahogany table. Enrique stood nearby, helping Arminda ladle steaming rice porridge into delicate glass bowls. The scent of vanilla beans curled through the air.

"Please, tell me about your Schubert quartet," said Josefina, declining the plate of farmer's cheese David held out to her. Her eyes searched his face. "Tell me about *Death and the Maiden*. What happens in the story, when you play this string quartet?"

David tore apart a piece of *marraqueta* bread. "The second movement's like a death march, you know. And Death is trying to entice the maiden. He's drawn to her tenderness, and he says he comes as a friend. But she says, '*Vorüber*! Pass me by.'"

"And then?" Josefina asked, her soft eyes almost imploring. "What happens to Death and the maiden at the end of the song?"

"That's easy." David stabbed a thick slab of cheese with his fork. "The maiden yields, every single time."

THE TAROT

The tarot reader wore jeans under her skirt. She squatted in the sprawling plaza outside the cathedral, surrounded by a sunny halo of auto exhaust, her dog-eared cards stacked before her.

She tugged at the hem of my black dress. "*Les leo la suerte.*"

"*No, gracias.*" I shook my head. I didn't need anyone reading my fate. Just a few stolen moments with the Stahler that morning had told me everything I needed to know. I was lost. I was sick with desire for the cursed instrument keeping me alive.

The stone arches of *Iglesia de San Francisco* loomed before us, waiting. Mikhail had called during breakfast with his usual excuses. This time, he admitted to waking up in Calacoto, nearly thirty minutes away. Rather than wait for him, we made a quick trip down the hill to light candles for Raysa Veizaga. But now, I wasn't sure I wanted to enter the cathedral. Was I an abomination in the sight of God? Would His angels strike me down?

"Come on," David hissed, following Lucia through the huge arched doorway.

I took a quick breath and crossed the threshold into the darkness. Cold, damp air bit my ankles, and hushed voices swelled around me. But the sky didn't fall, and the hand of God didn't strike me down.

I hung back as David and Lucia navigated through the echoing cathedral, gazing up at the saints. The churches I knew generally had a single altar in the front, but San Francisco was lined with smaller altars all along the sides, each one dedicated to a different angel or saint.

We passed an old woman kneeling before a painting of St. Anthony. I watched as her lips formed words, and I wondered how she knew which prayer to use, which saint to address.

I tried to remember what Enrique said about the miners, who made their offerings to *Tío* whenever they went underground. How did they know what to offer? And how did they know when they'd offered the devil enough?

Unexpectedly, a hand gripped my shoulder.

"Could you keep up?" David asked, tugging me away from the crowd of worshippers leaving Mass. "We don't need you wandering off."

I began to scowl and realized immediately that it wasn't a good idea with a fractured jaw. "Could you at least try to treat me like an adult?"

David came to an abrupt stop, his eyes fixed on Lucia, who was praying in front of a huge marble statue several feet away. "Could you at least try to understand we're in danger?"

"We're in danger?" I asked, pretending to be surprised. I followed David's gaze to Lucia's frail body. She stood with her hands clasped and her lips moving, oblivious.

"Do you see a pattern? First Lucia ends up in the hospital. Then Raysa's murdered outside the theater. Then this psycho attacks you."

"He's dead," I insisted. "Hurst is dead."

"That's what I'm worried about. He was butchered, Isobel. He was butchered like an animal."

I dragged my shoe along a crack in the weathered stone floor, my upper lip prickling with sweat. "I know. I saw."

David shot another glance at Lucia. "Then you know there's still someone out there."

We joined Lucia at the feet of the Archangel. She took three candles from the case beside the kneeling bench and slipped a handful of coins into the donation box.

"Do you have one for me?" David asked, for once almost

awkward, and I realized he had even less experience with prayers and churches than I did.

"Here," Lucia said, lighting David's candle and solemnly acknowledging the statue above her. "This is where we pray for the departed."

I held out my taper to Lucia's, and I wondered whose candle had given hers its spark. Dozens of candles were burning away in their holders, many already spent, each one marking some desperate prayer or treasured dream.

I lifted my face to see the placid marble features of the Archangel.

Let my father be at peace, I thought, recalling once more the bearded specter in the museum courtyard. Wherever he is, let him be happy and free.

I wanted to pray for my mother, alone in her hospital room, her eyes clouded with madness. But she was lost, trapped in another world, and there was nothing I could do to help her. Or was there?

Flimsy and insubstantial, an idea took shape in my mind. A hope. I whispered a prayer and placed the candle on the stand.

Outside, the sunlight was unnaturally bright. When I paused to put on my sunglasses, the tarot reader tugged again at the hem of my dress.

"*Les leo la suerte, señorita.*"

My hand drifted to my forehead. Under the beige latex surface of the Band-Aid, the smooth patch of leathery skin felt unchanged.

Enrique had called me a miracle. He didn't know the half of it. But why was I a miracle? Was *Tío* responsible for my existence in this world? Or was it simply the Stahler, winding me up like a mechanical toy?

The tarot reader's eyes were calm, without appeal. "*Señorita, usted necesita saber su futuro en el amor.*"

At this, Lucia broke into a smile. "Isobel, you do need to know your romantic future. Especially after spending the night with Enrique, under his protection." She crouched down next to the tarot reader, catching the back of her short black skirt and tucking it behind her knees. Pointing at me, she said, "*Cuánto cuesta?*"

"But I can't have my fortune read," I protested. "Not outside a church. I'm trying very hard to limit my acts of sacrilege."

"It's not sacrilegious," Lucia said. "It's just a bit of fun. And in case you haven't noticed, we need some fun."

David shrugged, still scanning the plaza for signs of danger. "Go ahead."

Lucia gestured excitedly to the fortune reader, pulling me down alongside her. I hesitated, half-afraid that I would find myself starring as Carmen in some tragic Bizet opera, drawing the Death card over and over again. Or maybe I'd draw the Devil.

But how could it matter? I'd spent the night at Enrique's house, under *Tio*'s protection. And I was safe there. Safer than Hurst was.

For a moment I imagined Enrique standing in the doorway of his guest room, his eyes shining, his lean body almost touching mine as he kissed me goodnight. *My romantic future.*

The woman held out the cards, like a battered blue and white fan.

"*Tres tarjetas,*" she whispered, her lined face impassive.

I selected one card, and another, then another. She took the tiny stack of cards and began laying them on the ground.

The VIII of Swords. A woman was bound and blindfolded, surrounded by swords.

The V of Cups. A figure looked down on three spilled cups. Two cups remained.

The Tower. Lightning struck the walls of stone. Two figures fell in terror.

With a deep sigh, the tarot reader pointed at the second card and began to speak. Her Spanish was so rapid that I couldn't even begin to follow.

"She's saying great happiness is coming, but you have to wait," Lucia translated. "You've met a man, but sorrow and darkness surround him. But you'll love again, and you'll risk everything, and you'll never be lonely again."

"Never?" The battered cards lay on the stones, inscrutable.

"Never." Lucia smiled brightly and handed the reader a coin.

"But what about the last card?" I asked in Spanish. I knew enough about the tarot to recognize The Tower. It signified ruin. Catastrophe and destruction.

The woman frowned at the card, avoiding my gaze. "*Ir primero a la torre.*"

"*Gracias,*" I said, a knot twisting in my belly. I would go first to the tower, whatever that meant.

"Very interesting," Lucia said. "And very similar to the fortune I had last time."

I tried to conceal my unease. "Really? Maybe everyone gets the same fortune."

"That wouldn't surprise me." Lucia flicked a sharp glance at David. "Every girl wants to think the next man will be the right man, that her future will be better than her present."

Beside her, David said nothing, turning his cell phone over and over in his hand.

"But what if you're not interested in your future?" I squinted up at the cross above the cathedral tower, shading my eyes with my fingers.

"Don't be silly." Lucia waved her arms with elegant scorn. "Everybody's interested in their future."

"*Señorita.*" The tarot reader interrupted, reaching for Lucia's hand. "*La mano.*" Lucia hesitated, then knelt down to offer the woman her hand.

"Fortunetellers are always interested in me," she told us complacently. "I have what they call a single palmar crease on my right hand, which is very unusual. The heart line and the head line are fused."

"Which probably means you're heartless," David said.

Lucia flared with annoyance. "No, it means I'm passionate and intense. Which *some* people don't seem to be able to deal with, but that's hardly my fault."

She tried to tug her hand away, but the fortuneteller held on, her chapped brown fingers tracing the base of Lucia's thumb. I heard a hissing breath. Under her thin wool coat, Lucia's back became rigid.

David and I exchanged a glance, and David bent down to intervene.

"That's enough," he said to the fortuneteller. "Let go!"

But the woman had already released Lucia from her grip and was hurriedly gathering her cards. Lucia's head slowly turned, and she lifted her chin to face us.

"My life line," she said, her voice strangely calm. "It's gone."

I seized her icy hand. "You mean you don't have one? Is it because of your palmar crease?"

Lucia shook her head, her eyes huge. "I had one. But I don't anymore."

GUARDIANS OF PACHAMAMA

"I'm going to die. I know it." Lucia was shaken to the core.

"You don't know that," David said, half-dragging her up the steep hill to Enrique's house for rehearsal. "You don't know any such thing."

She wouldn't believe him, and I knew better than to share what I knew. Still in the shade of the cathedral, we stopped to rest on a corner by the Witches' Market, next to an old woman selling tiny knitted finger puppets from a huge plastic trash bag. Up the narrow street on my right, I could just see the coffin-maker's shop where Enrique and I had found what was left of Hurst.

"It's a sign." Lucia panted with exhaustion and struggled to drink from her water bottle. "I'm going to die."

"That's a bunch of crap." David was fighting hard not to lose his temper. "I thought you were Catholic, Lucy. Weren't we just in a church? I thought you didn't believe in that stuff."

She looked up at him, a tiny bead of water trembling on her lower lip. "You think there isn't room in the church for the devil?"

"Lucia." I spoke with a sudden, surprising conviction. "Whatever this is, we have to stop it. We need to call Henrik Paulsen. He'll know what to do."

I don't know why I said that. I couldn't explain how I knew Paulsen would help. But the sun was shining on the streets of

La Paz, and I was sure.

It didn't matter anymore, what happened to me. But whatever had destroyed Raysa and my parents, I wasn't going to let it have Lucia. And if I had to ask Paulsen or the devil himself for help, I would.

Lucia took a deep breath and looked back at the stone arches of the cathedral. "You're right, Izzy. Henrik has all kinds of medical knowledge. He'll know what to do."

Hesitating, she screwed the cap onto her water bottle and slipped it into her bag. Then she brightened. "And he wants to have coffee with me anyway."

David's face darkened for just an eye-blink. Then he nodded, and we continued walking up the hill.

Our quartet rehearsal that afternoon was less than inspiring. The Stahler gave me nothing. It felt like an ordinary viola in my hands, as if all the magic had gone out of it forever.

Perhaps its power had fled, both for good and for evil. I wanted to believe that, but one look at Lucia's stricken face told me I was wrong.

"Jesus!" Mikhail exploded the moment we finished limping through Schubert's *Death and the Maiden* quartet. He looked around Enrique's drawing room in disgust. "What's the matter with you people? It's fucking anemic!"

David set down his bow and drew his broad shoulders back, spoiling for a fight. "Let's see? What could possibly be wrong? Oh, I know: Lucy just got out of the hospital. Izzy just got mugged. Our publicist is dead. And what are you doing? You're spending every night in a sleazy tourist bar. Or is it a coke den?"

Mikhail drew his thin lips together and scratched at his patchy eyebrows. "I'm not the one who's missing entrances. I'm not the one whose vibrato sounds like an old lady in a nursing home."

Lucia winced and cowered, something I'd never seen her do before.

I opened my mouth to say something and glimpsed

Enrique standing in the shadowy entrance to the dining room. How long had he been there?

He caught my eye and stepped into the room. "Don't worry," he said, giving Lucia a warm smile. "It'll come together for the concerts. It'll be magical."

"Do you really think so?" Lucia looked up at him, grateful.

Enrique reached out to touch the scroll of her violin, and the black phoenix on the crest of her Vuillaume gleamed for a moment in the winter light. "When I heard this quartet in Washington, the four of you sounded like a single instrument, like the voice of an angel. You'll sound that way again."

I exhaled, realized I'd been holding my breath. Enrique was certain. He knew.

He strolled over to the antique sofa and held up his Schubert score. "May I stay?"

"Of course." Lucia and I said in unison. Enrique sat down with a smile and opened the score.

David focused on Mikhail, his face tight with menace. "Three days until the concert in Sucre. Think you can get it together by then?"

Mikhail rolled his eyes and kicked David's digital metronome away from his music stand, sending it skidding into the faded apricot flowers on the woolen rug.

He needs a drink, I thought with sudden clarity. That's what's wrong.

David's bow flicked resentfully back and forth, like a horse's tail swatting flies. He and Lucia must have loved each other once, I was sure of that. And Mikhail must have been functional. But ever since I joined the quartet, everything had changed. It was almost as if we'd all been cursed.

Lucia hooked her left thumb into the frog of her bow and stared down at her right palm. I saw Enrique's shoulders straighten over his Schubert score. He was watching, waiting for the magic to return.

It was 2:00 P.M. by the time we broke for lunch. We settled at the table, where Enrique placed a spicy dish of *llajua* on the table, apologizing for his sister's absence.

"Josefina could have the baby any day," he confided as Arminda brought in a broad platter of seared trout. Hearing Josefina's name, Arminda set down the platter, her face conveying a silent message, and disappeared into the kitchen.

The meal was as exquisite as everything in Enrique's house, but I found myself anxious in his presence, unable to eat. I watched him toy with his pistachio tart.

What would it be like? To live in the shadow of a curse, knowing your sister is going to die, knowing your family can only sustain itself through death?

I set down my dessert fork and finished my mango juice in a single gulp.

Enrique swiftly poured me another glass. "You like mangos."

"I seem to be thirsty all the time," I confessed. "It's the high altitude." Fretful, I crumpled the napkin in my left hand, the fine linen catching on my calloused fingertips.

"It could just be that you like mangos." Enrique's eyes were as dark as the ebony fingerboard on my viola, and so alive, so very alive. He handed me the glass, and his slender fingers brushed mine.

I don't love him, do I? I don't know if I'm capable of love. But I could try to feel something besides my own pain. I could try to be like everyone else, just for as long as it lasts.

As we were leaving, Enrique stopped me on the landing above the stairs. "Isobel?"

I turned away, wondering what was wrong with me, wondering why it hurt so much to look at him. I pretended to take interest in the courtyard below, where Mikhail was using his cell phone to photograph the marble angels guarding the fountain.

Enrique took my hand. "May I see you again, tonight?"

We brought our instruments back to the Hotel Miranda, and Lucia crawled into bed and fell asleep right away. I showered and changed into a simple knit dress, then peeled away the Band-Aid on my forehead. The leathery patch of flesh had

140

deepened into a dark shade of gray, resembling a moldy mushroom. The pale, freckled skin around the edges appeared to be puckering, like the ripples of trapped air in a laminated badge.

I sighed. It was clearly getting worse, and it was probably only a matter of time before another part of my ear splintered off as well. My cropped hair hung around my face like jagged icicles. I lifted a few strands and stole a glance at the truncated rim of my ear, wondering why my rehearsal on the Stahler had done so little good.

I pasted a clean Band-Aid onto my forehead, used the tiny scissors in Lucia's manicure kit to snip a makeshift fringe of bangs, and decided to over-compensate with the eye makeup. Soon a stranger was looking at me in the glass: a thin girl with short blonde hair, dark, smoky eyes, and a fierce, grown-up look on her face.

I thought of the retro fashion sketches that Georgia Lamb had sent my father, and I had to smile. My father and his image consultant had gotten their way after all. Then my smile faded, and I remembered what the psychiatrist had said about my mother. *She says it isn't you, that you're not her daughter.*

She knew. On the day he died, she knew she'd lost us both.

I left the Stahler in the room with Lucia, and David and I walked down the hotel steps to the Café Miranda.

David signaled the waiter. "I'll wait here until Enrique comes to pick you up."

"You don't need to be my bodyguard," I said, inexplicably resentful. "We're in a café, after all, in a modern hotel."

David regarded me coolly. "I don't mean to cramp your style, Isobel. I just think we should stick together. Let's call Paulsen now, while Lucia's resting."

I nodded, regretting my acid tone. I didn't want to fight with David.

"I've got his number on my phone," I began, and then I realized I couldn't bear to leave the Stahler. For a moment, I considered running back up the stairs to my room, wondering if I should bring it with me to Enrique's house.

But what kind of a girl goes on a date and brings a cursed viola?

I opened my phone and dialed. Paulsen picked up right away.

"Isobel?" His voice echoed strangely, out of sync.

"It's me," I said through clenched teeth. "And David Weiss. We need your help."

"Hey, Paulsen." David abruptly stood as Paulsen entered the sunny cafe. "We were just trying to reach you."

I closed my phone. It was easy to see why Paulsen caught Lucia's eye when we first met. He had impossibly high cheekbones, pale gray eyes, and the kind of long, golden hair that seemed best suited to a dissolute artist. But Paulsen wasn't an artist at all, unless his art was interrogating the dead.

"You were saying you need my help," Paulsen said, looking steadily at me.

"Yes." I shot a glance at David, wondering how this conversation would play out. Surely, Paulsen wouldn't tell David the truth?

"We don't feel safe here," I said, hoping that would be sufficiently neutral.

"You heard what happened to Hurst?" David asked.

"I heard. When do you leave for Sucre?"

"In two days."

"Can you get an earlier flight?"

David pulled his backpack up from the floor. "Let me find out."

Paulsen dropped his gray canvas satchel next to David and strolled over to the window, tugging off his coat.

I got up from the table and followed. Through the glass, I could see the entrance to the archeology museum. Tourists entered the courtyard, their cameras flashing, while the mountain lions guarding the gates shone in the sun.

Then the impossible happened. One of the stone lions lifted its angular head, sniffing the city air, and raised its heavy body on thick, limestone haunches. I sucked in my breath, unable to look away.

The stone lion was searching for something.

"You understand, don't you?" Paulsen's voice was flat and cold. Impassive, he watched the stone lion. "You need to get out of this city, away from La Paz."

"You should leave as soon as possible," he told David, turning from the window.

David rubbed his eyes, consulting the itinerary. "If I can change the tickets, we should be able to leave in the morning. But Lucia—"

"What about her?" Paulsen asked.

David glanced at me, then lowered his voice. "She thinks something's happened to her. To her hand. She's lost the lifeline on her hand."

The muscles in Paulsen's jaw tightened. "Take me to see her now."

"But Isobel can't be alone—"

"I told you I'm fine," I insisted. "I'm just waiting for Enrique."

"He's here to meet you," Paulsen said. "I saw him in the lobby."

David and Paulsen went upstairs, leaving me alone in the sunny Café Miranda. Outside the museum, the stone lion arched its solid neck, snaking its head back and forth, and I knew then how Hurst had died. I backed away from the window.

You shouldn't be here. You shouldn't be here, but you are.

I should have died a long time ago. I understood that now. Somehow I'd been preserved, given the chance to see this city, to meet Enrique and feel his lips on mine, to play the most beautiful music in the world. Somehow, I'd been preserved.

A shadow moved up the open staircase from the lobby. As it came into focus, I saw it wasn't Enrique. It was the pale, gaunt man dressed in black. His bony fingers caressed the banister, and he came to a stop on the landing, turning to me with hollow, empty eyes.

I watched as his tightly stretched face tugged itself into a cruel smile. It was my own death I was seeing.

But I won't yield to death, I decided with sudden resolve. I had been saved for a reason, and tonight, at least, I was going to live.

THE SUNKEN TEMPLE

Someday, you'll need to know how to brush past your own death. I'll tell you this: it's as bitter as a winter night. If you move fast and stare straight ahead, the cold won't bite too deep. You'll still know what you love when it's all done. But something else will begin to fade, almost right away.

Enrique was waiting in the hotel lobby, poised and serene in his leather coat. When he raised his eyes to greet me, I had to remind myself to breathe. Across the room, people shuffled past him, all of them worn, sloppy, and fading. But Enrique seemed like a timeless treasure from a lost, golden age. Then the spell broke, and he held open his arms. He was just Enrique.

I hurried over to give him a hug. We went out to his car, and he surprised me by grasping my hand, drawing me close. "I've missed you, Isobel."

"Are you sure?" I said, trying to keep things light. "It's only been three hours." I fussed with the latch on my seatbelt, ignoring the dry tears stinging my eyes.

Enrique grinned and started his car. "I'm sure."

We drove to the Miraflores district and parked on a steep hill streaming with soccer fans. Enrique motioned to a trio of young men, who planted themselves possessively in front of his car. He gave them each a few bills and glanced at his phone.

"The *Hernando Siles* stadium holds forty thousand people," he said as we walked away. "And tonight it will be full. But we have reserved seating."

"Which team do we cheer for?" I asked, unfolding the tickets. I'd never been to a soccer game. Football game, I reminded myself. "Bolívar? Or The Strongest?"

"What do you think?" Enrique asked, with a mischievous smile.

I looked about. Some of the people on the sidewalk wore black and yellow scarves, signifying *El Tigre*, the tiger mascot of The Strongest. Others wore scarves of a brilliant blue, the color for Bolívar. Given Enrique's pro-indigenous politics, and the fact that he could speak Aymara, he probably wouldn't be cheering for a team with a yellow tiger and an English name. "Bolívar?"

Enrique reached into his pocket and pulled out a black and yellow grosgrain ribbon. "My neighborhood's a stronghold, you could say."

"The Strongest?"

"The Strongest." As he said this, he slid his hands under my cropped hair, tying the ribbon around my head. His fingers almost brushed my truncated ear, and I flinched.

The fans came from all levels of society. Around me, I could see tailored leather coats and modern business clothes, but also women in black bowler hats, with heavy shawls over their bright ethnic dresses.

"Enrique? The women wearing traditional clothes. I didn't see anyone dressed like that at my concerts."

"No," Enrique said with a slight frown. "It takes a long time to change things here. But football has a much broader appeal. That's why I thought you should see a game."

We crossed a busy street in front of the stadium and arrived in an empty park circled by the traffic roundabout. Then I caught my breath in surprise.

Directly below our feet was a sunken courtyard. Shaped like an empty swimming pool with walls six feet high, it was filled with stiff, rectangular statues. One statue loomed high above the courtyard, holding a scepter and a chalice. Seeing the towering statue, I felt a sudden chill, as if I'd been in its presence before. But that was impossible.

Enrique followed my gaze to the statue. "That's a replica of the so-called Bennett Monolith, named for the archeologist who discovered it in the thirties. It must represent a god, since it was found in the Semi-Subterranean Temple at the ruins of Tiwanaku. This sunken courtyard is just an imitation of that temple at Tiwanaku, but for many years this courtyard displayed the actual statue of the god."

"Here?" I asked, unsettled. "The god was here?"

Enrique nodded. "All 20 tons of it."

"What god is it?" I asked, wondering why it felt so important to know.

Enrique shrugged. "There are theories, and most are probably wrong. Some think it represents the earth mother Pachamama. Others say it's Viracocha, who formed human beings out of earth and stone. I know this much: it's not a god with an English name."

Surrounding the replica of Bennett's monolith were the steep walls of the sunken courtyard, ornamented with carved faces that seemed to be embedded into the walls of stone. The faces had rectangular mouths and big, staring eyes. Were they the chthonic deities, subjugated gods of the underground? Or were they just men and women, shaped by the god out of earth and stone?

There's power here, I thought, focusing again on the monolith. For years, the god itself was here in this city, bending the lesser gods to its will.

"It's strange," I heard myself say. "There's a movie theater in my neighborhood that rents out space to a church on Sunday mornings. And this place feels so much like that theater, like there's something sacred about it and yet wrong, somehow."

"It is wrong," Enrique said sharply. "The monolith is a national treasure. It never belonged here in a replica of its old temple, exposed to pollution and riddled with the bullets of forgotten revolutions. A few years ago, the statue was finally returned to Tiwanaku, the most sacred place in the Andes."

"More sacred than Machu Picchu?"

"Far older, and far more deeply rooted in the beliefs of the people. Tiwanaku is the home of the gods. If I could take you there with me, you would feel it, Isobel."

It puzzled me to hear Enrique speak so passionately, remembering his painting of the Virgin Mary and the angels guarding his fountain. What had Ambassador Melton called it, that merging of beliefs and mythologies?

Syncretism, I thought, savoring the unfamiliar word.

A paper airplane flew across the temple, sailing right past the blunt face of the statue, and a buzzer blared over the traffic, announcing the preparations for the game.

"Let's check out the temple before we go." Enrique stepped down into the sunken courtyard, his black hair gleaming in the sun. He spun about and grabbed my hand, and we walked easily together. I passed ancient statues and staring stone faces, and I felt a tight sensation hovering around my ribcage, almost like a phantom pain.

It shouldn't be real. But it is real. It shouldn't be true, but it is true. Tonight after the game, we'll return to his house in the old quarter of the city. I'll step out of my blue dress and my black leather shoes. And then— I pushed the fear away, but it came back, with all the force of a prophecy—*I will never see him again.*

My gaze shifted to the right, and I saw who had thrown the paper airplane. The pale man stood on the flagstones above the sunken temple. With long, bony fingers, he was making wings from another piece of paper. As if he could feel me watching him, he turned to me with his empty eyes. He opened his pale hand, and the paper demon sailed effortlessly away. I watched it fly, surprised I wasn't afraid.

I could be happy tonight, I thought, remembering the resolve I'd made in the Café Miranda. In spite of being lonely, in spite of being trapped between life and death.

After all, I was on a date with a beautiful man, wearing a ribbon in my hair, in the presence of an unknown god. Just for tonight, in spite of everything, why shouldn't I be happy?

As if in answer to my question, Enrique came to a sudden halt. Six feet above us, dressed in black and gold, a noisy crowd marched past the sunken temple, led by a man beating a large, cylindrical drum. Slinking along beside them, their eyes gleaming in the fading light, two stone lions were heading right for us.

ALFONSINA Y EL MAR

"Do you see them?" I asked, my heart pounding.

A harsh, thrumming sound swelled up around us, and the statues in the temple began to pulse with force and power.

"I see them," Enrique said, and then we were running for our lives.

We fled for the temple gate. We made it to the staircase, but the steps were gone, inexplicably blocked by a wall of stone. Trapped, we spun about, and the ground beneath our feet vibrated with a resounding crash. The stone lions were in the temple.

They'd come for me, just like they had for Hurst.

Breathless, I reached for Enrique, but he pushed me back with a firm hand, placing himself between me and the lions.

The lions slunk closer, their limestone bodies pitted with age and ruin. Their eyes were blank gleaming surfaces, without pupils. A deep crack gouged the forehead of the first lion. A growl rumbled in its throat like a cartful of rocks.

"Isobel!" Enrique lunged for the six-foot wall on our left. Using the carved faces emerging from the wall as footholds, he pulled himself out. "Take my hand!"

Paralyzed, I stared at the lions. They hadn't flinched.

They're blind, I thought, but that was no comfort at all.

I bolted, and the lions sprang into sudden motion. I scrambled up the rough wall and reached for Enrique, feeling the strength of his hand clutching mine, stone jaws snapping behind me. Then I was free. We ran out into the busy roundabout surrounding the temple, dashing for the stadium ahead of honking trucks, microbuses, and taxicabs.

We threw ourselves into a throng of soccer fans, their clothes bright with electric blue and gold, moving in a human stream towards the stadium. Elbows and shoulders nudged us along, the stone lions nowhere in sight. Through a gap in the crowd, I spotted a yellow sign advertising Inca Kola. I grabbed Enrique's leather coat, pulling him with me.

"What are those things?" We crouched between the concession stand and the entrance booths, searching the faces in the crowd for the stone lions.

Enrique shouted over the din, his voice distorted. "They're pumas, sacred to Pachamama."

"What can we do?"

His face hardened. "We have to get back to the house."

A few meters away, two men were carrying a huge banner, a garish cartoon tiger rippling across its yellow fabric. The banner unexpectedly pitched and swayed as one of the human tent poles lost his footing and stumbled to the ground.

"Enrique!" A stone puma burst out of the crowd and struck the concession stand, snarling with mossy teeth and scattering yellow bottles of Inca Kola.

I grabbed Enrique's hand, and we ran. We plunged back into the crowd, fighting upstream to get away from the puma. I felt my arms wrenched, my hair pulled, and my toes crushed, and I clung to the solid reality of Enrique's hand. It was the only thing I had.

At last we were free, gasping for breath in the thinning crowd.

"Go left!" Enrique shouted, skirting the traffic loop that closed off the sunken temple. "We might make it to the car."

Even from across the street, I could see the tall replica of the Bennett monolith looming above the sunken temple, at least twenty feet high. The god stared straight ahead, chalice and scepter in its hands.

The god knows I'm here. And it wants me gone.

The pavement buckled, and I swung around in panic. Soccer fans tumbled in confusion, jostled by a force they couldn't see.

"Isobel, run!" A stone puma leapt forward with a rattling growl, its ancient teeth bared. I turned to flee, but a wrenching snap shuddered through my body as musty stone jaws closed on the hood of my jacket.

I felt the fabric tear, and with a scream of pure terror, I dashed out into the traffic, dodging a minibus and plunging right into the path of a taxicab. Behind me, I heard the minibus slamming into the stone puma. Brakes screeched as the taxicab slammed to a halt, and I crashed onto the scorching hood.

It should have been agony. I should have been crushed on the pavement beneath the taxi. But I felt nothing. I lay sprawled on the hood, wondering why there was no pain. All around me, the puma's body was splintering, breaking. The minibus drove on.

Enrique yanked open the door of the cab, shouting at the angry driver, and then he was pulling me into the back seat, on top of a young man in a gray suit, an old woman in a black dress, and a tourist with a dingy backpack. "Get in!"

I clutched the doorframe as we drove away, seeing fragments of dust and stone falling like snow outside the window.

Back at the house, the air buzzed with a familiar, disquieting drone. *Tío* waited for us in the entrance hall. A thin scab of red paint was peeling from one of the devil's horns, and the voices of the dead pulsed and murmured around him.

Enrique called for Arminda, conferring quietly. He spoke his sister's name, and the old woman made a harsh sound in her throat and retreated into the recesses of the house. I watched her go, the music swirling around me.

Lost in the voices of the dead, I was startled to realize Enrique was speaking, asking me a question. "Are you okay, Isobel? That puma. I saw it tear the hood from your coat. And when the car hit you, I thought—"

"I'm okay," I said, but I couldn't look at him. "Really, I'm okay."

"I'll get you something to drink," Enrique said and called for tea. He pulled out a chair at the dining room table, and I placed my body in the chair, unnaturally calm.

Enrique gripped the mahogany table edge, his eyes fixed on the candelabra. "I didn't mean to put you in danger, Isobel. I didn't mean for any of this to happen. There are things about my life—" He trailed off, uncertain of how to proceed.

I searched his face. *He thinks they came for him.*

"It's alright." I touched his hand. "You don't have to tell me."

Enrique covered my hand in his. "You're freezing."

He wrapped a brown alpaca shawl around my shoulders, and I recognized it as the one his sister had worn when she arrived during the night.

"Where's Josefina?"

Enrique's gaze drifted to the entrance hall, to the statue of *Tio.* "She's resting."

Esperanza brought us a tea tray, with cold fruit and smoked oysters in little tarts. Grateful for something to do, I poured the tea into pale blue cups, and the girl disappeared into the kitchen, leaving as silently as she came in.

"Enrique?" I said his name before I even knew I had a question.

"Yes?"

"Raysa's maid, Esperanza. Is she working for you, now?"

He shook his head. "She's just staying here, until she finds a new position. When Raysa died, she had nowhere else to go."

Something stirred in my chest, a vague memory: Esperanza bursting into the drawing room, announcing Hurst's death, speaking a language that wasn't Spanish.

I watched Enrique spoon sugar into his tea. "Where did you learn to speak Aymara so well?"

He abruptly froze, eyes on his tea. "It's not Aymara, it's Quechua. And where do you think?" He shoved back his chair with a grating screech and left.

I hung back, aware that I'd said the wrong thing, wondering whether he was hurt or angry or both. I couldn't help thinking of Lucia's story about Enrique's mother, a young girl from the country. A powerless housemaid, with only a sixth-grade education, she'd died bringing Enrique into the world.

I looked down at the sugar bowl on the tea tray, suddenly wanting to put the porcelain lid on straight. There were so many things I wanted to make right.

Hesitantly, I picked up the tray and peered into the drawing room. A cold draft nipped my ankles as I passed the stone-mullioned window. Enrique was at the keyboard of his piano, a hand pressed against his forehead. Bathed in the lights of the entrance hall, the clay figure of *Tio* looked on, voices of the dead pulsing discordantly around him.

The pale man. Would he return for Josefina, or would he come at last for me?

Then I remembered: Death couldn't touch us here, and neither could the stone lions. We were under *Tio*'s protection.

I took a quick, shuddering breath, and the bile rose in my throat. I didn't *want* the devil's protection.

I shoved the tea tray onto the table and fled, pushing my way past Esperanza and the other maids in the bustling kitchen, darting out into the cold of the breezeway, and running the length of the stone balcony to the little guest room. Once inside, I pressed my weight against the heavy wood door and stared up at the painting above the bed. The Virgin Mary gazed down on me, her face serene. A gold halo surrounded her flaxen hair.

How did this happen? If the earth mother was benevolent and good, then why were her mountain lions hunting me? How did I become one of the damned?

Underneath the painting of the Virgin, the simple iron bed was freshly made, with clean sheets and pillowcases. I winced in disgust, remembering the elliptical curve of dust I'd found on the pillow. I lifted my hand to my mangled ear, and then realization slowly dawned: it didn't hurt. It never had.

My gaze fell to my legs, which must have made contact with the bumper of the taxicab when it struck. Heart pounding, I lifted the hem of my knit dress.

There was no bruise. Instead, a long, shallow curve dented the flesh above my left knee, the skin oddly warped and shiny, like cheap plastic that had melted in the sun. And I felt nothing. Nothing at all.

I pressed my hand against my mouth, and something hot splashed onto the top of my hand. I was crying. Behind me, the door briefly rattled, and I heard knocking. "Isobel."

"Enrique?" I brushed my eyes and opened the door.

Enrique stood on the breezeway, haunted and forlorn. "I'm sorry I lost it back there. I'm really sorry. Believe me, I'm not angry with you."

"You have every right," I began.

"Every right?" He glared at me, eyes nearly black. "I almost got you killed at the stadium!"

I looked at him, tears filling my eyes. The two of us: we were lost.

"Please, Isobel. You look like you've seen a ghost. Tell me what I can do."

"I need music," I told him, wishing urgently for my Stahler. "I just want to hear music. Let's not speak of this anymore."

"Of course." He stepped back from the doorway. "Of course."

Enrique sat at his Steinway, playing and singing a slow, quiet lament. In his soft baritone, he painted images of an ancient voice, lost in the sea forever. I tried to follow the lyrics, but they were only words, and words couldn't make my horror go away.

He reached a cadence and held a chord, and I took the opportunity to speak. "What's the name of this song?"

"*Alfonsina y el Mar*. It's about the Argentine poet Alfonsina Storni, who ended her life by walking into the sea. The ocean claimed her, and it sings endlessly of her suffering." Enrique's voice changed. "It's ironic that this song is so popular in

Bolivia, since we no longer have an outlet to the sea."

The song wended its way to its mournful conclusion, Enrique's gentle voice calling up visions of coral and sea foam and loneliness. Slipping to the floor beside the sofa, I carefully straightened each of the tassels on the faded needlepoint rug. When the song ended, the piano continued to resonate, and I closed my eyes, lost in sound, waiting until I was sure there was no music left.

"That was beautiful." I curled up against the cushion I'd pulled from the sofa.

"Thank you." He smiled with sudden pleasure and closed the lid on the piano. "My favorite line is in the second verse. *'qué poemas nuevos fuiste a buscar?'*"

I thought for a moment. "What new poems did you go to find?"

"Exactly." Enrique slid down beside me. As he settled against the velvet cushion, I reached for his hand and interlaced his fingers with my own.

"Why did Alfonsina kill herself?" I asked, still tethered to the music, almost hearing echoes of the melody. "Isn't suicide an unforgivable sin?"

I waited for his answer, remembering my father's razor blades, wishing I didn't have to care.

"Not suicide," said Enrique quietly. "Loss of hope."

"But why did she do it? Why did she walk into the sea?"

He sighed. "Why does anyone pull the roof down on their own head?"

Because her pain was too deep? Because the world was too hard?

Enrique straightened, his eyes on my face. "Your mother. She's a poet, isn't she?"

"She *was* a poet. She's not anything anymore."

I felt myself sinking into an endless mire of self-pity and recrimination. But I couldn't let myself sink any further, or there would be no escape.

"Life's too hard for lots of people," I said with a careless shrug. "Sometimes they can't take it. Georg Stahler was a bankrupt alcoholic, and he killed himself before the varnish was dry on my viola." I picked up my teacup and tilted it. Grainy traces of tea trailed down the pale blue porcelain. Could it show me my future? Did I want to know?

I could still see the tarot reader's final dog-eared card, its ominous warning. *Lightning struck the tower. Two figures fell in terror.*

"That explains it," Enrique said with a slight catch in his voice.

I set down my tea. "Explains what?"

"Why your viola sounds so beautiful." He closed his eyes, as if reciting from a poem. "They say the last wish someone makes before surrendering his life has a special power. Perhaps even the power to transform his life's work."

"What does that have to do with my viola?"

"Isn't it obvious?" Enrique asked, almost urgently. "Stahler's dying wish must have been for his music to live forever."

I searched Enrique's face. He should have been joking, but he wasn't. He seemed entirely earnest, as if he actually believed what he was saying.

For a moment I heard fragments of a familiar melody, and the desolate voice of the mother I loved.

My baby, she'd cried. My poor little girl.

I let the pain of my mother's madness sweep over me, and then a hope returned. It began to form and grow.

"How can you be so sure?" I asked. "That he'd want his music to live forever? Because if I were going to die, that's not what I would have wanted. That's not what I would have wished for."

SHADOWS OF THE PAST

Enrique looked up. Arminda was standing in the doorway, an apron over her pleated gray dress, weary brown eyes focused on Enrique. Dinner was ready.

We entered the dining room, where Esperanza was adjusting a small vase of roses sitting on the table.

"White roses." I leaned over the table towards them, taking in the sweet clarity of the scent. "These are my mom's favorite flowers."

Enrique pulled out a chair and slid it into place as I sat down. "I'm glad I got something right. But what are *your* favorites?"

I focused on a swollen blossom. "Gladiolus."

"Gladiolus?"

I touched the gilt edge of my porcelain plate, embarrassed. "When I was a little girl, I used to think they were called Glads, and I thought it was because people felt happy when they saw them, the way I did."

I could still remember the childish delight I'd felt over those bright, extravagant flowers. I really had felt that way. It wasn't all a dream.

"And then you found out they were named for a sword." Enrique spoke quietly, as if he understood. "And you were disappointed."

I shrugged, not knowing what to say. "I was just a kid."

Enrique sat down opposite me, and our eyes met across the table. "It's okay, you know. To miss the person you used to be." He reached over and touched my hand. "I know I do."

I watched as he poured wine into my goblet. "So do I."

After a rich dinner that mostly went uneaten, Enrique picked up his wine goblet and tilted his head in the direction of the drawing room.

"I almost forgot," he said. "I have something for you." We walked into the drawing room together, and he opened a long, narrow case resting on top of the piano.

"A gift," he said, lifting up a viola bow with ornate silver designs on its ivory frog. He placed it in my outstretched hands. "For your Stahler. It's by James Tubbs."

"Tubbs?" I was too shocked to respond. The bow was a nineteenth century masterpiece: weighty, smooth, and perfectly balanced. "Enrique, I can't accept this."

"But you have to," Enrique said, a hint of urgency creeping into his voice. "I almost couldn't bear to watch this afternoon, seeing you struggle with that old violin bow of Lucia's. I went to Aguirre's after lunch, and he said this was the best viola bow he's ever seen. He was looking for an international buyer. But why shouldn't it be used here, in Bolivia? And why shouldn't you be the one to play with it?"

Because I'm not who you think I am. Because I'm a monster.

I lowered my head, humbled by his generosity, yet unable to keep from imagining the new bow moving in my hands, caressing the cursed strings of the Stahler.

"I really can't accept this," I finally said. "You don't know how it is."

Enrique regarded me sadly. "You think I don't understand? You think I don't know where my money comes from? I *do* know how it is. Every treasure I own, every concert I pay for— it's all a legacy of centuries of barbarism. It was paid for years ago, in blood.

"Some people think I have no business supporting the arts when my country is so poor. But I can't change the past: I can only change the future. I've been surrounded by music and beauty all my life. And why shouldn't my people hear it, too: the most beautiful music in the world?"

The most beautiful music in the world. I curled my fingers around the bow, relenting. I loved it too, and I couldn't bear to give it up. Not yet.

"Thank you," I said, slipping the precious bow into its narrow case. "I'll use this in Sucre and La Paz. When I'm gone you can find a musician here in Bolivia, someone who'll treasure it."

"You'll take it with you when you go," Enrique insisted.

But I won't. I'm never going home.

"We'll talk about it later, Enrique." I placed the bow case on the table by the wall, where a bronze nymph gazed up at me, her lips placidly smiling.

"This is exquisite." I admired the nymph's long, sinuously twisting lines, but I didn't know enough about sculpture to express why it was beautiful.

"That one is by Carrier-Belleuse. It was my grandfather's." Enrique ran a hand along the top of the figure. It was disconcerting to see him touching such a beautiful work of art: I almost expected Arminda to descend upon us like an irate museum guard.

The sadness crept back into his voice. "These bronzes, my piano, your new bow—all gifts of *Tio*."

I looked up from the nymph, alarmed. "*Tio?*" The devil was in the next room. I had almost let myself forget.

Enrique shrugged, as if it were obvious. "The wealth in Bolivia's mines has always brought art and musicians here, luxuries for people with money."

"Musicians are luxury goods?"

"The very best kind."

I flushed, turning quickly to look at a delicate bronze depicting a fox.

Following my gaze, Enrique identified it, his voice casual. "Emmanuel Frémiet. A French work from the eighteen eighties."

"You have so many beautiful things."

"I know I do." His voice grew softer. "But they're not mine. I didn't choose them." He paused, as if struggling to get his words right. "I wanted things to be different, you know. I wanted to go to college in the States. But this house, and the old servants, and my sister . . ."

"I understand," I said. "You don't have to explain."

Enrique looked out the window into the darkness. "Your quartet, Isobel. It's the only important thing I've ever chosen for myself."

It should have bothered me, the way he said that. But musicians were a luxury that few could afford, and I understood.

We sat down together on the sofa, and he draped an arm over my shoulder. I leaned against him, feeling the warmth of his skin under his pressed gray shirt.

"Are you feeling better now?"

"I *am* feeling better," I said, looking up at his face, which seemed to have been crafted from molten bronze.

"I'm glad." Smiling, Enrique reached out with a gentle hand to touch my chin. "And I'm glad you're here. It seems like I've known you for years, but you've only been here for four days. And I still don't understand how it happened, how you appeared in my life, like a visiting angel. How did you end up here in La Paz, having dinner with me?"

I struggled to think of an answer that didn't involve the truth. But the warmth of Enrique's hand under my fragile chin had compromised all the communication pathways in my brain, my sense of incoherence increasing when he turned my head and lightly began kissing my cheek. I shivered, remembering what lay under the Band-Aid on my forehead, only inches from his lips.

The answer, I thought. What was Enrique's question? It was hard to remember.

Enrique's kisses grew more distracting. I heard my voice speaking, but the words seemed to be coming from a great distance away. ". . . because Rachel went to jail."

I sat up. *Oh, God. What possessed me to say that?*

Enrique lifted his head, replaying the conversation. "This is why you've come to La Paz?" he finally asked, a hint of laughter in his voice. "Because someone else went to jail?"

My face burned. "That was a rhetorical question, wasn't it?"

"Not really."

"I meant your earlier question." I felt horribly confused.

"Isobel." Enrique disentangled his arms and helped me to my feet. "I think you need some fresh air. Let's go for a stroll in the courtyard, and you can tell me who went to jail and why this has brought you to La Paz."

We left the drawing room and found ourselves in the entrance hall, where a red candle burned at *Tio*'s feet. A mound of coca leaves rested on a gilded piece of paper. The devil was smiling.

As we stepped outside onto the breezeway, I felt a twinge of alarm. And yet I also felt so completely new, as if the entire world had become another place, a different place, undiscovered before now.

Perhaps this was what a second chance felt like.

We strolled out onto the balcony, and I paused at the cold stone railing, looking down at the rippling surface of the fountain. Enrique touched a switch, illuminating the staircase with lights. I took his arm and walked down the steps.

"She was an animal rights activist," I told him. "The former violist in the quartet." I felt strangely drawn to the fountain as I explained this, reaching for an oval leaf floating on its surface. I'd never seen such a leaf in Minnesota.

"Ah! Everything is clear now." Enrique was trying to sound scholarly or detective-like, but he was laughing quietly, so the effect was ruined.

"She belonged to an animal liberation group that once destroyed millions of dollars worth of cancer research at the University of Minnesota. They set all the lab animals free, but most were later found dead, starved to death or hit by cars."

We sat down on the fountain ledge, Enrique no longer amused.

"Rachel and her friends were arrested in December, trespassing at a research facility at the U of M. She spent four months in jail, and now she's at an inner city diocese in South Minneapolis, doing community service with the nuns. David and Lucia and Mikhail were really upset. She played the viola really well."

Sighing, I tugged at the leaf I'd rescued from the water.

"I know that." Enrique said, becoming more serious. "I've heard your quartet's Villa Lobos recordings."

"Oh, right." I felt a sudden stab of dismay.

"Isobel?" Enrique searched my face. "What's wrong? You don't think I'm comparing her to you?"

"I think maybe they were happier when they had Rachel."

"But they needed you." Enrique touched my shoulder, and his voice dropped to a whisper. "You're a magical performer, and you've transformed this quartet."

I fought back a shudder. Transformed? Into what?

"You do realize, don't you? How much better you are?"

I shook my head. "Sometimes I wonder if they regret losing Rachel, choosing me. Things have been hard for all of them, since I joined the quartet. Sometimes I wonder if it's my fault."

That might not have been the best thing to say. A strangling sense of vulnerability began to tug and swell. But it was true, after all: my fear that somehow I'd contaminated them all, that my curse was bringing them down. I wondered what Paulsen had said when he saw Lucia's hand. I wondered if there was anything he could do to help.

Enrique brushed a few blonde hairs from my cheek. "They're lucky, Isobel, and they know it. I heard you play *Death and the Maiden* in Washington. That night, I heard something the old quartet never could have achieved. I heard something searing and visionary."

I thought of the many concerts that filled my heart, the ones that ended and took a part of me away with them. Each time, the only consolation for the silence that followed was memory.

Enrique understood. Somehow, he knew. He could feel the

magic when it was there.

"Isobel," he said softly. "I want you to stay with me tonight."

"Yes," I whispered, not meeting his gaze. "I know."

I wanted to feel some emotion—excitement, joy, or desire. But all I could feel was a numb sense that I was someplace far away, watching another girl, a girl who looked like me and spoke like me and played like me. And this girl was exquisitely talented, and she was worthy of love, and she was filled with life and joy and hope.

But she wasn't me. I was already gone.

I splashed my hand in the leaf-filled fountain, seeing David and Mikhail and Lucia, all of them dressed in black and gold, colliding and swallowed up in the glittering pool. The stone lions swirled to their death beside them. The cold water dampened my sleeve, and Enrique reached for my hand.

"Careful," he said, drawing my hand towards his face. "You'll ruin your dress."

I watched as his lips touched my fingertips, and for a moment I sensed that a labyrinth of options existed somewhere else, in a distant place. There, people weighed their decisions and made their choices and calculated their odds. But in this courtyard, there was only one path I could place my feet on, its surface a smooth mosaic of interlocking brick and stone. We went upstairs, and I stepped out of my dress.

In the shadowy half-light of Enrique's bedroom, I could faintly hear the droning voices of the dead. Threads of brightness filtered in through the window, splashing Enrique's moving form with gold. Then the music began to fade, and I lifted my eyes to muted lights unlike any I had ever seen: chandeliers over a hundred years old, fitted to use both electric bulbs and gas. And it seemed to me that I could easily take a single step and be gliding across that ceiling, stooping down to gather up those ancient lights.

I woke with ribbons in my hand. The black and yellow band had fallen out of my hair during the night, and it lay woven through my fingers.

Beside me, Enrique gripped the sheets and cried out, and I held my breath, wondering if I should wake him. The clock ticked slowly, the hour hand pointing to 3:00, and Enrique sank back into his dreams.

The room was quiet and cold. Moonlight arched in through the windows, bathing the room in an eerie glow. I felt achingly insubstantial, as if the core of my body had slowly begun to unravel or dissolve. I slipped out of bed, and the dissolving elements drifted away, lost to me forever.

Wrapping my naked body in the alpaca shawl, I tried to remember what had pulled me from my sleep. There were faces in my dream: faces emerging from a wall, each gazing at me with round, staring eyes of stone. One was the face of someone I knew.

I'm going mad.

I stepped up to the window and pulled the edges of the curtain apart. Outside, the city was dark and still, but the lights of the Prado glittered at the canyon's base. A shadow rippled in the darkness outside my window, and then a faint buzzing sound broke the silence.

I grabbed my purse and opened my phone before the buzz could become a full-fledged ring. It was Henrik Paulsen. "There's a plane leaving for Sucre at 6:00 A.M."

I stole a glance at Enrique's sleeping form. "Paulsen? What the hell are you talking about?"

"6:00 A.M." Paulsen repeated. "You need to be on that plane."

GHOSTS

There was a time in my childhood when I couldn't peel an orange. I couldn't play Bach either, and that single fact hollowed out my entire world. Tendonitis had crippled my hands, and for eight weeks, recovery was simply a matter of unpeeled oranges and unplayed songs. But I missed those oranges. I missed those songs.

Waking Enrique that morning, I remembered the bright Valencia oranges I'd tried to peel, the aching in my citrus-scented hands. I hadn't wanted to give them up.

"I have to go now," I whispered, watching Enrique's eyes flutter awake.

"So soon, Isobel?" He lifted a hand to touch my face.

My eyes dropped to the floor. "There's a plane I have to catch."

He slipped out of bed and reached for his clothes. "I'll take you to El Alto."

I stole a glance out the window. "I'm going alone, Enrique." There were two stone lions, but only one was destroyed. I wasn't going to put him in danger again.

"Don't say that." He drew me into his arms, and the warm scent of his skin nearly destroyed my resolve. "I'm coming with you."

I pulled away, hating myself when his face creased with bewilderment and pain.

"No, you're not."

I didn't want to spend another moment looking into his eyes, knowing what we were about to lose, what we could never have.

Enrique reluctantly called for a driver, and I remembered that his Audi was still in the *Miraflores* district. Left behind and unspoken, like our intimacy during the night, it was almost as if it belonged to another person's life.

I managed not to cry in front of Enrique, but as I climbed into his SUV, I dissolved into stinging, messy tears. What was wrong with me? Hadn't I resolved to face my fate? Perhaps this wasn't the end. Perhaps I was just leaving town for a few days. Perhaps I'd be back for the concerts on Friday, armed with stories and souvenirs.

I closed the door of the car and hid behind a curtain of butchered hair, feeling strands clinging wetly to my cheeks, hoping Enrique wouldn't see my face. And for a while, he missed it. He gave directions, nodded to the driver, opened the gate.

"I've made you reservations at the Hotel Sucre," he began, leaning into the open window. But then he saw my swollen eyes, and he stopped.

He brushed my hair aside with a gentle hand. "Don't worry. If everything goes well with Josefina, I'll fly into Sucre on Wednesday morning. I'll be there for your concert. I wouldn't miss it, Isobel. You know that."

My throat constricted, and I knew if I tried to say anything, I'd make a rasping sound. So I sniffed, nodded once, and tapped the driver on the shoulder.

Enrique stood by the gate, watching me drive away. Behind him, a magpie came to rest on the angel guarding the fountain, a piece of string caught in its beak.

David stood waiting by the airport entrance, his face grim. He handed me the Stahler and my new boarding pass, and we walked silently into the half-deserted airport.

I saw Lucia and Mikhail standing in the giant luggage room,

and a new hardness grew inside me.

Pull yourself together, I thought, clutching the viola case to my chest. You've got to face whatever comes.

Lucia was wearing too much makeup, and her face had an odd, waxy sheen. Mikhail was drinking airport coffee. He peered at me over the top of his glasses, the rims of his eyes a deep orange-red. I tried to think how I might ask him if he was sick, but I couldn't. I tried to read the signs around the airport, but I couldn't do that either. I made out one word. *Cuidado.* Caution. Be careful.

My mind skipped through a montage of images; each one featured Enrique, and each one hurt. I stood and waited and scuffed my shoe over a stain on the industrial rug.

"Are you okay, Mikhail?" I finally asked. "You don't seem very awake."

"Of course I'm not okay," Mikhail snapped. "It's 5:00 AM, and I'm a fucking musician." He slurped some coffee and scowled into the cup as if it had insulted him. "I've had enough of La Paz. I'll be glad when we get to Sucre."

"We're not done with La Paz," David interrupted. "We've got two concerts here this weekend."

Mikhail shrugged. "Henrik said we could visit his dig in Socorro. He said he'd show me a mummy."

David stiffened, his eyes on Lucia. "We're not driving into the mountains on a sight-seeing adventure. We're going to stay at the hotel and rehearse."

Lucia didn't react. Her face seemed thinner than before, and her full mouth had crystallized into something sharp and brittle. Seeing the emptiness in her eyes, I thought of my mother's madness, and my lungs wanted to collapse.

I tried to get her attention. "Enrique says we can rehearse at the concert hall in Sucre. He says it's the best hall in Bolivia, modeled after the Paris Opera House."

"The Paris Opera House?" David repeated, a bit desperately, but Lucia didn't respond.

Turning away, I caught sight of Paulsen. Dressed as usual in his shabby tan raincoat, Paulsen was dragging a large stainless steel case, bright red biohazard stickers emblazoned across its sides. The industrial-strength casters supporting its weight reminded me of the metal gurneys in the *Hospital Obrero*.

Typical, I thought. You can take the man out of the morgue, but he'll just take the morgue with him.

Seeing Paulsen, Mikhail pitched his coffee cup into a trashcan and trotted across the luggage room. "Hey, Henrik!"

Paulsen scanned the room, his focus flickering for a moment on my face. Then something strange and unexpected happened: he greeted Mikhail with a bright, devastating smile. "Mikhail!"

"Need some help?" Mikhail asked too-loudly, slinging his violin out of the way.

"I think I can handle it." Paulsen tilted his head, indicated the metal case. "But I can't even get close to the coffee shop with all this gear."

Mikhail held up a finger, as if to say: *Please, sir. Wait just one moment.* I watched as Paulsen nodded agreeably and sent Mikhail off in search of an Americano. Next to me, Lucia still hadn't moved.

"Excuse me," I murmured to David and Lucia and walked over to Paulsen.

"I saw what you did." I inspected the biohazard sticker on his battered metal case.

Paulsen frowned. "And what exactly did I do?"

"Do you enjoy manipulating people?" I hissed, more harshly than I planned. "You just snap your fingers, and Mikhail turns into your own personal errand boy. What else are you going to make him do?"

"That's very fine, coming from you," Paulsen said, his gray eyes flashing. "What have you done since you got here, but twist everyone and everything to your will?"

"Me?" I stared at him, aghast. "You think I wanted any of this to happen? You think I wanted Raysa dead, or Lucia in the hospital? Is that what you think?"

We glared at each other, the air thick with distrust.

He thinks I've cursed them. Maybe he's right. But I didn't mean to.

"What's wrong with Lucia?" I finally asked. "What does it mean, that she can't find her lifeline?"

"It means exactly what you think it means," Paulsen said, slowly and deliberately.

I looked over my shoulder at Lucia. She was stranded on an island of luggage, her skin like a waxy pear, dark chestnut hair blazing against her black wool coat.

"Come with me to the burial site in Socorro," Paulsen abruptly said.

"So Mikhail can see all the mummies you've been telling him about?"

Paulsen didn't blink. "So *you* can see something."

I took a step back. "What's in it for you? Why are you helping us?"

"Is it so strange to want to help people?" Paulsen asked with an inscrutable smile. He reached for the black handle on his metal case and gave it a tug.

"Miss Baigorria," he called. "You look radiant as ever."

Lucia looked up, her face flooding with relief.

Lucia sat by Paulsen on the plane, becoming more and more animated as he told her about his archeological site in Socorro, his mysterious graveyard filled with mummies, his research to help indigenous people with tuberculosis. Somehow, Paulsen had the power to inspire belief, and Lucia wanted to believe. I didn't want to hear a word of it.

Mikhail watched them from across the aisle, apparently spellbound. His body was hunched over into the aisle, his shoulders pulled tight. Every now and then his lips moved, as if he were practicing clever responses and rejoinders.

He was lonely. And Paulsen was on a big white horse, dressed in gold.

The plane took off at a phenomenal speed, racing down an endlessly long runway. My ears popped, and my face felt pressured and swollen.

Mikhail was still leaning into the aisle. "Socorro's in the mountains?"

Paulsen nodded. "In a narrow valley. On the slopes are small trees they use for drying hay. You'll see trees that are flattened down, with grass and hay piled on top."

As he spoke, Paulsen raised his scarred right hand and pressed down on an imaginary tree. I could see the trees, bent under their mounds of prickly hay, like old women who will never stand upright again.

He'll have them all convinced, I thought with dread. And we'll be spending the night with the mummies in Socorro.

David nudged the slender bow case at my feet. "You got a bow, I see."

"A gift from Enrique." I paused. "It's a Tubbs bow."

"A Tubbs?" David raised a dark eyebrow and whistled. "He must really like you."

"He does," I allowed. "But it's for the quartet, you know. Not for me." I took a quick breath, aware that I was close to tears.

David looked in my eyes, his lips briefly pressed together. "When you have a fling, you have to walk away. You do know that, don't you?"

I looked past him and his cello, staring out the window. Clouds swirled around the plane, stifling and uncontrollable. Perhaps they would find their way into the plane, and then how would we repair the breach? We would all die of oxygen deprivation.

David opened his magazine. "Enrique's a nice guy. But you can't let yourself fall in love with him."

The plane flew on, and the earth wheeled away from us, hidden by clouds.

"It's not love, David. I don't fall in love." But it really was the best I could do.

Sucre was a white city on the edge of the mountains. Filled with beautiful colonial buildings, it looked like an expensive movie set: all whitewashed stucco and freshly painted shutters. Palm trees stood in the cold winter air.

Sharing a van with Paulsen, we drove from the airport to

the Hotel Sucre. We passed a park with paddleboats in a moat, a small metal structure standing above it like a miniature Eiffel Tower.

The hotel lobby featured exquisite Andean weavings. Suspended above the registration desk was a thin bronze panel depicting the sun god Inti: a squat figure holding a scepter, with a halo radiating outward like the rays of the sun.

"Nice place," said Paulsen, checking out the lobby. "Too bad I can't stay."

Mikhail looked forlorn. "I don't see why we can't go to Socorro with you. I want to see the mummies. Lucia does, too."

"Well," Paulsen said, his eyes on me. "You're certainly welcome to visit the dig. But I think it's up to David. And Isobel."

"Sorry, Mikhail. We've gotta rehearse," David said. He began to check in, and Lucia took off her sun hat, shaking out her hair.

"What a gorgeous hotel," she said to Mikhail. "Enrique did all right, didn't he?"

Her voice seemed to float for a moment in the coolness of the hotel. Above Lucia and Mikhail, the bronze panel of the sun god wavered, as if caught in a current of air. Then a taut vibration filled the lobby, undercut by a faint, low-pitched drone.

I backed away from the registration desk, my eyes on Lucia and Mikhail, and felt a pair of hands come to rest on my shoulders. I turned, looking up at Paulsen.

"Do you hear them?" he asked, his eyes distant.

"I hear them," I whispered. They'd followed us to Sucre. The voices of the dead.

The pale man would come first, as a warning. And then the earth mother and her guardians would strike us down. We were no longer her children.

Ten feet away, Lucia was laughing, urging Mikhail to tuck in his shirt. "Straighten up! This isn't some sleazy backpacking hotel." The air around her rippled like a mirage.

"Why is this happening?" I whispered. "Why is Lucia's lifeline gone?"

Paulsen bent his head close to mine. "She must have played your viola. It took something from her."

"How do you know that? And how could you stay around to hear my encore, when no one else could?"

Paulsen reached into his coat for his cell phone. "I've heard that music before."

"But how?"

"There are things you can only hear, if you've learned how to survive." His hand tightened on the phone, the scar on his knuckles deepening white. "It's an achievement to survive. You know that. But it always costs you something."

The low, ambient drone intensified. I wanted to cover my ears.

"You said we'd be safe here," I accused.

Paulsen offered me a thin smile. "You mean you don't feel safe?" He raised his voice slightly, and the voices of the dead dissolved into silence. "Time to say goodbye, Mikhail. I've got to head for Socorro."

"No!" Mikhail rushed forward. "Why can't you stay for lunch? Or dinner? You could stay and watch us rehearse."

"I need to work. And the mountain roads aren't safe to drive at night."

"What's so important in Socorro?" I asked. "Besides your job, of course."

Paulsen gave me a measuring look. "Come and see."

Three hours later, there was an ambulance on the side of the road, and Lucia had nowhere to pee. After leaving most of our luggage at the Hotel Sucre, we'd placed our lives in the hands of Paulsen's reckless driver, heading south to Socorro. Now we found ourselves deep in the mountains, on a treacherous cliff-side road. Lucia and I were in the middle seat with the cello, Lucia's legs tightly crossed.

Paulsen stared out the front window, as if trying to memorize every nuance of the scenery. So he saw the rescue workers first.

The van came to a stop on the narrow road, and I looked up, expecting another excruciating series of back-and-forth maneuvers to pass an oncoming vehicle. But we were in a wide spot with plenty of room to get by, and the ambulance in front of us was parked and empty.

A man in a white shirt festering with an orange-red emblem approached and looked appraisingly into the van. He said something to Paulsen under his breath.

We all got out of the van. As I stepped down onto the dirt road, my left leg made a harsh snapping noise, like wood splintering, or ice breaking up. The hem of my long knit dress flapped against my knee in the breeze. I couldn't feel a thing.

The Stahler, I thought, torn between panic and despair. I needed to play again.

"A truck went over the edge last night in the fog," Paulsen said as David and Mikhail got out. "They're asking us to help pull up the driver."

David took Lucia's arm, shading his eyes with his other hand. "We'd better wait."

"You girls stay here," Mikhail said over his shoulder, following Paulsen with a hint of a swagger in his step. "This is guy stuff."

Lucia and David exchanged a disgusted look and leaned against the side of the van to wait, but Paulsen quickly returned in a swirl of blowing dust and sand.

"We'll need you, too," he told David, pulling off his tan coat and dropping it onto the seat by David's cello. "Someone's rappelled down and strapped the body to a stretcher. It'll take all of us to pull it up."

David followed, but not before grumbling under his breath. "We could be rehearsing right now, in a nice hotel with modern plumbing. But instead we're here, wherever the hell this is, dragging up corpses."

Looking oddly pleased, Lucia watched them go.

As Paulsen picked up the rope and got in line with the other men, I wondered at his matter-of-fact tone. Nothing seemed to surprise Paulsen, not the dead body below the road, not even me.

What keeps your blood circulating? I remembered his question at the hospital, the soft urgency in his voice. He'd wanted to understand, but he hadn't been surprised.

I eyed the weathered coat lying on the upholstered seat, wondering what secrets it contained. Paulsen had worn it on Wednesday night, when he met with Hurst. He'd taken the thing they called the Mother's Stone, and he'd slipped it into his pocket.

The men began to pull, and Lucia saw her chance. "Izzy, you've got to cover me."

"What?"

"They're all busy pulling up the body. Now's my chance to pee."

Impatient, I scanned the area. Directly behind us were the cliffs from which the road had been carved. In front, the road's non-existent shoulder, ornamented with white crosses.

"You get behind the van," I said. "I'll stay here and keep a lookout."

Lucia crouched behind the van, and I hesitated, wondering if I had time to look at my injured leg. But I might not have another chance at Paulsen's coat pockets. I slipped my hand inside a pocket. Nothing. I tried the other, my fingers closing around the firm right angles of a book. I pulled out a small black journal, filled with Paulsen's jagged handwriting.

Breathless, I paged through it. Diagrams, numbers, incomprehensible drawings. Words and symbols in languages I couldn't understand.

Hurst's grating voice echoed in my mind. What had he said to Paulsen? "You haven't used the stone. There's another price you'll pay for that."

Hurst had *known* what he was dealing with.

Paulsen's not a pathologist. He's a necromancer.

Ten yards away, a man shouted orders. Paulsen's boots dug into the ground. He was taller than any of the others pulling at the rope, and the sun striking his hair made it look like gold.

I hurried to tuck the journal back into Paulsen's coat, but something slid out: a cloudy glassine envelope containing a thin, coiled object I immediately recognized. I stared at it for a moment, my heart in my throat.

"Much better." Lucia was scuffing cascades of sand over her puddle, her movements as precise as a cat's. She returned, smoothing the front of her jeans, as I slipped the envelope back into the Paulsen's journal.

As if competing in a grisly tug-of-war, the struggling men finally dragged the driver's rigid body up to the roadside. The dead man's face and clothes were covered with fine dust, his skin drained of color. But his long black hair blew about in the wind, dark strands floating and shimmering as if they still had life.

One of the rescue workers draped a blue cloth over the dead man's head. I glanced at Lucia, whose face was expressionless. It seemed I should make some gesture, or in some way acknowledge that the man was dead. But I found I wasn't able to move.

Back in the van, Mikhail brandished his Bolivian guidebook. "This week's the festival of San Juan, and Wednesday's the winter solstice. We should buy firecrackers. We should have a bonfire after the concert in Sucre! What do you think, Henrik?"

But Paulsen wasn't paying attention to Mikhail. Instead, his eyes were fixed on me. "Isobel? Are you okay?"

I reluctantly looked up. "I'm okay." He waited for the rest, and after awhile I added, "I'm just—I thought it was weird that Lucia and I were taking a bathroom break while you were rescuing the body."

"Is that what you were doing?" Paulsen asked, smiling a little.

"That wasn't a rescue. That was a recovery," said David, as if that was that.

Mikhail seized the topic as his own. "Hey, isn't it disrespectful to be looking for a place to relieve yourself, when *we're* pulling a body out of a wreck?"

Paulsen regarded me quietly.

"Disrespectful?" David sounded exasperated. "Mikhail, you can't do anything for the dead. It's only the living you can do things for."

But maybe the dead man had a family. Maybe he had a beautiful wife.

I remembered my father lying prone on our kitchen floor, and a shudder passed through me. I looked out the dusty window at the mountains. Superimposed upon the white peaks and narrow valleys, I saw again the glassine envelope in Paulsen's journal. There was no mistaking the object inside: a thin coil of fine blonde hair, clotted together with human blood.

THE MADWOMAN

We drove on into the mountains, leaving everything certain behind. Paulsen sat next to the driver, turning from time to time to chat with Mikhail.

He didn't look like a murderer. He didn't look like the kind of man who could kill another man for a bloodied lock of stolen hair. But what else could he be?

Socorro was a dusty, isolated mining town, a disorganized pile of cheaply constructed buildings and unpaved streets, empty except for a few vendors, children, stray dogs. Broken bottles lined the tops of the walls. Llamas and goats grazed in the steep hills above town.

We checked into our hotel, which was not a hotel at all, but some kind of community center contracted to provide rooms for visiting researchers. Our room was shabby and cold, with a door that didn't lock. Mikhail and David put their bags and instruments into the room next door and came by to inspect ours.

"Just like our room," David sniffed. "But at least you got your own bath."

"The door doesn't lock. There's no security." I tried not to think of Paulsen, who'd checked into the room down the hall. What had we gotten ourselves into?

"We'll just have to take the instruments with us," David

said. "Everywhere."

"Oh my God!" Lucia called from the bathroom. "Isobel. Look at this! How am I supposed to take a shower?"

The windowless bathroom featured bare concrete walls, whose gray surface had long ago turned brown. David and I peered into the shower stall. A quarter inch of grime encrusted the floor.

"Do you have any plastic bags?" I asked. "You can tie them around your feet, like socks." Amazing, how cold I'd become. We were sharing a hotel with a killer, and I was calmly providing grooming tips.

"Nice. Where'd you learn that?" Lucia tugged her hair from its barrettes.

"My mom," I said, the phrase sticking in my throat. "She grew up on a farm."

"Come on, you guys!" Mikhail urged, pacing about. "There's an ancient burial ground on the edge of town. When are we going to see Paulsen's mummies?"

Lucia retrieved a plastic shopping bag from her suitcase. "When are we going to eat? And what are we going to eat? *Those* are the important questions."

"We'll have to settle for whatever they have down the street." David looked around our room, his disgust obvious. "Talk about a one-horse town. There's no Internet here. No cell phone service. Not even an ATM."

"It's not like we need money," Mikhail said. "The rooms are ten dollars a night."

"Not exactly a bargain," David said, gingerly picking up a pillow. "Look at this place. We could get bedbugs. We could get those beetles that give you heart disease."

"Chagas beetles," Mikhail informed us, with a superior air. "Henrik told me all about them. They're only in subtropical parts of Bolivia, so we don't have to worry. He told me all about the mummies, too. It's really weird. He says most of the time when you have a large burial ground, you'll see all different age groups. But there's no children here. And Henrik said he expected to find malnutrition and tuberculosis, or maybe some regional parasites. But he can't figure out how all these people died."

"That's not our problem," David said. "Our problem is making sure we don't miss the van service tomorrow. Because if we miss the van, we'll be riding back to Sucre in a truck full of mummies."

Mikhail scratched at his nose and grinned. "You say that like it's a bad thing."

Outside our open window, an old Jeep pulled up and honked. Lucia went to close the faded curtains. "Just what we need," she snapped. "Little kids spying on us."

"That's Jhimi," Mikhail told her indignantly. "He's going to drive us around."

Jhimi couldn't have been more than 13 years old. His 1940's-era Jeep had the word *Rambito* written in yellow letters across the top of the windshield. There must have been something wrong with the gas tank, because a large plastic container rested on the floor next to Jhimi's sandal-clad feet, a thin tube siphoning gasoline into the engine.

"Paulsen says this Jeep used to belong to Che Guevara," Mikhail announced.

David rolled his eyes. "Of course it did."

"Will you get out?" Lucia demanded. "I'm taking a shower here."

David and Mikhail left, and Lucia closed the bathroom door and turned on the shower. I hesitated, wanting to see what had happened to my injured leg, but afraid to know the truth. I lifted my viola case onto the stained polyester bedspread, my left leg creaking like a warped door as I bent forward to pick up the Stahler. The viola's orange varnish gleamed in the afternoon light. It was so beautiful, so perfect. And I was falling apart.

It wasn't the weird snapping noise that was bothering me. It was the fact that I couldn't feel my leg at all. Afraid to look at my leg, I wedged a heavy chrome mute onto the bridge of the Stahler. Could I repair the damage seeping through my body? Could I do so without hurting anyone else?

I plunged into the violently moody opening sequence from Schubert's *Death and the Maiden*. The Tubbs bow floated in my hand like a dream, but I couldn't stop thinking about the glassine envelope I'd found in Paulsen's journal.

Paulsen knows what I am. What does he want with my hair?

I continued playing, but something was wrong, terribly wrong. The Stahler sounded pinched and sharp, as if its strings were too tightly wound. I tried to relax and let the instrument play itself. I tried to slip into the haunting, unremembered music, as I'd done so many times before. But the forgotten melody eluded me. The magic wasn't there. Defeated, I slid the Stahler into the case and sat down on the bed.

Why couldn't I play the Stahler anymore? Why couldn't I find the forgotten melody? Is it because I'm not a virgin? Or is it because I've reached the end?

My eyes cautiously followed the line of my legs, taking in the indentation on my left thigh: a shallow trough just above the knee, hidden by the fabric of my knit dress.

Steeling myself, I pulled up the blue fabric and stared. From my upper calf to the place where my thigh disappeared under the dress, the flesh was brittle, shrunken and gray. My whole leg looked like a large piece of petrified wood.

I'm becoming a mummy. The realization arrived with a strange, uncanny calm.

Then a piercing scream turned my heart to stone. Soaking wet and naked as a baby, Lucia stood in the bathroom doorway, staring at my leg, screaming until I was sure my eardrums would burst.

I dropped the fabric over my shrunken leg and jumped to my feet, trying to reassure her, but she backed into the grimy bathroom, shrieking like a lamb in a slaughterhouse. Numb with horror, I couldn't look away. I saw it in her maddened eyes: the same devastating encounter with the truth that had poisoned my mother.

The door banged open, and David charged into the room. "Lucy!"

I picked up Lucia's towel and pointed helplessly into the

bathroom.

"Damn it, Lucy! Are you hurt?" David asked, seizing the towel.

"Get out!" she wailed, scrambling to hide in the shower. "Get out!"

"Lucy, it's me. It's David."

Lucia swung her head wildly as he inched into the shower. Then she launched herself forward and clung to him, her short nails digging into his dense black hair.

"A monster," she gulped, her face bright red. "She's a monster!"

She lapsed into hysterical shrieking, and David folded her in his arms.

"Help us, Isobel," David begged. Lucia's legs gave way in the slippery shower stall, and he struggled to hold her up. "Find Paulsen! He's at the burial site."

Turning my back on Lucia's torment, I threw myself out into the street, and I ran.

No wonder, I thought, as dust billowed around me. No wonder my mom went mad.

Paulsen was the last person I wanted to ask for help. But there was no one else. His office was a cluttered room in an antiquated Quonset hut, with slanted windows overlooking a pit filled with researchers. The diggers all wore hospital masks.

Struggling to catch my breath, I pleaded with him. "You've got to help us. Please. Lucia's gone mad. Just like my mom."

"I don't understand," said Paulsen, with infuriating calm. He hadn't stood up. "What do you mean, she's gone mad? How did this happen?"

I paced for a moment in front of his messy desk, then pulled up the hem of my dress, revealing the petrified expanse of shrunken gray flesh. "She saw this."

"Ah," he said, not batting an eye. He closed the laptop computer on his desk.

"I'm asking you for help," I said. "I want Lucia to have her lifeline back. I want my mom to have her mind back. I want all of this to be over."

"Over?" Paulsen asked, suddenly roused. He walked up to the window, his back to me. "You've given yourself to the powers of darkness. Do you really think it will ever be over?"

I felt it then: how hopeless it all was. But Enrique was right. The only thing the gods wouldn't forgive was loss of hope. And I would not lose hope.

"Lucia doesn't deserve this," I insisted. "She's not the one who destroyed her family. She's not the one who chose death."

Paulsen slipped his arms into his long tan coat. "I'll do what I can for your friend. Perhaps some medication may help. But what makes you think I can get her lifeline back?"

"Don't play games with me. You know what I am, and I know what you are."

He watched my face, his pale gray eyes cool and remote. "And what am I, Miss Linden?"

I met his gaze, unflinching. "You're one of those who interrogate the dead."

"Maybe I am." He slung his canvas satchel over his shoulder and gestured in the direction of the door. "But I'm also someone who's paid to tell the truth. So let me tell you this one true thing: Whatever you've lost in this world, you can never get it back."

He gripped the strap of his satchel in his right fist, and the stitch-marks on his long white scar shone brightly against his tan. "If you try, you'll destroy yourself, and you'll destroy the ones you love."

I threw myself in front of the door, blocking his exit.

"Please," I begged, "I know you can help me."

"I don't know why you think that."

He'd said he wanted to help. Why had he changed his mind?

Furious at his indifference, I took a gamble. "You have knowledge, Paulsen. And you have power. I know you have the Mother's Stone."

Paulsen abruptly swung his head, a single lock of golden hair clinging to his cheekbone. I'd succeeded in surprising him.

"The Mother's Stone?" he enquired, his voice taking on a

nasty edge. "Do you know even what you're talking about? Do you know what it would cost to use it?" His face was taut with an emotion I couldn't recognize.

I clenched my fists. "I don't care. I'll do whatever I have to. It doesn't matter what happens to me."

Paulsen's face darkened even more. "You think it doesn't matter?" Without warning, he seized me by the shoulders and shoved me hard into the metal doorframe.

"Stop it!" I cried, beating him back with my fists. "I know what you are! I know what you did to Hurst!"

Paulsen released me at once. For a long time, we stared at each other.

"Where's the rest of my hair?" I finally whispered. "What have you done with it?"

He shoved me through the door and locked it behind us. "Hurst didn't have it."

"You mean, he didn't have it when you killed him."

Paulsen headed out into the dusty street. "You can think that, if you want to."

THE PIT

It was getting dark. The village felt deserted, and the buildings all had a grim, desperate air, as if the people of Socorro were on edge. Perhaps a windstorm was expected. Everywhere I looked, they'd shuttered their windows.

Paulsen headed briskly for the makeshift hotel, ignoring my angry protests. We hurried past the burial ground. A few lights were mounted above the walls of the pit, illuminating the gaping holes where mummies had been found. The cavities in the sandy wall looked like huge, abandoned swallow's nests. They reminded me of something else as well, something I'd seen before.

Mikhail paced outside our cement-walled hotel, waiting.

"Henrik," he implored, showing us in. "You've got to help us!"

Lucia's screams echoed through the hotel. Her face was red and swollen, and she couldn't form words anymore. Not in English, at least.

"*Monstruo*," she wailed, whipping her damp hair back and forth, "*Monstruo.*" Her eyes stared straight ahead. David stroked her hair and whispered encouragement.

Mikhail's face was tense and pale. "What's happened to her?"

Paulsen took Lucia's swollen cheeks in his hands, gazing into her dilated pupils.

"She's in shock, Mikhail." He straightened and looked around. "I've got some sedatives in my room."

He slipped out the door, and Mikhail and I followed him down the narrow hall.

Paulsen's hotel room was tiny and Spartan, his stainless steel case nearly blocking access to the bathroom. He knelt down to unlock the case.

"They don't have a real clinic here," he said, rummaging through medicines and sterile wraps, "so I bring supplies to the nurse whenever I come into town."

He tore open a small cardboard box with his teeth. Tipping it sideways, he retrieved a vial of clear liquid.

Mikhail twisted his hands and watched Paulsen prepare a syringe. Hating the sight of the needle, I turned away and scanned the room. Paulsen's table held just one object: a small photo of a young woman with bright eyes and dark, glossy hair.

Paulsen followed my gaze to the photograph. Holding the syringe between two fingers on his left hand, he slipped the photo into the pocket of his trench coat, and grabbed a plastic water bottle from the bed.

"Let's go," he said, and we filed silently into the hallway.

Back in our hotel room, David winced as the tiny needle entered Lucia's thin, twitching arm.

Paulsen slid the used needle into the empty water bottle. "We'll take her back to Sucre in the morning, when the roads are safe. There's a storm coming."

"What can I do?" David asked, his voice cracking.

"Stay with her," Paulsen told him. "Keep her quiet and calm. No company, no conversation. The sedative should take effect soon."

He produced a metal key. "Isobel should stay in my room. There's a cot in my office. I can sleep there."

Mikhail hovered in the doorway, glasses framing bloodshot eyes.

Paulsen gripped his shoulder. "Come with me, Mikhail. Give Lucia a chance to rest, and we'll call the clinic in Sucre."

As they went out, Paulsen turned his head, his cold eyes

seeking mine. *You,* the eyes said. *You have done this.*

Numb, I followed him and Mikhail back to his office. We passed houses with metal roofs, noisy chickens, and scavenging dogs. A fierce wind had picked up, and a few villagers were gathering buckets and tying down tarps.

Between the burial site and Paulsen's Quonset hut, a modern generator hummed quietly, muffled by a painted enclosure. While Paulsen unlocked his office, I listened to the generator hum and recognized a D minor chord.

It was like a white noise machine, that generator. Its pulsing minor chord seemed to be masking another sound, something too faint to give a name. With a shudder, I cast one final glance at the burial pit and followed Paulsen into his office.

Paulsen called the clinic in Sucre, using his high-tech satellite phone.

"If the pass along the canyon were open, we could take her south to Potosí instead," he said when he was done. "But it's better to get back to Sucre."

Potosí? I remembered the drawing I'd seen in Enrique's entrance hall, and a memory rippled. The city beneath *Cerro Rico*, the mountain that swallows men.

"We need to call Enrique," I said, digging in my purse for Enrique's cell number. "We might have to cancel the concert on Wednesday."

"Cancel?" Mikhail's forehead filled with deep lines. "But she's gonna get better. She *has* to get better."

He looked to Paulsen for confirmation, but Paulsen simply punched Enrique's number into the phone. It rang and rang.

I felt some relief when Enrique didn't answer and his voice mail didn't pick up. *What would I say to him? What would I ever say to him again?*

"He's not there."

"Then we'll call the embassy," Mikhail said, abruptly galvanized. "Or we'll call Ambassador Melton."

Paulsen frowned. "I really don't think that's necessary. This is a medical matter, and Lucia—"

"The ambassador's one of our sponsors," Mikhail insisted.

"He'll know what to do." He dug in his pocket, spilling crumpled bills and shiny bolivianos onto Paulsen's desk. "I *know* I've got his number."

"Mikhail, I have it." I handed Paulsen a 3X5 card containing the ambassador's number. And Raysa Veizaga's.

Paulsen looked at the names on the card. His eyes met mine. "If that's what you want." He slowly punched the number into his satellite phone.

"I'll handle this," Mikhail said, seizing the clunky black phone as it began to ring. "I'm the one who knows Lucia."

"Ambassador Melton?" Mikhail pressed the phone against his ear, darting a quick glance at Paulsen. "This is Mikhail Leiberov. We're in Socorro, and Lucia's really sick."

Whatever the ambassador said, it made Mikhail's shoulders slump. He lowered the phone, and I heard the ambassador's faint, tinny voice coming through the speakers. "Is David there? Let me talk to David Weiss."

"He doesn't want us," Mikhail said, shoving the phone into my hand. His face was haunted and miserable. "Nobody wants us."

I cradled Paulsen's satellite phone as Mikhail sullenly pushed his way out the door.

"Hello? Ambassador?" But the line was already dead.

Paulsen hesitated, then called out through the open door. "Mikhail! Don't go into the burial site. Not without a mask."

"What's wrong with the site?" I asked, my eyes on Mikhail's departing figure.

"The bodies are still decomposing." Paulsen began to say something else and stopped. "You need to keep an eye on Mikhail. Take him back to the hotel. I'll bring you some food."

I shrugged, unwilling to agree too readily about anything. I didn't trust Paulsen. Every word he said filled me with unease. I could still feel his rough hands gripping my shoulders, the weight of his body slamming me into the doorframe.

"Isobel." Paulsen's voice dropped. "Who broke the ambassador's statue?"

I searched his face, taken aback by his abrupt question.

I remembered it so clearly: Mikhail stretched out his hand to touch *Tío*'s forehead, making the sign of the cross. I grabbed his arm as the devil shattered, and a current of emptiness passed through us, dry and cold.

"Mikhail did." *Or did he?*

Paulsen's eyes followed Mikhail's retreating figure. "Did you have a visitor?"

A visitor? Unbidden, the pale man appeared in my mind. I saw his cold smile, the withered llama fetus gripped in his claw-like hand.

"You could say that," I whispered.

Paulsen turned, his face blank. "I thought so."

Picking up his satchel, he stepped into his research lab.

I found Mikhail on an outcropping of rock overlooking the pit. Uninvited, I sat beside him. He peeled a narrow strip of bark from a stick and turned the bark over and over in his hand. As the generator quietly hummed, we watched the moths fluttering in the fading light.

Then Mikhail spoke. "This happened to your mom, didn't it? She went mad."

Something flooded my eyes, something too dry to be called tears.

The hem of my dress fluttered in the rising wind, and I rested my arm over the dented, shrunken part of my leg. "It did."

"What was she like before?"

Before? I wondered how far back he'd be willing to go. Before my dad died? Before I found the Stahler? Before I got tired of being a puppet?

"No one's ever asked me that." Strange. Of all the people who could have asked, Mikhail wasn't the one I'd expected.

Mikhail's red-rimmed eyes focused on the metal ramp leading down into the burial ground. A spotlight illuminated its shiny surface. "Was she like Lucia?"

"She was kind," I said, calling up images of the beauty she'd been when her eyes were still bright. "She wrote poems, and she believed in me. Not just my music. She believed in me. And she thought the whole world was magical and holy."

"Magical and holy?" Mikhail let out a sigh, his face like a wounded soldier. "God."

"What's wrong with that?"

"Nothing's wrong," he said, tossing his scrap of bark into the burial pit. "But I would have given anything. To have a mom like that."

I nodded, surprised by an unfamiliar emotion. It felt like gratitude.

Mikhail stood up, brushing the dust from his clothes. I glimpsed the reflected glare of my bandaged forehead, distorted in the cloudy lenses of his glasses. He took the glasses off, and I saw that his eyes were drowning.

"We can't give up on them, Izzy. We can't give up."

Back at the hotel, I sat on Paulsen's bed, holding the Stahler. The hands of the cheap alarm clock crept along. Through the thin wall, I could hear Mikhail practicing unaccompanied Bach. He rushed through the stately Chaconne at a furious, reckless tempo. When his arpeggios finally collapsed into confusion, he made a choking sound in his throat. He was crying.

I slipped into the hall and knocked on his door.

"Go away," Mikhail snarled. "Leave me alone."

"Let me help you, Mikhail."

"You can't help," he said, his voice tight and reedy. "Just go to bed."

I hesitated, looking at the white paint peeling on the door. Then I returned to my room, my leg creaking as I bent down to lift up the Stahler. I stroked the orange varnish with my fingers. I caressed the ebony fingerboard. I wanted so badly to play it. But every time I slid the instrument under my chin, I remembered Lucia's face.

I couldn't do this anymore. I had to let go.

Setting the Stahler back on the bed, I shut myself in Paulsen's bathroom. Alone at last with the truth, I pulled my dress over my bandaged face and gazed coldly into the mirror.

The petrified gray skin on my leg had spread upwards. Long, narrow threads of brittle skin reached upward over my hipbone and into my groin. The soft flesh of my belly puckered around a few taut gray lines, like hardened scars binding the tissue together.

I turned on the shower, careful not to look at my body again.

What will happen when it reaches my heart?

That night I couldn't sleep. I turned my pillow over, then turned it over again. It was too stiff and too high. Finally, I rolled into the middle of the bed and rested my head in the trough between the pillows. But now I was too far from the edges of the bed, and my mind wouldn't settle. I wanted to see things clearly, but nothing was clear. Lucia was lost and broken, and I was in a stranger's bed.

I heard the scraping of footsteps and a woman's laughter outside my room. Then I heard a man's voice speaking in Spanish. He was laughing as well. Had they always been that happy? I wondered if they were new lovers or a long-married couple, and if they'd ever felt suspended between one world and the next: between the world of possibility, and the world where people are lost and alone.

A series of blurred images twisted slowly before me, in ribbons of color and light. I felt a great urgency, as if some terrible crisis needed my attention. But I didn't know what the crisis was. Then the colors swirling in my vision coalesced into something I recognized. A field of prairie grasses, shot through with snow. I became calm again, and I entered the one place in the world where decisions could always be made, where possibilities could persist forever.

It was a cold day in Minnesota, and my father would soon be dead. Not even in my dreams could that be undone. But it had not happened yet.

For a long time I sat beside him at the anniversary party, eating pecan pie. After the pie had been eaten and the guests had all gone home, we found a place near the piano and listened to my mother sing. And when my father said, "Isobel, aren't you going to play your Stradivarius?" I opened up the violin case, and I played one perfect song.

THE MUMMY

"Isobel!!" Mikhail pounded on the hotel room door. "Wake up!"

I clawed my way back from oblivion and peace. The pounding intensified, and a fierce wind rattled the flimsy windows. Groggy, I reached for the bedroom light.

"Mikhail?" I stepped into my flats and tugged open the door.

"Lucia," he gasped. "They've taken her."

"Who's taken her?" I began. Then I heard a faint scream coming from outside.

Please, God. Not Lucia. Panicked, I followed Mikhail into the darkness. Dressed in our pajamas, we raced out into the street, the mountain wind coursing ahead of us.

A single electric light illuminated the entrance to Socorro's restaurant, less than half a block away, revealing David struggling to climb onto the back of a moving Jeep. A heavy-set figure crouching in the Jeep shoved David forcefully backward, and he fell.

The Jeep rounded the corner next to the empty restaurant, Lucia's screams echoing through the darkness. Then it picked up speed and was gone.

We rushed forward and lifted David to his feet. His black hair was glistening with blood, a huge gash disappearing into his hairline.

"Lucia!" The look on his face, a wrenching blend of remorse and disbelief, was something I never wanted to see again.

Mikhail began crying, openly and helplessly, big tears running down his narrow face. "Oh God," he cried, tugging off his glasses. "She's gone."

The four of us, I thought grimly. We're like a family.

Blood was dripping from David's eyebrow. "We've got to find Paulsen. He's got a phone that works here. He can call the police."

"Hold still," I said, using both hands to apply pressure to David's forehead. The wind tossed my hair in gusts, blowing it away from my face.

Mikhail straightened his shoulders. "I'll find him."

Then it hit me: Paulsen could have engineered this whole thing. "Mikhail, wait!"

"He's sleeping in his office." David shoved me aside and blotted his forehead with his sweater. Then he stared at my face, his eyes abruptly fixed on my ear.

I stepped back from David and covered my broken, mutilated ear. My hands were wet and red. Behind him, in the darkness beyond the deserted restaurant, I glimpsed a pale blur, moving toward the archeology site.

"Henrik?" Mikhail saw the figure too. Without another word, he bolted down the dusty road. But David stood frozen, gazing down at my face.

"Isobel," he whispered. "What's happened to you?"

"Not now," I begged. "We've got find Lucia. You've got to get that bleeding under control."

Then I heard the voices: the droning voices of the dead. They cut through the wind rushing across the high mountain plateau. They cut through the fluorescent hum of the flickering restaurant light. They cut through the beating of my heart.

My gaze dropped. Blood ran down my hand as Paulsen's voice surfaced in my mind. *Did you have a visitor?*

"Oh, God." My back stiffened, a hard wire tugging from my scalp to my spine.

I lifted my eyes to the restaurant, where the pale man was waiting. He put a bony finger to his lips, and his hollow black eyes creased with his smile. Then he glided away, his gaunt form heading for the burial site. Abandoning David, I followed, bloody hands clutching at my pajama top, trying to hold onto something real.

"No!" I cried. "Mikhail! Mikhail, come back!"

The voices of the dead rose up around me as I ran, pulsing in the wind like shimmering zephyrs of sound. I reached my destination: the looming burial ground.

The wind battered at my body, and I wavered, afraid to plunge into the mass grave. It stretched out below me, shadowy and dark. But I knew I had to go in.

Finally, I scrambled down the metal ramp, clinging to the armpit-high ropes anchored to the swaying light posts. Finding myself at the bottom, I skirted around scaffolding and plastic tarps, following the pale man with the hollow eyes. He wove through the obstacles with silent steps, glancing over his shoulder with a tight, frozen smile.

Then he was gone, as abruptly as he'd appeared. I'd reached the edge of the mass grave. Walls of clay and sand loomed before me. The air stank of dry, autumnal decay.

"Mikhail! Mikhail!"

A clump of dried grass blew past, striking my cheek.

Caught in the wind, a tarp pulled away from its moorings. A circle of human figures rested on the ground, their shriveled bodies laid out in a circle like bent spokes on a wheel.

I took a step backward and heard the crunch of glass under my feet. My hand reached down, retrieved a broken pair of glasses. Icy cold, the empty frame lay useless in my hand.

Turning slowly, I scanned the gaping holes gouged into the side of the burial pit. Then I froze. Beside the hollow cavities that held the mummies, there was something else embedded in the wall. I screamed, and my voice echoed through the graveyard.

Mikhail was trapped in a wall of rock, his mummified face contorted in agony. His dead eyes stared straight ahead, as hard and dry as stone.

THE SHADOW

Mikhail was always the one playing second fiddle. Always last to come onstage, trailing behind Lucia's beauty, behind my prestigious recording career, behind David's rock star smile. At the end of every concert, there was always a half-beat of hesitation, right before he joined us to share a bow. To the audience—even to the rest of the quartet—he was perpetually in the shadows, never quite coming into focus.

Clutching Mikhail's broken glasses, I sank to the ground in the dusty pit. An ugly refrain was pounding at the space behind my eyes: *Stop. Stop. Stop.*

But it was all out of control. Lucia was taken, Mikhail dead. I wanted it to be over, but it would never end.

The beam of a flashlight broke into the gloom, its gold circle of light tracking along the wall of the burial site, coming to rest on Mikhail's agonized face. I turned, straining to find the source of the light. Silhouetted against the spotlights hanging over the pit, I could see a tall form in a long coat. *Paulsen.*

"You found Mikhail," he said, a catch in his voice. He didn't sound surprised.

His canvas satchel slung over his shoulder, Paulsen descended the narrow metal ramp, edging past the circle of bodies exposed by the flapping tarp.

Wordlessly, I stood and held out Mikhail's broken glasses.

"Poor kid," he murmured, taking the bent frames from my hand.

"You bastard!" I swung my arm, catching him off guard. My knuckles cracked as they made contact with his jaw.

Paulsen rocked on his feet in the darkened burial yard. Then he was still.

I gripped my twitching right hand. It should have stung, but I felt nothing. "You knew he was going to die, and you did nothing to help him."

"Listen, Isobel—" he began, setting his flashlight on the ground.

"You wanted him dead, didn't you?" I snarled, indicating the shadowy circle of mummies. "A fresh specimen for your research. You lured us here so he would die!"

Paulsen's eyes gleamed unnaturally in the broken light. If it had been anyone but him, I would have thought he was in tears.

He held Mikhail's glasses, almost protectively. "You still don't get it, do you? You want to know why I brought you here? To show you these mummies. To show you what you'll become if you don't let go."

"I'll become like Mikhail?" I choked out. "Is that what you mean?"

Paulsen flinched at Mikhail's name. "It was a mistake," he admitted, "to bring Mikhail here. This place is a locus of power."

"A mistake?" I wanted to feed his body to the lions, one piece at a time. "You're a doctor! When you make mistakes, people die."

A harsh laugh broke from Paulsen's lips. "You've got that wrong, Isobel. When I make mistakes, people are already dead."

"Already dead?" I stiffened, not wanting to hear another word.

Paulsen drew closer, forcing me to look at him. "Mikhail was marked for death, and you know it. He was marked from the moment he touched the ambassador's statue. You know what powers he summoned at that moment, and you know what it cost him. When you touched him, you turned his visitor aside."

He paused, his eyes darkening. "But only for a while."

Only for a while. I braced myself against the crumbling wall, surrounded by earth and decay. The gusting wind rattled the scaffolds and tarps as I took in the full horror of Mikhail's desiccated face. His cheeks were withered and sunken. The whites of his eyes were the color of coffee grounds.

Paulsen's voice softened. "Isobel, there wasn't anything you could have done."

"You don't know that! You don't know me." A strange, unearthly feeling enfolded me. "If I'd understood the danger, I could have stopped it from happening." I glared up at him. "But you knew. You could have done something."

Paulsen shook his head. "Your friend David spoke the truth yesterday. There isn't anything you can do for the dead. It's only the living you can do things for."

"If you say you believe that, you're lying," I accused. "You don't believe that. If you did, you wouldn't be who you are. You wouldn't do what you do."

Paulsen didn't flinch. But something sparked in his eyes—something hot, furious, and desperate. "If you really know what I am and what I do, you should think hard about what you say to me."

"Are you threatening me?" I snapped. "Because I'm not afraid of monsters like you."

"Paulsen? Is that you?" An anguished voice interrupted our quarrel, carried across the burial site by the gusting wind. It was David.

"We've found Mikhail." Paulsen stood, looking up across the circle of mummies. "I'm sorry, David. Mikhail's dead."

"Dead!?" David stumbled down the metal ramp. "Mikhail?"

Paulsen slipped Mikhail's broken glasses into his coat pocket. He tilted his flashlight as David approached, directing the beam to illuminate Mikhail's tormented face.

"Oh, God." David whispered. He froze mid-step. "That's

impossible."

"David?" Paulsen's flashlight wavered, then shifted to David. The blood from David's forehead had dripped down his neck, soaking his shirt with gore. "You're hurt."

"They took Lucia," David said slowly, as if in a daze. His eyes never left Mikhail's shadowed face. "They took her away."

"Lucia?" Paulsen's neck muscles tightened. He swept his hair back from his face, revealing absolute, unfeigned shock. Finally, something had taken him by surprise.

Gripping David's shoulder, he tugged him back toward the metal ramp. "You're hurt, David. We need to get help. We need to call the police."

"But Mikhail—" David broke off. "What's happened to him?"

"We can't help him. We need to find Lucia."

Paulsen's Quonset hut quickly became a crisis control center. He called the Bolivian police and sent his helper Jhimi to wake the town, to find volunteers to search for Lucia. Then he contacted the U.S. Embassy and put David on the phone.

"Our friend Mikhail Leiberov is dead," David said into the ugly, impersonal satellite phone. "He was an American citizen."

He looked searchingly at me, his eyes on the jagged tuft of blonde hair covering my mutilated ear. His voice broke as he went on. "We don't know how he died."

I wondered how the embassy would deal with Mikhail's mummified remains. I wondered how we would go on living in the world. I tried to imagine the future, but there was a shadow concealing our path, blotting everything out.

"Lucia Baigorria was taken by four men," David told the embassy as Paulsen dabbed his face with antiseptic. "She's a U.S. citizen. They were wearing heavy jackets, driving an old Jeep. We don't know where they went."

Paulsen taped a gauze pad over the gash on David's forehead. He didn't speak.

"They're saying the men must have taken the road back to Sucre," David told us, after he hung up. "The mountain pass that leads to Highway One is impassible this time of year. They're going to block the road outside Sucre."

Jhimi came back in, having sent forth the volunteers. He stood close to David as Paulsen applied the last of the bandages.

"*Quiero ayudar.*" Jhimi's jaw was set, his eyes steady. He wanted to help.

"You're going to need sutures," Paulsen told David, shaking his head at Jhimi.

David touched his fingers to his bandaged forehead. "I can't bear to think about Mikhail trapped there, alone. Somebody should dig him out of there!"

"Jhimi can help us," I interrupted.

I remembered what Mikhail had said about the burial site. There were no children there. "Someone should stay with Mikhail's body. Someone should stay with him."

David and Paulsen exchanged a glance.

"*Quédate con Mikhail,*" I said to Jhimi. It was an entreaty.

Half-hidden under thick bangs, his eyes met mine. "*Sí.*"

David nodded. "*Gracias*, Jhimi."

Paulsen retrieved the flashlight from his desk and gave it to Jhimi. I watched him go, watched the rest of his childhood walk away.

"Jhimi will stay with Mikhail's body," Paulsen said, after a pause. "And we *will* find Lucia."

David fought back tears. "I don't understand why they did this. They broke into our room and kidnapped her. They even took her violin. Why would they do that?"

"Her violin?" A look of alarm flashed across Paulsen's face, a volatile mixture of fear and shock and rage. For the second time that night, he was taken by surprise.

"You're sure it was the violin?" he asked David. "They didn't take the viola?"

"It was the Vuillaume."

Paulsen grabbed a tightly rolled black tarp, with a thick metal zipper standing out oddly from its edge. Shoving the tarp into his satchel, he patted the pockets of his tan coat, as if checking to make sure something was there.

"Isobel. You and David need to stay together. In a public place. I'll be back. I think I know where she's gone."

He unlocked his desk, removing a wooden box the size of a chess set, ornately carved with elliptical spirals. Seeing the box, a sudden distrust coursed through me.

"You'll be back?" I hissed. "You expect us to believe that? You're leaving town."

"Isobel!" David stared, appalled. "He's trying to help!"

Paulsen took his satchel and the wooden box, headed outside. "I said I'll be back, and I will. Take my phone. Wait for me in the restaurant in the morning."

I followed him into the deserted street. "How can I trust you?"

Paulsen stopped in front of the battered Jeep. "You can't, Isobel. You can't ever trust me. But Lucia can."

He climbed into the Jeep, started the engine, and drove away.

BETRAYAL

I returned to the Quonset hut to see an unfamiliar look in David's eyes. Guarded and wary, his gaze flicked from my bruised, bandaged face to the hair covering my mangled ear. As if he'd never seen me before. As if he wasn't sure he was really seeing me now.

He nodded curtly and picked up Paulsen's satellite phone. "I'm going to make some more calls."

I paused on the threshold, then turned slowly and went back out.

He doesn't trust me anymore. But neither do I.

Jhimi was crouching in the half-shadowed burial pit, unsurprised to see me. He held the flashlight in his lap, his eyes on Mikhail's tormented face.

I slipped to the ground beside him, wondering if he was cold. I couldn't tell anymore if the night was bitter or if the sun was warm. I couldn't tell anymore if I was in pain. It didn't matter, anyway.

Jhimi regarded me solemnly. *"Mikhail está libre."*

He is free.

Jhimi didn't look to me like an old soul, like one who knew the ways of the spirits. He was just a kid. But as my eyes took in the torment written across Mikhail's face, I knew that Jhimi had got it right. The agony etched there was of something passing from this world, passing into freedom.

He's right. I thought. Mikhail is on the other side.

Jhimi and I sat there together as the sun came up and the wind went down.

When morning arrived at last, David descended into the pit with a trio of researchers. David glanced at the circle of mummies laid out in the pit. He stared hard at Mikhail's mummified face. But he didn't look at me.

"We'll take over from here," he said. The men covered their features with hospital masks and dusty bandanas, and they began to dig Mikhail out.

One of the workers looped a rope through the grommets on the flyaway tarp, tying down the heavy plastic to cover the circle of mummies once more.

I tried to speak and realized my mouth was parched. Touching my fingers to my lower lip, I felt a tough, leathery surface, split with long cracks of tender skin. Beside me, Jhimi swallowed, his eyes dull. He looked thirsty, and he probably needed a good meal.

I nudged his shoulder. "*Desayuno?*" I asked, thinking of the restaurant where I'd last seen Mikhail alive.

Then I remembered Paulsen. And the Stahler.

The walls and ceiling of Socorro's restaurant were covered with stains, the only evidence I'd seen of water so far. Humidity had warped the edges of the room's sole decoration: an advertising poster featuring an alcoholic beverage and a trashy-looking girl, whose upper arm featured a water stain as well. Everything else in the village was horribly dry, like the stretched, desiccated faces of the mummies. Like Mikhail.

I couldn't think about Mikhail. I couldn't let myself remember. We had to trust that Paulsen would find Lucia. Or we had to find her ourselves.

The restaurant was empty except for Jhimi and the stocky, blunt-faced proprietor, who poured lumpy batter onto a griddle to make a round of cornmeal pancakes. The air smelled faintly of burnt sugar.

Jhimi was eating heartily, and I wondered where he got his meals. Did he go to school? Were his parents alive? Something told me the answer to both questions was no.

I took a bite of cornmeal and tried to chew, but the texture of food in my mouth felt strange and wrong. I knew I needed to swallow, but the mechanics were unclear.

I'd forgotten how to eat.

Defeated, I spat the mush into a tissue. Jhimi eyed my plate, then casually speared the rest of my pancake with his fork.

A harsh gust of wind blew open the front door as David came in, lugging his cello and Mikhail's violin. We looked at each other, and then he set the instruments down.

Rigid with fatigue, David went through the motions of ordering food and drink. His injured face was hard and set, like a boxer waiting for the last round to begin. He hadn't mentioned my mangled ear. He hadn't mentioned Mikhail's mummified body. He hadn't said a word about what might be happening to Lucia.

He returned with a bottle of Coke. He unzipped his jacket, and dumped it on the floor next to Mikhail's violin. Then his gaze flicked to the Stahler.

"Isobel," he said, as Jhimi cut into his pancake. "Is there something you want to tell me?"

My hand stole involuntarily to the bandage covering the leathery spot on my forehead. It was unchanged, but I was not the same anymore.

Jhimi believed that Mikhail was free. Somehow, I trusted in Jhimi's solemn faith that it was over now, that Mikhail was at peace. But I didn't see any peace ahead for myself.

You've given yourself to the powers of darkness, Paulsen had said. Could I really hope it would ever be over?

"No, David."

David didn't blink.

"Can you tell me honestly this isn't your fault?"

I saw a hazy vision of a girl my age. Carried away by sorrow and grief and the music that time couldn't hold, she was setting down the Stahler, reaching for an old-fashioned set of razor blades. I wanted to call out to her, to send a warning. But the gulf between us was too great, and she was already gone.

"All right, then," David said, and pushed back from the table. My silence was the only answer he needed.

He went to the counter and returned with a plate of cornmeal pancakes and a smudged pitcher of clear syrup. He handed the pitcher to Jhimi.

"I don't like this," he said briskly, as if nothing had happened between us. "We should be searching for Lucia. We should be doing something."

"What else can we do?" I asked, grateful for the change of subject. "We've called the police. We alerted the embassy. We've got to wait for help."

David frowned at his pancakes. "I don't understand. Why would they take her? And why take her violin? If they knew how valuable it was, then they weren't just local thugs. But why didn't they take my cello as well? And how did they know we were here?" His Coke bottle fizzed faintly, but he didn't drink.

"No one knew we were here," I said. "No one but Paulsen."

Besides the ambassador, there was no one else.

Our eyes met, and David frowned. "Where the hell is Paulsen, anyway? He said he'd meet us at dawn. He said the police would be here by now."

I thought of Paulsen driving into the wind-swept mountains, his pale gray eyes empty and cold. "He won't come back. He's gone."

And Mikhail would always be dead.

"What do you mean, he won't come back?" David's brow furrowed, the bandage on his forehead seeping fluid. "And why did he ask about your viola?"

I took a breath, wondering if the time had come to tell the truth.

Outside, a canvas-covered Jeep drove by. It must have had a damaged tire or axle: a harsh clanking came from its undercarriage. As the Jeep rounded the street corner next to the restaurant entry, the clanking was accented by a loud thump.

"That Jeep," David said, his voice urgent. "Something fell out of that Jeep."

He got to his feet and hurried for the door.

"David, wait," I said, pushing back my chair. "We've got to stay together." But David had already disappeared.

"David, come back!"

Jhimi straightened up, listening for something.

"*Vigile esto, por favor*," I said in a rush, waving my hand at Mikhail's violin, at David's cello. Jhimi nodded, still chewing.

If I had known that I would never see Jhimi again, I would have said something more. Thank you, for starters. Also: goodbye. But I was already picking up the Stahler.

I left Jhimi with the other instruments and hurried over to the entry of the restaurant. David was kneeling on the ground several meters away, just a few steps from a broken crate made of flaking strips of wood. A black object lay on the ground at his feet. My leg creaking and snapping, I ran out to join him. As I got closer, I recognized the object. It was Lucia's violin case.

"Her violin." David was breathing fast.

I hobbled forward as he picked up the case. If the Vuillaume was here, then Lucia must be close. I reached for David, but he flinched and pulled away.

"Let's get help," I said. "There's Jhimi, and the cook in the restaurant. I saw some women by the church. That must be the same Jeep. Maybe Lucia was in there."

Another sound filled the air, coming from behind us. Tires crunching on gravel.

We rotated slowly, David holding the Vuillaume to his chest. A large black SUV pulled up. It came to a stop in front of the ramshackle restaurant, its rugged new tires flattening pieces of twine and bits of animal manure. Behind dark tinted windows, the passengers were obscured from view.

It wasn't the police. That car didn't belong here.

One of the back doors opened, and for a moment we glimpsed a thick shock of jet-black hair above the top of the door. Then a man's legs showed beneath the open door: dark jeans and dusty leather shoes. The shoes turned back toward the SUV, the man reaching in to lift something out. Above the door, a brief snapshot of dark chestnut hair.

"Lucy!" David lunged forward as the door swung shut, revealing Enrique Rodriguez, holding Lucia in his arms. Lucia was dazed and wobbly, her delicate face streaked with powdery white dust. Her long hair was at least six inches shorter than before. She wore Enrique's leather coat over her pajamas.

David clasped her in his arms. "Lucy," he said brokenly. "You're safe."

"She's not hurt," Enrique said flatly, staring down at Lucia. "Let's get her inside." He and David helped her into the restaurant.

I wavered outside the doorway, wanting to greet Enrique or embrace Lucia or do something, but consumed by the fear that everything was wrong, wrong, wrong.

I watched them ease Lucia's shivering body into the restaurant. Then I heard a metallic clang behind me. I whipped my head to see two men step out of Enrique's SUV. One of them gripped a rifle in his hands.

"Enrique?" My voice came out in a squeak. "What's going on?"

Enrique exited the restaurant and pulled the door shut behind him. He walked back toward me, his eyes on the Stahler slung over my shoulder.

"I'm sorry, Isobel. I didn't want it to be this way." He took the Stahler with his slender, perfect hands, and he pulled it away, still not looking at my face.

Somehow, I managed to speak again. "You! You took Lucia! Why are you doing this?"

"There's nothing else I can do." With a curt nod, Enrique signaled his men. They approached, and a thick hand closed over my wrist.

Faintly, I heard Enrique murmuring instructions. I felt my heels dragging through the gravel. But I didn't know where I was going. I could barely see the arms lifting me into the car. Time had folded back on its hinges, and once more it was Sunday, and the moonlight was shining on my skin. I was in a warm bed in Enrique's cold stone house, seeing his hands on my body, and the things I'd let him do.

I won't be able to bear this, I thought. I'll tear myself apart.

Enrique got into the seat beside me and rested the viola at his feet.

"*Vámonos*," he told the driver. A door slammed, and the car jolted forward.

I heard my own voice, paper-thin, coming from a great distance. "Where are we going?"

Enrique's eyes finally met mine. "To the *Cerro Rico*," he said. "Into the mine."

THE DEVIL'S MOUNTAIN

We drove southwest on the dry dirt road, heading uphill into the wind. White dust spun through the air. After several minutes of silent travel, the village was behind us.

Enrique took a breath. "Isobel, I can explain—"

"Don't you dare," I hissed. "After what you've done? You have no right."

I dug my nails into a seam in the leather upholstery and stared out the window. Enrique lapsed into silence. My ribs tightened around my lungs, each breath searing as it entered my body. I felt my chest rise and fall. It was the end of the world, and my stupid heart still wanted to keep beating.

Buffeted by cold, reckless winds, we drove on. The road climbed steeply, following tight switchbacks above narrow gorges and leafless trees. Soon we were driving through snow, following the deep grooves left by a few previous tires.

I watched the sheer cliff wall unfurling outside my window, and I saw again the tortured agony on Mikhail's mummified face.

No one expects to be betrayed. But it can happen anyway, and when it does, there's no option to forget. I'll always know it was a Tuesday. The broken glasses lying on the ground: I'll remember them forever.

An hour must have passed. The SUV slid through dense snow as we crossed a windy saddle, a sheer thousand-foot drop on either side. A busy paved road carved through the valley below us. In the distance, I could see a looming, cone-shaped mountain.

Enrique straightened in the seat beside me. An inarticulate sound escaped his lips. He gripped the door handle, focused on the mountain.

It was the *Cerro Rico*. The mountain that swallows men.

We merged onto the paved road and entered the old colonial city of Potosi. Filled with crumbling cathedrals and narrow cobblestone streets, the city stretched out in the shadow of the great mountain. Street vendors with woven shawls and wide-brimmed hats crowded the edges of the roads. Bonfires darkened the air, signaling the winter festival of San Juan. The air smelled like cotton candy.

We took a series of switchbacks out of the city, heading for the mines that honeycombed the mountain. The staccato of firecrackers and dynamite followed us. I waited until we'd begun the long climb up the side of *Cerro Rico*. Then I spoke.

"Mikhail's dead," I said. "He died last night, searching for Lucia."

Enrique's mouth opened in shock. A vein pulsed in his slender throat.

Relentless, I pressed on. "We have *you* to thank for that."

Enrique swallowed hard. "Isobel—"

"I know," I interrupted, my voice biting. "You had no idea."

"I didn't!"

"You have no excuse, Enrique! Taking Lucia like that? You have no soul."

Enrique buried his face in his hands. "It would be better for me," he choked, "if I didn't."

"This is about *Tío*, isn't it?" I accused. "You're trying to appease a ruthless devil. A monster that doesn't love anyone."

Enrique didn't reply.

We came to a stop in an open area clinging to the edge of a sheer rock wall, facing a stone archway opening into the mountain. Eight men stood beside the narrow-gauge rail track that led into the darkness. A carved stone cross was embedded above the archway, as if guarding the entrance and trapping the devil underground. The cross was stained black and red, a dark pool of blood collecting beneath it on the frozen ground. The corpse of a llama lay sprawled over a nearby wheelbarrow.

I stared at the slaughtered llama, appalled. "You brought Lucia here?"

Enrique's eyes were sooty and dark, an abandoned campfire. "My sister's in a coma, Isobel. She's dying."

He seized the Stahler and got out of the car. "I don't expect you to understand."

"Oh, I understand," I snarled, sliding to the ground. My black pajama pants billowed in the wind. "You're willing to sacrifice anything or anyone to protect your family. Your thugs beat up David. They kidnapped Lucia. Mikhail *died* trying to get help. You don't care?"

"They're not thugs, they're miners. They live in the shadow of this mountain. They live with the same curse that I do." He slammed the car door shut. "I can't do anything about the hold *Tio* has on this mountain. He rules every mine in this god-forsaken hill. I can't change any of that. But I must find a way to help my sister, and the men who work this vein. I must find a way to break my grandfather's curse."

Another round of fireworks went off in the city below, distant explosions echoing in the afternoon light.

"Do you even know what you're doing, Enrique? Do you know what powers you're dealing with?"

"What do you know?" Enrique snapped, his eyes blazing. "You've been in this country for a week. You don't know a word of Quechua or Aymara. You barely speak enough Spanish to order French fries! What do you know about me, about my life?"

I held my ground. "I know there's nothing in that mine but death."

Enrique pulled a dented helmet from his rucksack. "Believe me, I know that already. When my mother died, Arminda came to La Paz to raise me. My father knew she was my grandmother, but he didn't know she was a *yatiri*. She taught me to see the spirits and to know their names."

Enrique shoved the crude helmet onto my head. Then he slung my viola case over his shoulder.

"You kidnapped Lucia," I accused. "You think *anything* can justify that?"

He pulled me forward. "When Josefina got pregnant, I was in despair. Jack tried to convince her there was no danger, but I knew she would die. Just like my mother. Like her mother. Like my father's mother."

Stepping across the rusty rail tracks, he tugged me toward the entrance to the mine. "I was in Washington when she was hospitalized. I thought her future was written, that there was no hope. Not even music could take my pain away. But I went to the concert hall at Strathmore, and I heard you play *Death and the Maiden*."

I stopped. "You saw the pale man?"

He nodded, his jaw clenched. "I saw him. An old man sitting near the aisle was struggling to breathe, clawing at his tie. And Death came for him."

Enrique tipped back his head, gazing at the bloodstained cross carved above the archway. "I knew him at once. I'd seen him when my father died. Waiting on the breezeway, staring at the fountain. But something happened, when your quartet began to play. Death was caught up in the music. He passed on by."

"But he didn't pass on by," I said, remembering the darkened concert hall, the visionary performance. "He never does."

Someone else must have died that night. A different old man. A music student. A woman with a houseful of children.

Enrique ignored me. "I called Josefina, and I told her there was hope. We thought it was Lucia's violin, the famous Vuillaume. I'd read about the black phoenix painted on the back. I convinced myself it was an artifact of great power, something with the power to summon Death. But there was nothing there. Nothing but silence when we entered the mine. It was always you, wasn't it? It was the Stahler."

We'd arrived at the entrance to the mine. As Enrique carried the viola over the threshold, a mournful sound filled the air. To me, it sounded like a viola string, snapping and breaking. But I'm not sure we all heard the same thing, since two of the men still appeared to be listening, long after the sound had ended. All eyes turned to Enrique, who nodded in satisfaction.

"We've got it right this time," he said, almost to himself. "*Tío* is waiting for our sacrifice."

The miners put on helmets and lit old-fashioned acetylene lamps. One of them handed Enrique a stained black ski jacket, with feathers and goose down spilling from a rip in the shoulder. Enrique tried to make me put on the jacket, but I refused, arms folded across my chest. Finally, he pulled on the jacket himself.

I stared at the ground, realized my shoes were stained with llama blood. Boot prints tracked around the railroad ties, dark and rusty red.

Enrique reached into his canvas backpack and opened his hand. It contained a braid: Josefina's brown hair, interwoven with locks of Lucia's chestnut, my pale blonde.

"Please, Isobel. Play the music that summons death."

"You could have asked me, Enrique. There was a time when I would have done anything for you." That time was yesterday.

One of the miners reached for my arm, but I shook him off. "But now? After what you've done? After you've abducted Lucia?"

I fought to repress the memories of my night with Enrique: his tenderness as he touched me, the wonder in his eyes. But the memories came back, filling me with shame.

"Were you planning this all along? Was this what you were thinking when you lured me into your bed? And my hair: did you pay Hurst to take it from me?"

Enrique recoiled. "No! I didn't! I never wanted—"

When he spoke again, his voice trembled. "I didn't want to

take that road. I never did. Not even when they told me I had to. But there's no time anymore. Josefina's on life support. There's no time."

We followed the men into the mine. One of the miners, probably the foreman of the cooperative, trailed along behind us. His rifle slung over his shoulder, he stuffed dull green coca leaves into his swollen jaw. He breathed heavily, and I remembered that the miners seldom lived very long. Most succumbed to silicosis in their thirties and forties. I looked back over my shoulder, and our eyes met.

He's not really so old, I thought, my eyes on his weathered face. Younger than my dad was. But he's given his entire life to this mine. There were more ways to give up your life than I ever thought.

The tunnels twisted and descended, and soon we separated from the railroad tracks and entered a narrower tunnel. The curved ceiling was so low the men were stooping. Brittle pieces of toxic-looking calcification wafted downward, green and blue, as their heads brushed the top. Surprisingly bright, the acetylene lamps threw harsh, distorted shadows. The air smelled metallic, thick with dust.

We arrived at a slight widening in the tunnel, filled with debris. Broken liquor bottles, cigarette wrappers, coca leaves, strings of confetti. In the middle of the debris sat a devil on a throne.

It was *Tio*. The uncle underground.

"This mountain has hundreds of mines," Enrique whispered, handing the foreman a plastic bag filled with coca leaves. "And every mine has its own throne."

The miners were all staring at me, silent. Finally, one of them spoke. I picked up just one word: *ch'alla*.

"What do they want?" I asked, uneasy and fearful.

"You have to offer something before we go," Enrique said. "A gift."

My entire body tightened with rage. "For *Tio*? Never!"

The foreman and a younger miner exchanged a glance, fear transparent in their eyes. The miner spat a blackened gob of coca leaves against the wall, his face half-hidden by a clumsy haircut. He was Jhimi's age.

These men aren't criminals, I realized. They're here because they're desperate. Because they believe that *Tio* can protect them. Because he'll punish them if they don't offer enough.

I had nothing to give *Tio*. Enrique had my Stahler and the bow. My purse and my money were in Socorro. All I had were my black pajamas and my dusty shoes.

I lifted my hands to my ears: there was just one other thing.

The black pearls were a gift from my father, the last thing he gave me when we were still friends. When I was still his little girl.

I can't do it, I thought angrily. I won't give them up. I won't give up my past.

My eyes fell on the young miner, fear written across his face. He was afraid for his family. And he'd lived with that fear for his whole life.

I don't have a future anymore. But maybe he does.

I took off my left earring, carefully sliding the gold post through the backing. I handed it to the boy. He took it without speaking.

The fabric of my pajamas seemed heavier than before, weighing my shoulders downward, tugging at the back of my neck. But it was nothing compared to the heaviness in my heart.

"We'll go on," Enrique said, and nodded to the miners. "They need to perform the *ch'alla*, to make an exchange. We have an exchange of our own to conduct."

"An exchange? Where?"

"At the heart of the mine," Enrique said, his expression unreadable. He coughed, wiping his eyes. Then he adjusted his acetylene lamp and ducked through the aperture leading from the throne.

It occurred to me that I could flee. The foreman with his rifle, all the other miners, they were all intent on preparing for their ritual. There was nothing left to make me stay with Enrique, or even to stay in this world.

I could get away. But there's nowhere left to go.

Alone, we descended down the central tunnel, following the narrow-gauge rail tracks. Above our heads, long, calcified metal pipes stretched along the roof, emitting sharp, hissing noises. We reached a fork in the tunnel, and I asked a question.

"Tell me something. Did you help kill that llama?"

"Why should that matter to you?" Enrique asked, his tone angry and defensive.

"It does matter." It mattered to my heart.

Enrique directed the light into the mineshaft. "The men in the mining cooperative sacrificed the animal at dawn. It's what they do sometimes on feast days, as part of the *ch'alla*. To honor *Tio*, to restore the mine."

"*It's what they do*? Do you even hear yourself, Enrique? They killed a helpless animal to appease the devil. That's barbaric!"

Bitterly, I visualized the miners sacrificing the helpless beast, but my mind recoiled. I would never forgive them. I would never forgive Enrique. Most of all, I would never forgive myself.

"Barbaric?" Enrique frowned, his skin half-shadowed by the sharp blaze of his lamp. "You know what's barbaric? Your blindness, Isobel. You don't want to know, do you? Where your silver comes from. How your treasures are made. Whose hands took your pearls from the sea. You don't want to know how it's paid for, how many lives it has cost. You don't ever want to know!"

"You know something, Enrique? You can go straight to hell." I dug my feet into the rock, and I ran ahead of him into the darkness.

"Isobel!"

I ran and ran, barely glimpsing the rail tracks at my feet, hearing only the hissing pipes stretched above my head. Then I stumbled into a spur of rock, dislodging a cascade of toxic dust. It spun around me, choking my lungs, and for a moment I couldn't breathe.

Then Enrique found me, and I felt him pulling me deeper into the mine. The brightness of his acetylene lamp revealed a cloudy arch, the faint outline of a long narrow pipe clinging to the roof of the tunnel. I tasted something bitter and dry, deep in the back of my throat.

Enrique coughed. Narrow streaks of sweat cut through the white powder covering his dark skin, making his face look like the pale flesh of an apple eaten by worms.

"We're almost there," he choked. "You're going to summon Death. We're going to stand in his presence and end this curse. We're going to save my sister's life."

I remembered my last attempts to play the Stahler. Nothing happened. The forgotten music never came. The magic wasn't there.

"Even if I can play the music you want to hear, it will be the last thing you ever hear. The pale man will come, and he'll take you instead. You'll die, Enrique!"

Enrique's eyes were hooded and distant.

"I know," he said without emotion. "That's the whole point."

I stared at him, aghast. *Death. It was his plan all along.*

I opened my mouth to protest, but no sound came out. Instead, the ground abruptly trembled as an explosion shook the mine. First came the thunder-like crash, then a booming series of echoes. The walls of the tunnel rattled, dislodging powdery white dust.

Enrique froze. "That was dynamite."

"Dynamite?"

Enrique retraced our steps for about thirty feet, his body tense. "This isn't right. It's a feast day. It's San Juan. There shouldn't be anyone here." We rounded a corner and dimly glimpsed the passage ahead. It was blocked with rubble, dust fuming everywhere.

Enrique bent forward, deep bronchial spasms racking his body. He rubbed the powder from his eyes. Two brown patches gleamed in his ghostlike face.

I clasped my fingers together and realized I was praying.
Please, God. Not yet.

"We'll follow the rails." Enrique backed away from the

debris. "They lead to the heart of the mine. Then out to the other exit. You'll still be able to get out."

"Me?"

"I want you to be safe, Isobel."

"Safe? What about you?"

"It's not about me. It's never been about me."

The sound of the air pipes grew louder, piercing my ears. I could barely hear Enrique's shouted directions as we ran. We must have gone a quarter mile from the entrance when we finally arrived at the edge of a gaping pit. Enrique's lamp glanced off the walls as I leaned forward to see down. Nothing but darkness. Forced air was spilling from the screeching oxygen pipes, stirring the dust into rounded plumes.

"I don't understand." Enrique's face registered bewilderment. "He said it would be okay. He said the mine would be clear."

"Who did?" I yelled. "Who said that?"

He set down the viola case. "The ambassador."

The ambassador? My mind flashed to that moment in the green room before the concerto: the gleaming black phoenix, the ambassador's hungry eyes.

He's the one who took Lucia, who paid Hurst to take my hair.

I opened my mouth to protest, but the air pipes guttered and belched, dwindling into eerie silence.

"Oh, God," Enrique breathed, moving toward the end of the pipe.

"Enrique," I could feel his panic beginning to infect me. "Why is it so quiet?"

He knelt beside the faucet-like attachment at the end of the pipe, struggling to turn the large metal wheel.

"They've turned off the air."

THE AMBASSADOR

The silence of the air pipes was sickening and absolute. Enrique slowly got to his feet. His breath came in short, shallow bursts, reminding me uncomfortably of the foreman's blighted lungs. Torn between anger and concern, I inched closer.

What was wrong with him? There was plenty of oxygen in the cavern. I took a breath, aware that something was in the air, mixed with the plumes of toxic dust. It tasted like ashes.

It's begun, I thought, as the acetylene lamp flared across the low ceiling. Enrique's already in the hands of Death.

"Play the Stahler," he gasped. "We need to finish this."

"We're running out of clean air!"

Staggering backward, Enrique took in the dimly lit cavern, the plumes of dusty powder. "There's still time, Isobel. You can still get out of here."

I hugged the viola case to my chest. "If we've still got time, then we should come back later, when we can breathe."

Enrique's temper flared. "We don't have that kind of time. My sister's dying!" He succumbed to a fit of coughing, his entire body straining as he hacked and wheezed.

"But the Pale Man will come for you."

"Just play it!" Enrique sank to his knees, breaking the weight of his fall by grabbing at the wheel attached to the silent pipe. His acetylene lantern sputtered in protest as it fell. The flame wavered, then brightened once more.

I slipped the Stahler onto my shoulder. Crouching beside Enrique, I gazed into the darkness of the pit. Was this how it would end? Was I brought to this place just to watch Enrique die?

I touched his cheek. His skin felt cold and damp. "Enrique. We've got to leave this place."

I had to help him. It didn't matter what he'd done. What mattered—the only thing that mattered—was what I could live with.

Enrique tipped his head back, his neck as fragile as the stem of a flower. "Arminda told me. The last wish of the man who summons his own death will transform . . . "

"Don't talk like that!" I cried. "You don't know what I know about Death. You don't know what you'll leave behind."

"My sister," he murmured, his eyes glassy. "The miners." With a trembling hand, he held out the braid of hair. He let it fall, and the darkness swallowed it up.

"They got out," I soothed. "The miners got out."

Enrique leaned against the rusty wheel, his chest rising and falling with every shallow breath. "They'll never get out. *Tío* will hold them to my grandfather's bargain. Unless I end this now."

His unfocused eyes stared straight ahead. "I'm sorry I brought you here. I'm sorry you had to suffer. Because of me."

Because of me, I thought. And Mikhail and Raysa died because of me. They were caught up in my wake.

Abruptly, Enrique slumped forward, his chin striking the ground. His hand clutched at the collar of his padded coat, and he sucked in a rapid series of breaths through his nose.

"I don't expect forgiveness. But I hope—" His body shuddered and grew still.

Numb and disbelieving, I looked down at his motionless form.

"I'll forgive you anyway," I whispered. "If not in this lifetime, in the next."

I picked up the scorching acetylene lamp and brought it close to Enrique's face. The vein in his neck pulsed faintly. He was still alive.

I pulled myself to my feet, aware that a choice lay before me. I could play the Stahler, as Enrique wanted. I could summon the Pale Man. Enrique would die, and *Tio* would have a willing sacrifice. The curse might finally end.

Or I could do something else.

Stepping away from Enrique's body, I directed the beam of the hot lamp onto the rail tracks. The tracks divided, one set looping back into the collapsed mine tunnel, the other heading out to freedom. But which was which?

Not sure which way to go, I turned down the acetylene lamp and peered into the darkness. The trail to the left revealed a faint haze of light. Left, then.

At my feet, Enrique's chest jolted in brief spasms, his lungs still struggling to do their work. I turned the lamp back up, but the flame sputtered and faded. It was running out of carbide fuel. I would have to follow the rails in the dark.

I tugged off my helmet. It clattered against the metal rails. Then I gripped the nylon strap of the viola and slung it across my back. Sliding my fingers under Enrique's arms, I began pulling, dragging him toward the exit. His legs grazed the railroad tracks.

With the pipes turned off, the cavern was quiet, but plumes of dust continued to float in the air. I inched along the tracks, aware of something moving in the cavern's fading light. I hoped it was only dust.

Bent over Enrique's body, I tugged and pulled. He was too heavy, and the Stahler kept sliding forward, bumping into the side of my leg. I tugged again, and the brittle tendons in my shoulder gave way. Then, coming through the viola case, I heard the unmistakable sound of a string snapping.

It was no good. I would have to leave one of them behind.

I slid the viola off my shoulder and rested the case beside Enrique. I tried to remember who he was. I tried to remember his love for his people, the way he'd stepped in front of the stone lions to shield me from harm.

But it felt unreal. All I could think about was the Stahler.

"It's keeping you going," Paulsen had said. He didn't say it was keeping me alive.

What would I be without the Stahler? Dead? Or something worse?

I wondered suddenly how Jhimi knew that Mikhail was free. He could only have known that if he was sure the mummies in the burial ground had suffered a worse fate. What if those mummies were still in torment? What if they were still waiting, forever bound to their brittle flesh, unable to move or speak or escape their pain?

Paulsen had gone there for a reason. Because the dead were in bondage, in torment forever. I took a breath, unwilling to think too hard about what this meant.

I gripped Enrique's limp arms and began dragging him once more. The Stahler lay beside the rail tracks, slowly receding from view.

I'll come back for it. I won't abandon the Stahler. I won't abandon myself.

When the tunnel curved, I looked back one last time. Illuminated by the fading acetylene lamp, a pale, shadowy figure stood over the Stahler. Reaching down, it stretched out a hand as the light went out. He was waiting for me. He'd be there waiting when I got back.

The tunnel seemed endless. I tugged at Enrique's arms, wishing I were strong enough to throw him over my shoulder, the way the firemen did in the movies. My hands were numb, but they held on. My leg creaked and protested, but it kept moving. Finally I reached the light I'd glimpsed from the cavern. In the dull light at my feet, I saw blackened gobs of chewed coca leaves; I smelled a rotten, latrine-like odor. I was getting closer to the world of the living.

His eyes half-closed, Enrique breathed in irregular fits and starts. Under the dull coating of fine white dust, his face felt clammy.

Don't die, Enrique. Don't let Death claim you.

"Come on," I whispered, sinking my fingers into the greasy nylon of his worn-out jacket. "Let's get out of here."

After what seemed like hours, I finally glimpsed natural light. A burst of energy surged through my body, and I hobbled faster and faster. Light poured through the archway, half-blocked by a small rectangular mining car. I propped Enrique against the rusty car and straightened my creaking back.

"Breathe, you idiot," I whispered. "Try to breathe."

His face streaked with sweat, Enrique mumbled incoherencies and subsided into delirium. His lips were cracked and dry. He needed water.

Leaving Enrique propped against the rail car, I headed for the entrance. The sun was blinding, savage. Squinting, I inched forward, shielding my eyes with my right hand. Then I stepped into the light.

When I was small, I burned my hand on a sparkler one Fourth of July, and blisters sprang up all across my thumb. Now my hand seemed to be scorching, and suddenly the long-forgotten sparkler fluoresced in my memory—its fizzing noises, glittering brightness, the sharp smell of cooking flesh. My skin was on fire.

With a scream, I yanked my body back into the shadow of the mine, staring at the blackened flesh of my right hand. It looked like the skin of a charred corpse. Breathing hard, I slowly backed toward Enrique.

"Interesting," a voice said. A broad-shouldered body appeared under the arch, outlined in stark silhouette. "That worked even better than I'd hoped."

Ambassador Melton stepped into the mine. He was carrying a gun.

"You realize," he said casually, "you can never leave this mine."

I glared at him. "I can do whatever I fucking please."

"Really?" The ambassador trained the gun on Enrique's slumped body. "Go ahead, then. Walk through the arch. But I'm guessing your hair burned up in the spell Hurst made to bind you to the mine. So you'll find your journey rather warm."

I cradled my smoking hand. "You're a monster."

The ambassador laughed. "Me? I'm a diplomat."

He shrugged, and his broad pink face made a grimace of disgust. "Hurst, on the other hand… well, he did good work. And we shouldn't speak ill of the dead."

"It was you," I accused. "You paid him to take my hair."

Above my head, I heard the pipes shudder and groan as the air turned back on.

"He told me the music was keeping you alive, so I paid him to take you out of the equation. But you *were* the equation, weren't you?" He pursed his lips, stepping closer. "Where's your viola, Miss Linden?"

I held his gaze. "I don't know what you're talking about."

"You don't?" He hit me across the face, hard. Something snapped.

"Don't play games with me. If it wasn't the black phoenix, then it must be the Stahler." He took a breath, impatience rippling through his body. "I need it now."

I maintained a stony silence.

He watched my face, his tongue briefly grazing his upper lip. Then his eyes dropped to Enrique. "Fine. Enrique will know where it is."

"Leave him alone," I hissed.

Squatting on his thick haunches, he nudged Enrique's cheek with the gun.

"Poor kid. I convinced him that *Tío* is just a music lover. But the music alone is not enough. You can charm Death: you can put him off. But the devil doesn't work that way. At the heart of the mine, the devil has to have blood."

He gripped Enrique's chin, lifting his head. "You've had a hell of an inheritance, kid. But your niece will have a better one."

Groggy, Enrique squinted upward, black hair falling into his eyes. "Jack?"

"Come on." The ambassador tugged Enrique to his feet. "Time to meet your uncle."

DARKNESS

Staggering to his feet, Enrique twisted his neck, taking in the ambassador's gun, the proximity of the exit. His nostrils twitched, and then he saw my blackened, claw-like hand. He recoiled in horror. "Isobel, what's happened to your hand?"

I set my teeth together. "Ask your brother-in-law."

"Jack? What have you done to her?"

The ambassador's voice became oily and ingratiating. "Only what I had to do. Be reasonable, Enrique. We've got your sister and her baby to think about. We can save them. We can help your precious miners. We can revitalize this mine. Surely you understand."

"No, I don't!" Enrique shouted. "Put down that gun. You think I don't know what you had planned for me? You think I didn't know how this would end? *I knew.* But we weren't going to hurt anybody else. Josefina wouldn't want that!" He collapsed into a desperate fit of coughing, pressing the dirty sleeve of his coat against his mouth.

"It doesn't matter what she wants, or what you and I want," Ambassador Melton said. "The only thing that counts right now is what the devil needs."

He turned his bulging eyes on me. "Where's the viola, Miss Linden? And where's that asshole Paulsen?"

"Paulsen?" I froze, remembering the shadowy figure stooped over the Stahler. Wasn't that the Pale Man? Or had I been hallucinating?

"His Jeep's outside," Melton snapped. "He must be after the viola. Where is it?" He drew closer, brandishing the gun as if to strike my face.

"Don't!" I held up my charred hand to protect my eyes.

Enrique slipped into the space between us. "We took it to the pit. I'm sure it's still there." Seeing my outrage, he shook his head. "I'm sorry, Isobel."

"I'll be damned if I'm going to let that twisted little body snatcher have it." Ambassador Melton reached into the rusted mining cart and pulled out a dust mask and an industrial-strength flashlight. "Let's get a move on."

Defeated, I couldn't even speak. I turned my face to Enrique, beseeching him with my eyes. But the ambassador tilted his heavy black handgun, pointed it at Enrique's head.

Enrique spoke quietly. "Come on, Isobel."

"But Enrique," I protested. "Don't you understand?"

"I understand." Enrique said, his face calm. "Very soon, I'm going to die."

Nudged along by the ambassador's gun, we stumbled through the tunnel, Enrique wheezing and coughing. The burnt stench of my charred hand traveled with us into the darkness, blending its notes with the dry odors of dust, metal, and toxic gas.

There was something else as well, a faint scent I couldn't identify.

"Enrique," I begged. "We can't let him do this." But Enrique limped along like a condemned man, his eyes fixed on the rail tracks.

I spun around to confront the ambassador, who was pulling a paper mask over his mouth, his flashlight tucked under his arm. "You've got to stop this now, before it's too late!"

Above the mask, Ambassador Melton's eyes were watery and pale. "Too late?" His voice echoed. "It's been too late for you ever since you broke my wife's statue. The old gods have you in their crosshairs, you and your whole quartet."

"But you don't believe in the old gods!"

Ambassador Melton nudged the cold metal of his handgun into my sternum. "I believe in paying attention. I believe in knowing who's in power. Now turn around. Keep walking."

We arrived back at the pit. The oxygen pipes belched out clean air, hissing and screeching. If serpents reigned in hell, then I could believe I was already there.

The viola case lay open on the rail tracks. The Stahler was nowhere to be found.

The ambassador scanned the cavern with his flashlight, his masked face dark with wrath. "Where the hell is it?"

"Are you looking for this?" Illuminated by the beam of the flashlight, Henrik Paulsen emerged from the collapsed tunnel on our left.

"Thanks for the light," he added. I saw he had replaced the C string on my viola, and was now tightening the carved ebony peg with slow, careful turns.

He arrived in front of the viola case. A zippered black plastic tarp lay crumpled near his feet. That's not a tarp, I realized with growing dread. It's a body bag.

"Give me the viola!" the ambassador hissed.

"I have my own plans for this thing," Paulsen spat out. "And for Isobel."

I approached Paulsen and extended my blackened hand, wondering why I wasn't afraid. "That's mine. It belongs to me."

Paulsen laughed coldly. "Are you sure it's not the other way around?"

The ambassador's eyes narrowed. "What are you talking about?"

Ignoring the ambassador, Paulsen plucked the C string of the Stahler. Then he plucked the C and the G together. Both perfectly in tune. The pizzicato notes echoed off the low ceiling of the cavern, augmented by the screeching of the air pipes.

His face streaked with sweat, Enrique was breathing too fast. He stumbled forward and crouched close to the edge of the pit.

The ambassador tipped the beam of his flashlight into the

pit, revealing dust swirling in the darkness. I drew a breath, and a faint scent rose up from the deep. It was the scent of something I knew. Something I wanted to remember.

There was power here, and it was coming out into the world we knew.

I drew closer to Paulsen, stepping over the dull black plastic of the body bag. Then I reached into the viola case and withdrew the Tubbs bow.

"It doesn't matter if I belong to the Stahler or if the Stahler belongs to me. It's mine, Paulsen."

I remembered the photograph Paulsen had slipped into his coat at the hotel. A young woman—barely out of her teens—with smooth beige skin and dark sculpted brows. Eyes like a lost painting of Scheherazade.

I tightened the bow, my eyes on Paulsen. "She was a musician, wasn't she? The woman you loved. And she's still not free."

Paulsen froze, agony distorting his face. He wavered, as if trapped in his memories and grief. I pulled the Stahler from his unresisting hands.

"Yes!" The ambassador crowed. "Play it now!"

Here in this dark place, there was no room for hope. But a desperate hope flared in my heart. If I had any power over this cursed object, I needed to wield it now.

The bow pulsed and quivered in my blackened hand, and the Stahler sang out. The entire world backed away from me, receding until there was nothing left. No vicious ambassador, no mercenary Paulsen. No haunted, traitorous Enrique.

The hissing air pipes were replaced by silence. Enrique's body was motionless, crouched over the edge of the pit. The ambassador was caught in mid-gesture, his gun raised, his face exulting. And Paulsen stood still, his eyes far away.

I played the forgotten music, knowing it was for the last time. I played until I knew the power had awakened. Until I knew it could not be ignored.

The Stahler's plaintive alto sang through the cavern. The music was still echoing through the tunnels when the ambassador began moving again, extending his arm, taking aim at Paulsen with his gun.

Paulsen regarded me sadly, as if he knew what I had in mind. I held the Stahler out over the pit. Still vibrating, it fell into the abyss.

Your maker dreamt it, I thought, watching the viola fall. It was his last wish. A voice that would sing forever.

"No!" Ambassador Melton howled. "You've got to play!"

Enrique's mouth opened in horror, but only Paulsen understood what I had done. He leaned forward, pale eyes searching the pit. "She already has."

An echo rattled through the mine, building and climbing like demonic architecture, rising over the sound of the screeching air pipes.

I hadn't summoned death. I'd summoned a greater power.

I smelled the devil before I saw him. The sharp scent of fresh varnish rose up from the deep, canceling out the odors of burnt flesh, metallic grit, and acid dust.

Enrique backed instinctively away from the pit, but the ambassador dropped his flashlight and seized the collar of Enrique's coat, dragging him forward.

"Time to close the deal, kid. Save your sister. Restore the mine."

Enrique stared into the swirling dust below, as if in a trance.

"Enrique," I shouted, my voice shattering, breaking. "You told me once, that if you believed in the devil, you'd have to contend with his power. But you could believe in something else. You could believe in forgiveness. You could believe in letting go."

I couldn't be sure he'd heard me. His eyes were fixed on the pit, where a figure was rising, summoned by the music that time couldn't hold.

People say many things about the devil. That he's a hideous serpent. That he has pointed ears, red horns, and a tail. But here's the truth about the devil. He is beautiful.

He wasn't named the most glorious of angels for nothing. He rose up out of the darkness, shining so brightly he illuminated the entire mine. His skin glowed like the polished surface of a priceless violin. Tendrils of attenuated hair floated in the swirling plumes of dust, each strand made of gold.

The scent of varnish filled my nostrils, drawing me back to the happiest, most treasured moment of my childhood: a luthier's shop in Minneapolis, my chubby toddler hands gripping the tiny neck of my very first violin.

Gazing up at the devil's beauty, I felt something take hold of me, something more powerful than anything I'd ever known: a longing to embrace that beauty, to give myself entirely to his service.

I took a step forward and grasped Enrique's hand. We'd die together, and it would all be over. For both of us. We'd be in peace.

Then I saw Paulsen's face. It was ugly with anger, twisted with hatred and revulsion. He looked like a demon ready to destroy his prey.

What had Paulsen said to me in Socorro? "You've given yourself to the powers of darkness." It would never be over.

He sees it, I thought. He sees the devil as he really is. Not as I saw him. Not as Enrique saw him.

Captivated, Enrique stood poised on the edge of the abyss, gazing upwards in rapture. I sank my nails into his palm and pulled hard. He looked back.

"Isobel." Blinking, Enrique reached out to touch my forehead. I felt his fingertips trace a spider-web of hard, brittle lines, spiraling out from the bandage above my eyebrow. I tried to speak, but my throat was hardening, turning to stone.

Under a coating of white powder, Enrique's face was haunted, ghostly. "Did I do this to you?"

I managed to rasp out a few words. "I did this to myself."

My eyes were clouding, turning dark. Dimly, as if through a film of gray jelly, I glimpsed the ambassador crying out in a divine ecstasy, joyously throwing himself into the pit.

For a moment, there was a terrible silence. Then a pandemonium of sound ruptured my eardrums: *Tío* had accepted the sacrifice.

I sank to the ground. My extended fingers seemed to lengthen. My wrists became twigs. Flesh shriveled back as my limbs darkened and grew thin.

"Isobel." Enrique was crying. His voice grew softer and softer.

I wanted to tell him he was forgiven, but my tongue dried up, receded into my throat. Paulsen's arms cradled my head.

"Be still," Paulsen said, his voice cold and far away. "Try not to move."

But I wasn't listening anymore. I wasn't seeing anymore. I had entered the last dream of my heart. My mother was feeding songbirds. David and Lucia were playing duets. And somewhere in the silence, a dark-eyed woman whose name I didn't know was casting off her shackles, clawing her way to freedom.

THE GODS OF TIWANAKU

At first, I heard only the voices of the dead. They swelled around me in a faint, pulsing drone, punctuated by fragments of something human. They sounded so welcoming, so comforting, I couldn't imagine why I'd ever feared their song.

I glimpsed a dim light, and relief lifted an impossible weight from my heart. It was over. I was free.

The music changed, the drone diminishing and subsiding, while the human voices grew stronger. One of the human voices repeated a hissing, sibilant phrase, over and over, like a distant incantation. It sounded like a woman's name.

Joy leapt inside me. It was my father, calling to me. It had to be.

I wanted to speak, to see his face and call his name. But I couldn't move. My eyes took in the faint gray light, and I felt a scraping of dry tissue and membrane as my eyelids slowly blinked.

We'll be together, I thought. And he'll understand that I was broken, that I never meant to hurt him. And I'll understand he did the best he could. We won't ever have to explain. We would speak again, and we would speak only of good things.

Fine white dust was falling. It clung to my eyelashes, settled onto my cracked lips, found its way to the tip of my hardened tongue. It tasted like smoke and blood.

I felt life come back into my throat, felt the solid form of my tongue against the roof of my mouth. Life spread through me, channeling through my dried-up veins, carried along by blood and ash. But it wasn't *my* life. It was something new.

Cold air filled my nostrils, and I felt a stirring in my heart. Yet something was wrong. The resonant baritone continued chanting. But my dad's voice was an unforgettable, melodious tenor.

My eyes opened with an audible snap, and I saw a human figure above me in the dull gray light. It wasn't my father.

No! I wanted to scream. *Not him!*

The voice broke off mid-incantation. Henrik Paulsen stared down at me, his pale eyes wide with shock and recognition.

"Ayesha," he breathed, "you've come back to me."

But Ayesha wasn't my name. It couldn't be. My name was Isobel.

Paulsen raised a clenched fist, as if to shield his face. Clasped in his blood-smeared hand was a stone the size of a plum, its surface bright red.

"I've done such terrible things," he whispered. "But I couldn't abandon you. Every night, I heard you calling for help."

My eyes scraped against their sockets as I took in the scene. I was in a hollow place at the top of the world. Walls of limestone surrounded me. Emerging from the nearest wall were staring faces, carved from stone. I wanted to cry out, thinking of Mikhail's ruined, frozen eyes. But my throat wouldn't open, my body wouldn't move.

Above me, the dawn sky was threaded with pink and gold.

I'm at the ruins of Tiwanaku, I thought. *In the sunken temple in the mountains. This is the home of the gods.*

Paulsen's gaunt face was unshaven, his eyes bright. A layer of white dust dulled the surface of his long hair. The same dust creased the corners of his eyes. He was old. Older than I'd ever thought.

Behind Paulsen, a monolith stood in the sunken temple: a tall, rectangular statue with a human face. Carved in low relief, two pumas crouched at her feet.

With dread, I remembered the stone pumas I'd seen at the replica temple in La Paz. They would come for me, as they'd done before. I didn't belong here anymore.

I tried to speak, but a dry burr rattled my throat.

"I thought I'd failed," Paulsen said, his ageless eyes searching my face. "When I bound your ashes to her bones, there was no sign the stone had done its work. But her spirit held on, and it brought you back."

He pulled away the plastic tarp covering me, and the cold metal of a zipper scraped against my shoulder. "Take my hand, Ayesha. We don't have much time."

I'm not Ayesha, I tried to say. *I want to be with my dad. Let me go!*

But my shriveled gray hand reached up, animated by a force I couldn't fathom. It clasped Paulsen's hand. He pulled my body upright, and I felt the cold air on my skin. I saw the carved wooden box he'd taken from Socorro. It was a funerary urn, traces of ash still clinging to the sides.

"At last," Paulsen sighed, clasping my gaunt body in his arms. "You're free."

There was a force inside me that wanted nothing more than to say his name, to return his embrace. The force grew stronger, until I couldn't remember I'd ever wanted anything else. There was only Paulsen. There had never been anyone else.

My throat scraped, fighting against itself, as I formed a single word. "Izzy."

Paulsen released me at once.

"You!" His eyes hardened.

I stared at him, felt my sunken chest rise and fall.

"Please, Isobel. You have to let go."

I drew a shaky breath, wondering if it would be my last. Hadn't I wanted peace? Hadn't I wanted to see my father again? It was time to let go.

But the cold air filled my lungs, and carried with it a trace of memory. Songbirds. A magpie. Someone I needed to love.

I shook my head.

Paulsen's face twisted with despair. "You cannot stay in this body. One of you has to let go."

I felt my chin incline toward my chest. A gesture of assent, almost a bow. Then something I couldn't see or name peeled away from my withered body, like layers of winter clothing, one piece at a time. The last layer slipped free, and I glimpsed a woman's form, shadowy and pale. She drew close to Paulsen, touched two graceful hands to his face. He cried out, in joy and pain.

"Ayesha!" He reached for her, but she was already gone.

My eyes fell to my dry, shrunken body. As I watched, my hands began to change. The webbing between the gray, leathery fingers extended. The flesh grew firm, forming slender hands with tapered fingers. On the third finger of my left hand, an indentation remained, as if a wide band had rested there for a long time. My arms grew strong, covered with smooth, healthy skin. Hair tumbled over my shoulders, obsidian-black.

The girl in the photograph.

Sadness creased Paulsen's face, an expression of peace. Behind him, the statue was changing. One of the pumas carved onto the surface began to expand, becoming solid and real. Extending one clawed foot, then another, the stone puma emerged from the side of the monolith. Eyes gleaming, it padded silently toward Paulsen.

A deep crack jagged across the puma's forehead. Pitted limestone rippled over its moving thighs. I tried to speak, to cry out a warning, but my tongue was still too hard. A harsh rasp emerged from my mouth. I gestured at the puma, frantic.

Paulsen didn't even bother to look.

"I know, Isobel," he said calmly, his eyes still on me. "I know." He lifted the bloodied stone, his face weary and expectant.

With a snarl, the stone beast lunged for Paulsen's exposed throat.

"Paulsen!" I threw up my left arm, desperate to block the puma's jaws. But it flung its massive head against my arm, snapping the bones in my wrist with a sickening crack. Then it seized Paulsen with a swift, killing blow.

Paulsen's eyes were drawn upward, his throat torn open like an unwrapped gift. The puma regarded me with cold eyes of stone. Then Paulsen dissolved into powdery gray dust, taking the puma with him. I was alone with the mother earth.

When the pain reached me at last, it was real pain—so raw and so true, it almost shattered me. It blazed through my body, as if a vibrating current had surged from the base of my scalp all the way to my broken wrist.

The torment was unbearable, but I never wanted it to end.

I bent over double and wept real tears, not knowing how many tears were from agony, how many from gratitude. Somehow, I knew the puma's blow would never heal, but it didn't matter. I could *feel* again.

Cold gnawed at my skin, and I remembered it was the solstice, the longest night of the year. Paulsen's tan coat lay beside me on the ground. Weeping and shivering, I wrapped the coat around my naked new body and looked for the way out. The black tarp lay abandoned. Beside it, the wooden box and the blood-dark stone.

I picked up the stone, then let it fall. *Goodbye, Paulsen.*

I crossed the sunken temple, feeling each tiny pebble, round and cold under my bare feet. A steep row of steps led up to the surface. Empty-handed and free, I climbed out of the temple into the sun. I found myself on a long platform: Kalasasaya, the great temple of standing stones. Ahead of me was the legendary Gate of the Sun. Carved into the top of the gate, the sun god Viracocha greeted the dawn, rays of light surrounding him like a halo.

High in the Andean *altiplano*, I could see mountains, a broad lake, and a windswept plain. My pulse quickened. I felt the sun on my new skin, tasted the grit of sand on my new tongue. I looked around me, and I realized it was true: the entire world was magical and holy.

EPILOGUE

By the time Enrique finished meeting with the board members, it was almost noon. Too late to buy *salteñas*, but he could still grab a cup of coffee before driving to Josefina's for lunch.

He ducked into the Hotel Illimani and took a seat at the quiet bar. The barista was an efficient woman in a crisp white blouse. She saw his eyes on the tiny metal pitchers and immediately filled one with coffee, another with steamed milk.

Enrique nodded wordless thanks and inspected his notes from the meeting, aware that he was close to his goal. With a few more flutes and a handful of donated violins, the most talented students in La Paz would finally have instruments of their own.

And why not? Why shouldn't his people hear it as well: the most beautiful music in the world?

Enrique sighed, remembering the girl he'd said that to, the fading magic in her eyes. He still couldn't believe Isobel was gone.

He slipped the symphony papers back into his satchel and checked for the felted rabbit, safe inside. He couldn't visit Flavia empty-handed.

Another gift from Enrique, he thought with satisfaction. The only uncle she was ever going to have.

He finished his coffee and got up to leave, taking in his surroundings for the first time. A young woman was sitting at the corner table. Her beige skin was as smooth as fine parchment, her hair a rich shade of black. She typed slowly at her laptop computer, using only her right hand. Her left hand rested stiffly on the polished wooden table, not quite covering a concert program from *Teatro Municipal*.

She was alone.

A tan coat draped across her chair, and he guessed from the exposed label that she was British, or maybe from the States. Her clothes were simple, but a black pearl earring gleamed hauntingly against her skin. As she wrote, her left hand slipped from the edge of the table, dangling uselessly at her side until she stopped typing and used her right hand to lift it back up. He saw then that her program was from last night's Erik Satie concert.

She kept the program, he observed with a strange sense of kinship, wondering what she'd thought of the *Gnossiennes*. He considered going over to talk to her, but her eyes were fixed on her computer, and he didn't want to intrude. He picked up his satchel, paid for his coffee, and walked away.

She would come back to hear the Beethoven. And if she did, he'd see her again.

If he had stayed to talk, Enrique would have seen the woman's computer open to an email account, and he would have seen she was writing a letter.

Dear mom, congratulations on finishing your new poem. Thanks so much for sending me a copy. I love the image of the magpie searching for strings and ribbons at the end.

I saw an article about Lucia in The New York Times. She and David are auditioning a pianist for their trio. It sounds like they're doing well, though I doubt they'll ever play quartets again. They say they miss Mikhail. I miss him, too.

As for me, I'm still helping out at the shelter in El Alto. Last week they had me painting everything, even the stairwell. I haven't replaced my passport, but it's difficult, for reasons I can't explain. There's someone here who might help me, but I'm not ready to ask him yet.

I'm so excited you're coming to Bolivia! Please tell me when you get your tickets. I can't wait to see you, and there's so much I want you to see.

After all these months, you'll probably say I've changed. But I think you'll know me when you see me.

ACKNOWLEDGMENTS

This book owes its existence to my sister Naomi. Several years ago, she invited me to accompany her to Bolivia for a classical music festival. Since then, I've returned Bolivia again and again, and my love for the country has grown and grown. I'm also deeply indebted to my brother-in-law Javier, whose knowledge of Bolivian culture and society proved invaluable as I wrote *Requiem in La Paz*. He saved my manuscript from many mistakes. Any errors that remain are my own.

Every writer needs someone who believes in her, absolutely and completely. My husband Steve is that someone. He read many drafts of this novel, and he encouraged me to become a full-time writer. Thank you for giving me the courage to pursue my dream.

Requiem in La Paz would not exist in its current form without my wonderful writing group. Thanks very much to Kate Lansing and Zachary Milan. Thanks also to Benjamin Carrancho for interior formatting and to Damon Za for his evocative cover design.

I owe a huge debt of gratitude to Kelly McCullough and Michael Levy, two professionals who have offered me support and advice, every step of the way. Thanks for being mentors, allies, and friends.

An extra special thanks goes to my fellow authors at Wooden Stake Press: Jeff Chacon, Jack Maness, Floyd Jones, and Kim Baack. Besides being creative and tireless and delightful, you helped me get this novel into shape.

Finally, I want to acknowledge my parents, John and Marjorie Gjevre. My father showed me how writers get things done, and my mother taught me to listen to music, to hear all the notes. My two great loves—music and writing—come from you both. Thank you.

AUTHOR'S NOTE

In writing this novel, I've made every effort to represent the culture and topography of Bolivia accurately and respectfully. Many of the novel's scenes are set in real locations in La Paz, including the Witches' Market, *Teatro Municipal*, and the sunken temple near *Hernando Siles* stadium. The ruins of Tiwanaku lie on the high plains outside La Paz, and many shrines to *El Tio* inhabit the mines of Potosi. You can find all of these places if you visit Bolivia, which I hope you'll have a chance to do.

For the sake of structuring the story, I've taken liberties with three particular facts and locations, and for these liberties, I ask the reader's forgiveness. First of all, although Bolivia's National Museum of Archeology is in fact located just east of the Prado, there isn't a Hotel Miranda right next door. Secondly, the isolated village of Socorro in the mountains north of Potosi is a town entirely of my own invention. Finally and most importantly, while there is a Valley of the Moon on the outskirts of La Paz, the U.S. Ambassador does not have a home nearby. The last U.S. Ambassador was expelled from Bolivia in 2008. At the time of this writing (April 2014), the position of U.S. Ambassador to Bolivia remains vacant.

Several parts of this novel required extensive research, and I want to acknowledge a few sources that were especially valuable to me. My father introduced me to the work of his late colleague, Arthur C. Aufderheide, who inspired the character of

Henrik Paulsen. Dr. Aufderheide's book *The Scientific Study of Mummies* (2003) is comprehensive and astonishing.

A number of sources address the experience of Bolivian miners in Potosi, also exploring the miners' relation to the devilish spirit, *El Tio*. A good place to start is *I Am Rich Potosi: The Mountain That Eats Men* by photojournalist Stephen Ferry, with contributions by Eduardo Galeano (1999). Kendall W. Brown takes an academic approach to the Bolivian mining industry in his book *A History of Mining in Latin America: From the Colonial Era to the Present* (2012). The last source I'd like to acknowledge is a film. Kief Davidson and Richard Ladkani's documentary *The Devil's Miner* (2005) offers a sensitive treatment of child laborers in the dangerous mines of *Cerro Rico*. This film provides a vivid and accessible portrait of the miners who work in *Tio*'s shadow.

ABOUT THE AUTHOR

Jonna Gjevre writes fiction in sunny Colorado. A former professor, she has taught creative writing in Scotland and film studies in the United States. *Requiem in La Paz* is her first novel.

ABOUT THE PRESS

Wooden Stake Press LLC publishes fantasy, magic realism, and more. The Storyador affiliate specializes in literary fantasy.

Visit us on the web at www.woodenstakepress.com and www.storyador.com

www.ingramcontent.com/pod-product-compliance
Lightning Source LLC
Chambersburg PA
CBHW022036240626
47154CB00007B/2432